250

Twice Born

by
Edward Sanders

Bloomington, IN · authorHOUSE™ · Milton Keynes, UK

AuthorHouse™
1663 Liberty Drive, Suite 200
Bloomington, IN 47403
www.authorhouse.com
Phone: 1-800-839-8640

AuthorHouse™ *UK Ltd.*
500 Avebury Boulevard
Central Milton Keynes, MK9 2BE
www.authorhouse.co.uk
Phone: 08001974150

*This book is a work of fiction. People, and situations are the product
of the author's imagination. Any resemblance to actual persons,
living or dead, or historical events, is purely coincidental.*

First published by AuthorHouse 12/5/2006

ISBN: 978-1-4259-7340-7 (sc)

*Printed in the United States of America
Bloomington, Indiana*

This book is printed on acid-free paper.

Cover design © Copyright Alison Mitchell 2006

The author wishes to acknowledge and thank Kate Taylor for her meticulous copy editing, Patrick Taylor, Edythe Hannon, Karen Petersen, Elaine Huot, and Alison Mitchell, for reading the manuscript and offering me their sage advice. I am also indebted to Alison Mitchell for her inspired photography and cover design.

I am grateful to the talented staff at Author House, for making the difficult journey of publishing my first book, so much easier.

Edward Sanders. September 2006.

*

Prologue

They were identical twins, sharing the same placenta and floating in the same amniotic sac. In this close, dark, and liquid environment, they were doomed to constantly drift into each other. There came a point, when all the touching, bruising and sharing the same cramped space, was mutually threatening. Both of them needed to increase their capacity, to not only survive, but also thrive. This lead to one of them needing the whole placental universe to himself.

There being no predetermined morals that dictated behavioural niceties at this stage of life, he managed to wrap his twin brother's umbilical cord firmly around his twin brother's neck, effectively cutting off his nourishment from the placenta, and choking the outgoing elimination of his waste. His twin brother gradually withered away to a lifeless form. If this was a conscious act on his part, or an accidental entanglement, he might never know.

After his twin brother's untimely demise, he had a womb of his own. In this seemingly endless world, he had all the fluid that his little heart desired. He could at last drift freely, except, he still occasionally bumped into the deadhead that was his twin brother. These unsanitary conditions progressively lead to the poisoning of his entire environment. In the twenty-eighth week of his mother's pregnancy, they were cut out.

Imagine his consternation when he was untimely ripped from his mother's womb to face the brilliant, cruel light of the operating world. He was naked, cold, and virtually alone; the soft, wet-warm protective darkness of his past existence, was shockingly shed.

*

Two years before the outbreak of World War Two, at 2.00 a.m., on Sunday, April 18th, 1937, a tiny boy and his stillborn twin brother, were introduced to this tumultuous world, by a Caesarean birth.

He was screaming hysterically over his brother's dead silence. He weighed a mere three pounds. They didn't bother to weigh his unmoving twin. Despite his survival, the poisoned atmosphere within her womb had arrested his growth. He was born a mere slip, but a perfect little specimen, except for his unblinking, wide-open eyes, and the two middle fingers of each hand, which were joined together.

Chapter One

THE SPIDER'S WEB

To look at Eleanor Shafto for the very first time, one would be impressed by the way she carried herself. She was a slim woman, standing ramrod straight at about five foot seven. A certain inflexibility in her carriage suggested the weight of her thirty-seven years was prematurely pressing heavily upon her. Her brow wore the wrinkles of apprehension. Her eyes were a dull blue, and had the propensity to blink rapidly, as though they didn't quite believe what they saw and were trying to refocus. Her thin lips seemed to be on the verge of a small, nervous smile. She walked cautiously with small steps, warily picking her way through life. However, in a quirky way, all of those characteristics, of fragility and uneasy tension when viewed as a whole, added up to an attractive image of dignity and regal bearing.

*

After spending ten days at the County Hospital, Eleanor is now at home, in the quiet English village of Wilmington, Kent. She is lying in her own bed, luxuriating in the golden warmth of April's early morning sun, which is shafting through the open window onto her pale and drawn face. Her room overlooks the walled garden where she can see Hobbs the gardener, meticulously spinning out rows of string over the freshly turned soil, in preparation for spring's first vegetable planting. Her gaze is drawn to the vibrant yellow daffodils strolling on the dew-drenched lawn, and the shocking pink, purple and red of the bursting rhododendron bushes lazily leaning against the old, grey, dry-stone wall. Beyond the rhododendrons, etched against a cerulean sky, there are snow-white clouds of apple blossoms. She loves this time of fresh and fecund growth, this glorious season of new life.

She looks down at her tiny, ten-day old boy, snuggling in the crook of her arm; his unblinking, wide-open eyes are staring into the sun. The sunbeams, streaming through the window, are alive with dancing dust motes; their golden rays highlight the Madonna and Child.

With her right hand, she shades her baby boy's eyes and watches his pupils dilate. "What do you see, little one?" she whispers. "What are you thinking?" She is concerned that, since birth, he hasn't closed those unblinking eyes. Taking her hand away, to allow the sun to penetrate his vision, she notices, with relief, his pupils contract again. "I know you have been through a difficult time, my baby, but it's all over now, I'm here to take care of you." He keeps staring ahead, and she wonders what he sees, or indeed, what he has seen. Only *he* can really know the depths of that momentous struggle for life within her womb.

He squirms, and as his cheeks grow red, he smiles; she knows it is wind, but she prefers to think that he is smiling. Holding out her little finger to him, his tiny webbed hand instinctually grasps it. "Welcome to this beautiful world, my little darling. You are home now, you are safe." For a lazy moment, she stares out of the window, listening to Nature's morning song. "Do you hear the birds singing your praises? Look at the squirrel running across the top of the garden wall. And there, do you see the spider in the window, weaving its web?" He squirms and smiles again, his gaze shifting along the line of her finger that is pointing to the web.

Eleanor thinks of the son she has lost. Perhaps, the perfect life is not possible. Perhaps, he transmuted into perfect immortality, before the struggle with parents, siblings, friends, enemies, bosses, debts, lovers, children, illness and ageing, could make him as mortal as any of us. His stillborn body is buried in the graveyard of the old village church in Wilmington. Resolving to visit the grave, as soon as she is strong enough, she grieves for her lost child, but she is extremely grateful that his twin, this exceptional child she now holds in the crook of her arm, has survived.

The industrious spider continues spinning its web, and Eleanor is fascinated by the enormity, ingenuity, and complexity of its task. It is an intricate work of delicate splendour, designed explicitly to entrap an unwitting prey, a work of terrible beauty. How can something so perfect and so exquisite be designed for the sole purpose of entrapment and death? She knows that in order to survive, all things bright and beautiful must attract their prey, and then destroy it. Even humans are destined to ensnare, to conquer, to victimise, to render helpless and ultimately, to consume. Looking into the indefinable web before her, she marvels at the spider's single-minded dedication to the achievement of its definitive purpose.

Gazing down at her imperfect son, she is well pleased. His tiny webbed hand tightens around her little finger, and he squirms and squeaks, his unchanging stare remaining fixed on the spider's web. The sun's rays move across the plane of the web's gossamer surface as its delicate strands become more clearly defined; she falls under its spell.

The sunlight, reflecting off the dressing-table mirror, illuminates the room with its radiance. The light reflecting off a photograph on the bedside table attracts her attention. It is of Edward and herself, when they had first moved into this house. She remembers the first time they met.

*

Everything had happened so fast. They had met only two years ago, in Foyle's bookstore on Charing Cross Road. It was her lunch hour; she was working as a telephonist in the nearby Strand Hotel. They were waiting to get a ticket for the books they each had selected. She had often wondered about that bizarre procedure, whereby, you had to queue up to obtain a ticket, in order to purchase your book, and then join another queue, where you then submitted your ticket with the money, to gain possession of your book.

She was standing in the queue to get her ticket, in order to purchase 'An Actor Prepares', by Constantine Stanislavski, and was immersed in the opening chapter, when the man who stood behind her, without physically intruding, spoke over her shoulder. She was immediately conscious of his voice; it had a dark and rich timbre that resonated and rumbled through her.

"That's a very good book," he intoned. "Are you an actress?"

The query startled her. Keeping her index finger on the page she was reading, she closed the book. Turning to look at her inquisitor, she was presented with a slightly balding, but suave looking, middle-aged man. He was dressed in a casual, dark-brown, corduroy suite which he wore with re-laxed confidence. He sported a cream-coloured linen shirt which was open at the collar, displaying a maroon, green and yellow, paisley-patterned cravat. On his feet, he wore highly buffed, brown, brogue shoes. Her gaze travelled back to his smiling face, his raised eyebrows begged for an answer.

She was immediately captivated by his iridescent, dark-blue eyes; they were exceptionally penetrating and hypnotic. She caught herself staring at him, and wondered at herself for her bold appraisal of this stranger. Gathering her composure, she quietly answered, "I'm sorry, you startled me. What did you say?"

He pointed to the book she carried. "Excuse me, but I couldn't help noticing your book. I too have a keen interest in the theatre." Her curiosity was piqued. He continued, "I asked if you were an actress."

His question attracted the attention of the fidgety woman behind him, who like a startled squirrel, popped her little head out from behind his back to stare quizzically at Eleanor.

Eleanor was caught off guard, her mind went blank, and her cheeks felt flushed as she focused on his mesmerising eyes. As she withdrew the moist finger that marked her place, the palm of her hand felt clammy against the hard cover of the book. She then crossed her arms and clasped the book to her breast, in a defensive gesture. "Yes," she answered, in a voice that she didn't recognise. "What I mean is I am *studying* to be an actress."

His hypnotic eyes held hers. "How interesting," he replied. "You see, I happen to have written a few plays, some of which have even been produced."

This was not stated in a boastful manner, but merely as a matter of fact.

As he moved towards her, she retreated. Their contact was broken as his look shifted over her shoulder. She turned in the indicated direction to see that a long space in the queue had materialised; the assistant at the desk was glaring at her; Eleanor moved quickly to fill the gap. As she approached the desk to acquire her ticket, she was searching for something to say to cover her embarrassment. Over her shoulder, she remarked diffidently, "This is such a silly system don't you think?" She was aware of the assistant's disapproving glare.

"I agree," he responded.   "But do you know what is funny?"

She felt relieved that the stream of conversation had become shallower; she no longer felt out of her depth. With her ticket in hand, she turned to face him, "What is funny?" she answered, with a pinched and cautious smile.

His eyes met her gaze.   "I find it strange that I have never questioned the system."

Eleanor could see the squirrelly woman behind him, impatiently nodding her head in jerky motions and emitting small, strange, squeaky sounds as she shuffled forward demonstratively.   Ignoring the squirrel-lady, Eleanor moved passed him on her way to the other desk to pay for her book, their sleeves gently brushed and a shiver ran through her.   From the back of her queue, she watched with anticipation as he obtained his ticket and walked confidently towards her; she was aware of her breathing becoming slower and deeper.

As he took his place behind her, he continued his seductive conversation.   "I do have a question for you."

She felt the warmth of his voice trickling down her back, like melting chocolate pouring over vanilla ice cream.   She remained looking ahead, not wanting to meet his eyes.   "Oh? And what would that be?"

"I was wondering if you would do me a great favour and read my new play, I have a feeling it might interest you."

She was somewhat taken aback by this request, but at the same time felt rather privileged that he would ask.   Turning to answer him, with a small smile, she met his gaze and responded, "I would be honoured."

"Excellent," he exclaimed.   Then reaching into his inside jacket pocket, he pulled out a thin silver case, which he opened. "Here's my card. If you phone this number, my secretary will send you the manuscript. The play is called *Escape to Nowhere.*"

Their eyes broke contact as she looked at the card. *Edward Shafto, Playwright/Painter;* there was no address, just a telephone number. Putting his calling card in her handbag, she looked up at him. "Well, thank you, Mr Shafto. It was a pleasure to meet you."

"Yes it was," he remarked.

She nodded slightly, noting his ambiguous narcissism; she took a deep breath, bemused by his reply. Turning to the clerk, she handed in her ticket with the payment for her book, and as she was walking away from the desk, he raised his voice, attracting the attention of everybody in their immediate vicinity, and shouted. "Goodbye, and don't forget to call, will you?"

"Goodbye," she answered timidly, without committing herself, and quickly made her way out of Foyle's, onto the crowded pavement of Charing Cross Road, where she felt relieved to be part of the anonymity of the river of faceless people swirling around her.

It wasn't until she had seated herself, with her coffee, at the Lyons Corner House in the Strand that she opened her handbag to look at his calling card again; *Edward Shafto Playwright/Painter.* Amongst the clatter of crockery and the chatter of the crowd, she marvelled at his confidence and poise, yet she felt a little uneasy about his aggressive pursuit of her. She also wondered why, at no time during their brief encounter, had he asked her name, and if he had asked, would she have offered the information, and how much more would she have offered? All she really knew was that Edward Shafto had made an indelible impression on Eleanor Martin.

Chapter Two

ROBERT AND EDWARD

Lying in her bed, the colour is gradually returning to Eleanor's cheeks as she relaxes into the future. The birds resume their song of spring, the squirrel continues its chirping, and scampering back and forth across the wall, and the spider, having completed weaving its web, withdraws into the corner of the window to await its prey. Marvelling at the spider's ingenuity, she whispers to her wide-eyed son, "Do you know what I am going to call you?"

Breaking out into a smile, his face grows red; he moves his legs and arms energetically, like a bug on its back trying to right itself.

She laughs delightedly. "Yes, I think you do know. You shall be named, Robert; after Robert the Bruce, of Scotland."

He stops moving, but continues to gaze upon the spider's web.

"I will tell you why your name is Robert." She watches the little bubbles dancing on his lips. "Long, long ago, when England was at war with Scotland, at the Battle of Methven, the armies of Edward the First of England, 'the Hammer of the Scots', defeated the brave soldiers of Robert-the-Bruce of Scotland. Robert then went into hiding and became a hunted outlaw. He retreated to a cave on a remote Scottish Isle, and in this cave, he spent the winter alone in contemplation. As time passed, he became fascinated by a spider, just like the one we are watching in the window, trying to build its web. On a single, long thread, the spider attempted to swing across the cave to reach the other side, but it failed. Five more times it attempted to reach the other side, still without success. However, on the seventh attempt, the spider was victorious, and continued successfully to weave its web. This became a decisive turning point in Robert's life; he was tremendously impressed with the spider's courage and tenacity. This redoubtable insect was the inspiration for Robert's reawakening; his motto became, 'Never despair'."

Looking down at her wide-eyed child, she murmurs affectionately, "That is why your name will be Robert, because, despite the adversity you have suffered in your heroic struggle for life, you never gave up. What do you think of that?"

There is no reaction from the tiny creature; he has fallen fast asleep, with his wide-open eyes still fixed on the spider's web.

Feeling the need to conclude her whispered legend, she continues. "The next day, armed with arachnid courage, Robert emerged from the cave and set out to recruit and train an army of five thousand men. And on June 24th, 1341, at the battle of Bannockburn, Robert, against overwhelming odds, defeated a vastly superior English army, numbering twenty thousand strong. The English army was commanded by the effeminate Edward the second, the son of Edward, 'the Hammer of the Scots'. And you, my little Robert, will also prevail against insurmountable odds." Kissing him lovingly on the top of his tiny head, she declares, "What's more, what I find ironic is that Edward is your daddy's name?" She remembers Edward Shafto's powerful and tenacious pursuit of her.

*

In 1935, she lived on the first floor of a small family-owned house in Ealing, in north-west London. The ground floor was occupied by her older sister, Theresa, and their older brother, Jasper. They were all products of a strict Catholic upbringing; the ingrained fear of the Lord, being translated into a shyness and timidity towards the world around them. None of them had ever been married; they preferred the familiar, familial proximity of each other. "Marriage is not in our blood," was the oft quoted, defensive humour that they shared. Consequently, when any of them received guests, it was an occasion of great interest, and was duly noted and conscientiously monitored by their siblings.

Four days after first meeting Edward Shafto, Eleanor phoned the number on his calling card, explaining the purpose of her request. She was informed by a refined and distant, female voice, that it would be necessary for her to leave her name and address, in order for the script to be delivered.

One day later, Theresa Martin answered the ring of the front door bell at 17 Neville Road. Eleanor, who was dressing for an appointment, heard her older sister calling up the stairs, "El-ean-or, you have a vis-i-tor. Shall I send him up?"

Eleanor went to the top of the stairs, and looking down to the front hallway; she was greeted by the smiling face of Edward Shafto. He was carrying a large, brown, manila envelope, a bouquet of colourful spring flowers and a bottle of white wine.

He looked up at her. "Hello, Miss Martin, forgive me for being so presumptuous, but I do like to deliver my own manuscripts."

Eleanor was at a loss, she couldn't speak, she couldn't move.

"May I come up?" he persisted, smiling slightly with his eyebrows raised.

She would become very familiar with that particular questioning expression. "But of course, Mr Shafto. Please forgive me, come right up."

As he glided up the stairs, he set his deep blue eyes on her.

Theresa's gaze followed him, as she remained standing and smiling at the foot of the stairs. Jasper's voice could be heard calling from the parlour, "Tedie, don't be so rude, leave them alone." Eleanor opened the door of her room and stood aside to let Edward in; their sleeves brushed against each other as he walked passed her; that slight shiver ran through her again.

The walls were white; she loved purity. An old, green, brocade settee stood in the middle of the room. At one end of the settee was a plain looking standard lamp, with a large, fringed, yellow parchment shade. In front of the settee squatted a low veneered wood coffee table. A worn Persian carpet, that had seen better days, covered most of the wood floor.

In her dark-purple suit and white pearls, her stocking feet and hairnet, Eleanor felt vulnerable. She had planned to go out to lunch with Theresa and Jasper, and then she was due for an appointment with a theatrical agent in the early afternoon; she was obviously ill prepared for this visit. Edward was still wearing his brown corduroy suit, and seemed to be in no hurry to leave.

Politely indicating the settee, she said, "Please take a seat, and forgive my appearance, I wasn't expecting you."

Edward moved to the settee and awkwardly seated himself. He put the large envelope on the coffee table in front of him, and still clutching the flowers and wine, he disingenuously apologised. "I am so sorry to intrude, but I thought it might be a good time to discuss the play."

She stood with her back to the recently closed door and looked uneasily at her intruder.

"Would you care for some wine?" he offered, raising his eyebrows as he looked at her.

Crossing to where he was sitting, she relieved him of the flowers and wine, replying, "Thank you for the flowers, but no thank you for the wine, I think it is a little early to be drinking, and besides, I was on my way out to see my agent." Without waiting for a reply, she continued, "If you would excuse me, whilst I put these flowers in water."

Edward silently watched her open the glass door of the cabinet and take out a crystal vase.

Going out to the landing, she left the door of the room open and entered the bathroom, closing the door behind her. Looking in the mirror above the sink, she removed her hairnet and quickly powdered her nose; she felt discombobulated. She was flattered that he had personally brought his manuscript, but she felt ill prepared, and was thrown off balance by his unannounced arrival. Looking into the mirror for some reflection of direction, she leaned on the sink and waited for her breathing to return to its normal rhythm. Pouring some water into the vase, she haphazardly dropped the flowers in and returned to her room to see him standing in front of the bookcase, scrutinising her collection.

He turned around to face her, and immediately asserting control, he said, "Here, give me that vase, allow me to arrange the flowers."

Bending to his will, she silently handed the vase to him.

He strode over to the table under the window that overlooked the vegetable garden, and with a few authoritative flourishes, expertly rearranged the flowers. Turning to look at her, he nonchalantly asked, "Where is your agent?"

"Soho," she immediately replied, closing the door behind her and crossing to the settee.

"Ah! Good," he said, keeping his eyes on her, and elegantly bending his head to inhale the flowers' fragrance. "Would you like a lift? I have my car outside."

"No, really," she hurriedly responded. "I have to meet someone for lunch first." She felt pressured by his assertiveness. A ripple of irritation moved through her.

Raising his eyebrows, he asked rhetorically. "You're meeting someone? I see." The vowel of the last word was drawn out before it decayed. He moved fluidly towards the door and stated, "Well in that case, I'll be on my way." Then pointing to the large brown manila envelope on the coffee table, he pronounced, "I'll leave the script with you, Eleanor. I would be very interested to hear your comments." He was opening the door as he turned to look at her; his dark-blue, iridescent eyes were glinting. "Maybe you would be interested in playing one of the roles in *Escape to Nowhere*? I am currently in preproduction planning; let me know if you are interested." With his hand on the doorknob, he faced her, audaciously expecting her to acquiesce.

She leaned on the back of the settee, feeling intimidated by his controlling expectations, she would not submit so easily. Her voice was quiet and, she hoped, controlled. "Thank you, Mr Shafto. I will call you when I have read your play." She remained standing stiffly behind the settee. "Let me show you out."

"Edward, please. Call me Edward. It's all right; I can find my own way out." He opened the door and stepped into the hallway. Then, looking around the edge of the door, he raised his eyebrows and smiled, "Now don't forget to call, will you?" Without waiting for a reply, he swiftly withdrew his head and gently closed the door.

"I won't forget," she whispered grudgingly to the closed door. She listened to his light-hearted footsteps skipping down the stairs. She heard the *thrum* of the front door closing behind him. She wanted to go to the window to look down on him, but she knew he would look up with those penetrating, hypnotic eyes, and catch her off guard. She heard the *thunk* of the car door closing, and the whine of an expensive motor changing pitch as it disappeared down Neville Road, into the sonic distance.

Chapter Three

BECAUSE, THE RABBIT DIED

Eleanor is watching the spider sinking its poisonous fangs into the captive fly, immediately paralysing it and sucking out its life force. Her reverie is interrupted by the soundless appearance of Edward in her bedroom; she senses his presence from the smell of his ubiquitous pipe.

At the age of 51, he is fourteen years her senior. This tweedy man, with the fixed smile, has lost the firmness of his flesh and is going soft in the middle now. He is a partner in a chain of grocery stores and an accomplished writer and painter. Maybe, because of his success in business and the arts, she feels unworthy of him, she is intimidated by him, and this bothers her. He has the annoying habit of striding into a room unannounced with a sense of entitlement. It is as though he is master of all that he surveys; everyone and everything is subject to his wishes. Paradoxically, it is this air of arrogant confidence that had first attracted her; she had fallen in love with his image.

Before the Caesarean, Edward had been constantly by her side. He had been attentive to her every need, perhaps because it was also his need. Now, she feels his bitter disappointment with the less than perfect, tiny child that has survived. She suspects that Edward's anger is directed both towards her and at this tiny innocent she now holds in her arms. He seems to blame both of them for the strangulation of his unbegotten son. At times, she feels the inexplicable chill of fear; this is one such time. She remembers his reaction of shock and anger, when he first saw his strangulated stillborn son. She knows that if she had carried the twins to full term and a natural birth, he would have been overjoyed, because he would have been blessed with two ideally wonderful sons. Now, he is denied what he considers to be rightfully his -- perfection.

She resents his overbearing intrusion into her room, not even having the time to powder her nose and brush her hair. In the dressing-table mirror, she sees the reflection of her wan face, her eyes have lost their sparkle, her dull, auburn hair lies limply on the pillow, and she has lost the vigour and vitality that once had so attracted him. She is acutely aware of her weakened body, it is a pale reflection of her former self; her previously complete beauty has disassembled into its individual, unattractive parts. A weak smile slouches around her mouth, begging for approval; it is not forthcoming. Through his frozen smile, she is acutely aware of his penetrating eyes, and she shivers.

Easing herself up to a sitting position, being careful not to disturb the sleeping child, she instinctually reaches for her compact and starts to powder her nose. She greets him apologetically, "Hello, Dear, we didn't hear you come in. Come; sit on the bed with us."

Edward clears his throat; he is obviously uneasy in the presence of this tiny, imperfect child, with the unblinking, wide-open eyes and webbed hands. 'No, thank you, Dear. I won't be staying long; I think I would prefer to stand." He draws deeply on his pacifying briar and exhales a puffy, white cloud of aromatic smoke, which she defensively disburses with the rapid sideways motion of her hand. Taking a small step forward, then leaning back slightly on his heels, he announces, "Eleanor, I couldn't help but overhear the last part of that story you were relating. Am I to understand that you wish to call our son Robert?"

Closing the compact, she gives him her undivided attention. "Yes, Edward, I do. We were watching the spider in the window weaving its web, and it reminded me of Robert the Bruce, and what a brave and tenacious spirit he had. After all our son has been through, to be here with us now, I thought it appropriate to name him Robert, after Robert-the-Bruce."

"I see," says Edward, the vowels of the last word drawing out until they decay.

"Do you like the name?" she asks.

He doesn't answer.

She repeats the question. "Edward, do you like the name?"

A hard edge cuts into his tone, "Yes, Eleanor, I like the name, Edward, but I don't like the name, Robert, particularly in the context of that story you were telling him."

She doesn't have the strength to argue with him, her shoulders slump, tears moisten her limpid eyes, and her bottom lip quivers. She re-opens her compact.

Edward exhales a long, drawn-out sigh and raises his eyebrows. "Now don't cry, ducky. Why don't we just compromise and call him Bobby? Then we will all be happy." With pipe in hand, and wearing the same set smile, he bends over the sleeping child. "After all, everyone has heard of Bobby Shafto."

Submitting to his demand, for she knows it is not a request; she wipes away her tears and powders her nose. "All right, Dear, we will call him Bobby."

Staring down at her, he pulls himself to his full height. She watches in trepidation as his smile fades. Pursing his lips, he hesitates before declaring, "My dead son's name shall be Bunny."

Until that moment, she has not given much thought to naming her stillborn son; she is curious. "I suppose we should put a name on his headstone, but why Bunny?"

Turning on his heel, he declares flatly, "Because, the rabbit died."

Watching him disappear through his cloud of smoke, she hears him emphatically close the bedroom door behind him. Had she made a terrible mistake by falling in love with this all-consuming man? Before Bobby was born, he had been so considerate and generous, and they were so much in love. Now, he has turned. She can never meet his demanding expectations; she is always under his control. From the very beginning, she had wanted to impress him, even to the point of deception. She remembers that first time in Ealing, when he left her room unsatisfied.

Chapter Four

Escape to Nowhere

As the privileged whine of his departing car faded into the silence of Neville Road, Eleanor realised she hadn't exactly told the whole truth about going to see her agent. Actually, she didn't have an agent; she had made an appointment with the Nate Schreiber Theatrical Agency, hoping that, as an aspiring actress, she would be represented by them.

After eating lunch with Theresa and Jasper, she took the Tube from Ealing Broadway to Tottenham Court Road and started to read '*Escape to Nowhere*, a drama in three acts, by Edward Shafto. By the time she arrived outside the agent's office in Tottenham Court Road, she had read the synopsis of the play and the first act. She was very impressed by the plot, and particularly by the part of Ruth, the protagonist, to whom she felt an indefinable affinity.

The play was set in the 1860s, in Bedlam, or Bethlam Royal Hospital, a lunatic asylum for the criminally insane, in London. Ruth, an inmate, was in her early thirties and was the wife of a London publican. She was found guilty of the murder of her husband, a domineering man, who constantly abused her, both physically and mentally, until she eventually snapped, and slashed his jugular with a broken bottle.

Ruth was arrested and certified insane. She was diagnosed as suffering from acute mania, and subsequently was committed to Bedlam Asylum for the Criminally Insane.

Whilst in the women's ward of the asylum, part of her treatment was to be constantly photographed, the theory being that she might observe and confront the various stages of her insanity/sanity. During this process, Walter, the photographer, fell in love with Ruth, and together they planned her escape. This feat was accomplished by the ingenious method of Walter bringing in his unsuspecting, new assistant, Dolly, who bore a striking resemblance to Ruth. Ruth, who was dressed in similar clothes to Dolly, took the place of his assistant. The conniving couple simply walked out of the asylum, leaving the innocent Dolly inside to protest her sanity. Having gained her freedom, Ruth was then confronted with the disturbing realisation that there was no difference in the behaviour of the people on the outside of the asylum, from the behaviour of those on the inside.

Eleanor pondered the questions raised by Edward Shafto's play. Who is sane? Is it those on the inside of the asylum, or those on the outside? Are we all insane? On the other hand, do we all posses our own individual and immeasurable sanity/insanity quotient? Did Ruth escape *from* nowhere, only to discover that she had escaped *to* nowhere?

Eleanor was still mulling over these questions as she walked up the dimly lit and creaking stairs to the Nate Schreiber theatrical agency. She timidly opened the opaque, glass-panelled door, on which was stencilled in bold gold letters, **The Nate Schreiber Theatrical Agency,** and stepped into a virtually empty waiting room. Seated behind a small desk, in front of a closed and grimy window, overlooking Tottenham Court Road, Eleanor saw a pencil-thin, grey-haired woman, with tight curls and a tiny pinched mouth. She wore tortoise-shell rimmed glasses and a pale-blue knitted shawl. Beside her, on the floor to her right, was a bowl-shaped electric fire. Worn, green linoleum, with white specks, covered the floor. It seemed to Eleanor that every inch of wall-space was filled with photographs of the luminaries of British stage and screen, from Judith Anderson and Brian Aherne, right through the alphabet, to Googie Withers and Emlyn Williams. Whether Nate Schreiber actually represented these artists, was pure conjecture, on her part. Along the wall to Eleanor's left, there was a high-backed wooden bench and two straight-backed chairs. To her right, was a door that was ajar, that presumably led to the inner sanctum of Nate Schreiber. Either side of the door stood low, wooden bookshelves which held various trade magazines and theatrical reference books. The room was small, narrow, and cold. However, despite the cold, Eleanor was feeling rather flushed; this was her first time in a theatrical agent's office, and she wasn't sure of the protocol. She looked at her watch and noticed it was nearly half-past-two.

She closed the door gently behind her, hesitantly announcing to the pencil-thin, grey-haired woman behind the desk, "Eleanor Martin to see Mr Schreiber. I have an appointment for half-past-two."

Without looking up, the woman, with the small pinched mouth, silently consulted her watch.

Eleanor, standing with her hand on the doorknob, and clutching her script, was straining forward for acknowledgement. To make her presence known, she emitted a quiet and courteous cough, before stating, "I'm afraid I might be a little early."

The shrivelled little woman looked up, slightly opening her dry, pursed lips, and in a rather put-on theatrical accent, spoke with forced civility. "Yes, Miss Martin, we have been expecting you. Don't stand in the doorway. Come in and be seated. Mr Schreiber will be back shortly."

Eleanor sat uncomfortably on one of the straight-backed wooden chairs and resumed reading *Escape to Nowhere*. After, what seemed a long time; she checked her wristwatch; which indicated it was nearly twenty-to-three.

Hearing the outer door of the inner office close, the blue-shawled woman put down her book and shuffled around the desk to stand at the door of the inner office. She condescendingly asked Eleanor, "What did you say your name was?"

Eleanor impatiently frowned and looked directly at her inquisitor. Raising her voice, she enunciated firmly and clearly, "My name is Eleanor Martin, I have a half-past-two appointment to see Mr Schreiber."

"Miss Martin, there is no need to raise your voice. I know who you are, I know why you are here, and I know whom you are here to see. I do work here you know."

Eleanor nibbled her bottom lip impatiently and slowly nodded her head.

Then, the self-important receptionist announced, "Mr Schreiber will see you now, Miss Martin, this way please." With a flourish, she opened the door to the inner office, and with her back to Eleanor, she trumpeted, "Eleanor Martin is here for her twenty-to-three appointment, Mr Schreiber."

From the inner office came a smoky, whisky-soaked voice. "Thank you, Mildred, send her in please."

Mildred stood aside and curtly nodded to Eleanor, "You may enter now, Miss Martin."

Eleanor, tensely walked passed the stiffly standing Mildred, and into the inner office.

Standing behind a large wooden desk, she saw a man who looked to be about Edward Shafto's age. Nate Schreiber was immaculately dressed in a dark-blue suit, a light-blue shirt with white collar and cuffs, accessorised by a blue and red diagonally striped tie, which was secured by a single Windsor knot. He wore a red carnation in his buttonhole, a maroon silk handkerchief peeked out from his breast pocket and in his left hand, he held a large cigar. Nate Schreiber was talking on the telephone.

Glancing around the room, Eleanor immediately noticed that it was far more opulent than the waiting area. Hanging on the white walls, instead of photographs, was a series of Picasso and Dali prints. She vaguely recognised a Picasso drawing, *La Mort d'Orphée* that hung behind Nate Schreiber's desk; it looked to her to be from Picasso's Blue period. A solid wooden door led out to the hallway, and over the single window hung white, diaphanous curtains. A royal blue, short-pile, carpet covered the floor. In addition to the two armless chairs in front of his desk, there were, arranged in the centre of the room, two upholstered arm chairs, flanked by cherry-wood veneered side tables. Eleanor was duly impressed with her surroundings.

Nate Schreiber expansively waved her to a chair in front of his desk; the ash from his cigar was raining down over the desktop, like dust from an erupting volcano. She assumed he was talking to one of his clients on the telephone. His whisky-soaked voice was raw and rasping.

"Yes, Daaarling, ...of course I will.......as soon as the cheque arrives, I will forward it to you........no I haven't heard from him yet...... yes, Darling, I will let you know as soon as he phones.......leave it with Uncle Nate, Daaaarling...... I love you too. Ta ta, Darling...,Ta ta."

He put down the telephone and directed his attention towards Eleanor. He looked debauched; his red face was fleshy and thick, dark eyebrows hovered over deep-brown eyes, resting on puffy bags of wrinkled skin at the top of his red-veined cheeks. He had a shock of thick, unruly brown hair that was completely out of character with his conservative clothes. As he smiled, he displayed a set of small yellowing teeth, which were encircled by full, pink lips.

He remained standing. "Ah! Miss Martin, Eleanor is it not?"

She opened her mouth to answer, but was not allowed to continue.

Waving his hands magnanimously, causing further ash to scatter over the desk, Nate Schreiber laughed hoarsely, "Of course it is, I never forget a name," and with a wink, "or a pretty face."

She was not quite sure what to say, but she needn't have worried, because Nate persisted.

"I can only give you a few minutes as I have an appointment at my club. Now, I assume that you would like me to represent you." Looking up to the ceiling, as though he was pondering a deep problem, he slowly paced back and forth behind his desk.

She remained silent, not wanting to interrupt his thoughts.

Eventually he stopped pacing and returned his attention to her. "Well, Ducky, am I correct in my assumption?"

Not knowing where she should look, she kept staring ahead at the blue Picasso. "Yes, Mr Schreiber."

From deep within his belly, erupted the sound of thunder rolling down a mountainside; he laughed. "Never wrong, Ducky, never wrong."

She smiled sweetly.

He glanced at his watch. "Well, Ducky, if you will let me know what play you are in, I will endeavour to come and see you, that is, if it's in London; I seldom travel to the Provinces. Just give Mildred the name of the play, the theatre, the dates and performance times."

Eleanor was about to explain that she wasn't actually in a play, but Nate looked at his watch again, in the process, scattering more ash. "*Tempus Fugit!*" he exclaimed, "I must dash. Goodbye, Ducky." With that, he turned his back on her and swiftly exited upstage right.

Eleanor was left sitting alone in the room, blankly staring across the ash-strewn desk at the print of Picasso's *La Mort d'Orphée*. She looked at her watch; it was nearly five-to-three. Throughout the entire interview, she realised that she had spoken just three words, "Yes, Mr Schreiber."

The door opened behind her, and she was assaulted by the shrill, theatrical, and pompous tone of Mildred, "If you will step into my office, Miss Martin, we will conclude the interview."

Eleanor exhaled a deep sigh, and reluctantly followed behind the overbearing Mildred. She crossed the uncomfortable expanse of green lino floor, and resumed her seat in her original chair. The waiting-area was still empty, except for the silent images of the theatrical elite of the British stage and screen. She felt so disheartened.

Mildred officiously seated herself behind her tiny desk. "Now, Miss Martin," she trilled, as she extended her skeletal, blue-veined hand. "May I see your résumé?"

Eleanor almost snapped, she fought for control and answered Mildred in an exaggerated slow, and level voice. "But I do not have a résumé. This is the whole point of being here. I was hoping to audition, so that I would get representation, in order to get work, so that I might be able to obtain a résumé."

Mildred leaned back in her chair; she seemed to be enjoying herself. She looked over the top of her tortoise-shell rimmed glasses, pointedly. "Miss Martin, I am afraid you don't understand. Mr Schreiber is not going to take on a new client who has never acted before." She sat erect, and disdainfully announced, "And even if you have worked before, it would be preferable if you were currently in a production, otherwise, how on earth do you expect Mr Schreiber to judge your talent?" Mildred was on a roll, and would not stop her pompous and pedantic diatribe. "I have been with Mr Schreiber for fifteen years now, and I can assure you, he only represents the very best in the profession." Spreading her arms wide, to embrace the luminaries on the walls, with a triumphant smile she crowed, "Just look around you."

Eleanor caught herself tightly clutching the script of *Escape to Nowhere*. She felt herself shaking; she wanted this pompous old woman to shut up. She wanted to throw the script at her and walk out. Raising the envelope in her right hand, she suddenly recalled that Edward Shafto had intimated that there could be a role in his play that would interest her. Before Mildred could say another word, Eleanor withdrew the script from the envelope, waving it triumphantly at Mildred, she firmly stated, "I may not be currently working, but I do have a role in Edward' Shafto's new play, *Escape to Nowhere*."

This revelation seemed to deflate Mildred a little. Her shoulders drooped, as she said, "And when and where is this production going to open, Miss Martin?"

Eleanor slowly lowered the script onto her lap. Speaking in a quasi-nonchalant manner, she mumbled, "Oh, it's still in the preproduction stages, a venue has yet to be chosen, so there are no firm dates as yet."

A tiny, arid smile of triumph hovered around Mildred's pursed lips. "Well, my dear, if you don't know when or where it will be produced, don't you think it's a little premature to be wasting Mr Schreiber's and my time?" In a final demonstrative gesture, putting both hands on her desk, Mildred raised herself to a standing position and straining for equilibrium, shuffled out from behind the desk, to walk haughtily to the office door. With her white, blue-veined hand grasping the brass doorknob, she looked down her nose at Eleanor. "May I suggest, Miss Martin, that you make an appointment to see us when you *are* in production? I am sure Mr Schreiber would be delighted to see you perform." With a flourish, a slight, slow nod of her head, and a superior smile, she fired her parting salvo. "But only in London, Miss Martin, only in London. Mr Schreiber seldom goes to the Provinces." Opening the door to the hallway she crowed, "Goodbye, Miss Martin."

Eleanor slowly stood, and with downcast eyes, sheepishly exited downstage centre.

*

That night, she dreamed she was in Bedlam. It wasn't in the refurbished women's ward of the 1860s, with the expansive glass roof, hanging flower baskets, smartly dressed people and strolling dogs; it was well over a century earlier. She was haunted by the terrible, mind-wrenching, dark images of Bedlam in the Hogarth paintings of the *Rake's Progress.*

Dressed in rags, she lay on the filthy, cold, stone floor, surrounded by lunatics in various stages of insanity and undress, when inexplicably, the cacophony of insanity that engulfed her, suddenly ceased. In front of her, the disturbing press of altered humanity parted like the bow wave of a great ship, to reveal a fleshy dandy in a red velvet suit and a white ruffled shirt, which was secured by a glinting, ruby pin at his neck. He was carrying a silver-topped cane and was laughing uproariously in a deep, whisky-soaked, thunderous voice, generously scattering his hilarity from side to side. On his arm, rested the immaculate white glove of an expensively clothed, crinoline swaying, society matron; they were relentlessly bearing down on her. As they drew nearer, Eleanor recognised the jocular singularity of the splendiferous Nate Schreiber, and the dry, pinched lips, tortoise-shell rimmed glasses, and small tight, mean steps of, Mildred. The intruding couple floated to a halt in front of her. Mildred looked down on Eleanor and accusingly pointed, releasing a loud and harsh cackle. Her finger was as long and straight as a broomstick, with an extended, sharp, brightly shining red fingernail. Eleanor felt the tip of the hard and pointed fingernail pricking her pale cheek, sending her body into uncontrollable spasms. The finger brusquely withdrew, the crazed cacophony resumed, Mildred and Nate vaporised, and the wonderfully depraved and chaotic life of the lunatic asylum, returned to its insane normality.

Eleanor awoke, shivering in a cold sweat. She could still feel the imprint of Mildred's sharp fingernail on her cheek. With her fingertip, she tentatively touched the phantom wound, but there was no blood drawn. Being fearful of re-entering the dark world of insanity, she made another pot of tea and remained awake to greet the pale, sober light of dawn.

Chapter Five

He will consume you

With the chaos of the nightmare still shadowing her mind, Eleanor phoned Edward's number, and the same, precisely clipped, female voice answered.

"Hello."

"This is Eleanor Martin. May I speak to Edward Shafto please?"

There was a three second pause … "I'm so sorry Miss Martin, Edward is not in right now, would you like to leave a message?"

"It's about his play, *Escape to Nowhere*, he asked me to read it and get back to him."

"I see." she said, the echo of the extended vowel lingered. "Would you like him to ring you back, or would you rather meet with him personally?"

"Whatever is convenient for Mr Shafto."

"Well, I know Edward would prefer a meeting, you see, he has an aversion to telephones. I will let him know you called and get back to you."

"Thank you. My telephone number is …."

"We have your telephone number, Miss Martin."

"Oh, I didn't realise that. Thank you very much."

"Thank you, Miss Martin, goodbye."

"Goodbye." Eleanor was sure she hadn't given Edward Shafto her telephone number. She also thought that his secretary was being a little too familiar, and was going far beyond her station, by referring to her employer by his first name.

Within the hour, Eleanor's telephone rang again. She let it ring three times, not wanting to seem too anxious. With the telephone in her right hand and a glass of sherry in her left, she answered, "Hello? Eleanor Martin speaking."

There was a brief hiatus …

"Oh, hello, Miss Martin," announced the tersely polite voice, "Edward would like to set up a luncheon meeting with you for tomorrow, would that suit you?"

"Yes of course, and where would that be?"

"Do you know the Prospect of Whitby in Wapping?"

"Yes, I do, I mean, I have never been there, but I've heard of it."

"I'm sure you have, Miss Martin, he will meet you there at one o'clock."

"One o'clock. Thank you very much. I am sure I will find my way."

"Yes, I'm sure you will, Miss Martin."

There was a gap, a silence …

"Miss Martin," the voice flatly continued. "I know what is happening, so let me warn you. Edward will try and seduce you; he will consume you, because he knows he can."

There was emptiness, a shift, a missing frame …

"It is when he has finally captured you that he will try and make love to you, and he will fail, because he is impotent. He will then blame you and quickly lose interest in you, and then he will ultimately reject you. I know this to be true. You cannot win, Miss Martin."

There was a moment unsaid, an infinitesimal time unstated …

Eleanor gasped audibly. She was dumbfounded by what she was hearing. She was unable to reply.

.The voice continued, "Edward cannot accept failure, it is not in his nature, he always needs be right. Goodbye, Miss Martin."

Eleanor didn't have time to respond, she listened to the dismissive click on the other end of the line as the conversation was abruptly terminated. She clumsily replaced the receiver on its cradle, sipping her sherry and lighting a cigarette; she was feeling a little unstable.

*

Taking the Underground to Wapping, she walked the short distance to the Prospect of Whitby. It was a beautiful spring day, luminous green sprouts were thrusting their way through the rich black loam, sticky buds were unfolding on the tree branches, and starlings were twittering on the rooftops. There was a slight chill in the air, but people were eagerly sloughing off their winter greatcoats, in anticipation of warmer weather.

Script in hand, she entered the Prospect of Whitby from the street doors, and stepped into a very large, dark room. On three sides, through leaded windows, she could see the river Thames as it curved around Wapping Wall. The room was cluttered with shipboard paraphernalia; lanterns, wheels and rope. The long bar counter, with an unusual pewter top, had barrels built into it. There was a wealth of timber beams and dark wood panelling; the upright pillars looked to be sections of an actual ship's mast. The air was layered with blue tobacco smoke, the warm hum of conversation rose from the lunchtime crowd, and the fragrant aroma from an

Irish stew that had been gently simmering for hours, greeted her at the door. She loved the ambience of pubs.

On adapting to the dim light, her eyes searched the crowd for Edward Shafto; he was nowhere to be seen. Crossing the well-worn flagstone floor, she stepped out onto the terrace, which overlooked the Thames and the Isle of Dogs. The river traffic was light; a dirty British coaster was heading upstream towards West India Docks. Her attention was caught by a bulky Thames barge plying the river; its large red sail was luffing as it moved effortlessly with the downstream current. Seagulls were swirling in circles above, looking askance at her, whilst cruising for discarded scraps of food, their raucous and aggressive screeching, marking their territory.

At first, she thought that there was nobody on the terrace, and then she saw him sitting at the far end, at a table by himself. He was absorbed in his newspaper; a half-empty pint glass of beer was in front of him. He didn't see her at first, which gave her a chance to appraise him. He was dressed in a thick, greenish, Irish-tweed, three-piece suit with dark-brown, leather buttons. She watched him sipping his beer and lazily puffing on his pipe. Again, she noticed his relaxed, confident, almost glibly arrogant manner. She walked towards him, the syncopated click of her high heels on the flagstone attracting his attention. Looking up, he lazily smiled. Again, she was immediately drawn to his magnetic eyes. As she approached, he arose from his seat, and walking around the table, he graciously pulled out a chair, and with his eyebrows raised, he silently held the chair for her until she was seated. As he resumed his seat, she watched his elegant smile creasing the corners of his dark-blue eyes.

"Good of you to come, Eleanor."

She hadn't been aware of it before, but she now noticed, that he tended to clip his words when he spoke. He would precisely complete a word, before embarking on the next one, except, as she had previously noticed, on a word with a double vowel ending, which he would extend, until it decayed.

Nodding her head in a gesture of involuntary deference, she apologised. "I'm sorry if I have kept you waiting, Mr Shafto."

"Please, call me Edward. And no, you didn't keep me waiting; actually, I arrived a little early." Opening his arms in an expansive gesture to display their surroundings, he turned to look at her. "Do you approve?"

"Of the time, the place, or you, Edward?" She was surprised by her precociousness.

He chuckled and held her gaze. "Why? All three, of course."

She felt the hot flush of embarrassment rising in her cheeks. "Yes," she sighed ambiguously.

He beckoned the waiter, who had followed Eleanor out onto the terrace, and without asking her what she would like to drink, he ordered another pint for himself and a gin and Italian vermouth for her. She was about to protest, but was unable to formulate her thoughts.

Putting his pipe on the table, Edward announced. "Since it is such a wonderful day, I thought that it would be pleasant to eat outside, and what more appropriate a place to conduct business than the Devil's Tavern."

Before she could ask the question, he pedantically provided the answer. "That was the name of this place in the sixteenth century. There were many nefarious deeds planned here. In the eighteenth century, the present name, the Prospect of Whitby, was derived from a collier boat that brought down coals from Newcastle to the Wapping power station." The waiter, arrived with the drinks, timely interrupting the discourse, and then placing them on the table, silently withdrew. Edward raised his glass. "To our health!"

Remembering the recent telephone conversation with his secretary, she had the feeling that she was being drawn in by him, and yet, she wasn't resisting. Peering into the deep brightness of his stare, she acknowledged his toast, "Our health." Looking over the top of her glass, she nervously sipped her gin and It.

Putting his pint down, he enquired, "Now, where were we?"

"We were talking about the history of this pub." She was conscious that she had used the inclusive word, 'We'.

He was looking at her and still smiling. "Please forgive my ramblings, enough of my arcane banter, how about you Eleanor? How and what have you been doing since I last saw you?"

The gin and It was bringing a warm glow to her forehead, and as she slid back into her chair, she was beginning to feel a little more at ease. "Well as you know, I saw my agent, his name is Nate Schreiber." She searched his face for any sign of recognition, but it remained inscrutable. She saw that she had his full attention as he relit his pipe and cocked an eyebrow.

She didn't like to namedrop, but she wanted to impress him. "Have you ever been inside Nate's office?" Not waiting for an answer, she continued. "I do like his collection of Picasso and Dali prints, particularly the Picasso behind his desk, *La Mort d'Orphée*. I believe it is from his Blue period."

She noticed his back stiffening as he looked out at the river. He then drew on his pipe and leaned back in his chair. He turned his head towards her, in a patronising gesture. "No it isn't," he answered flatly, and lazily blew a billow of smoke across the table towards her. "Picasso's Blue period was at the turn of the century. *La Mort d'Orphée* is one of his most recent drawings, where we see him experimenting with Classicist Representational Surrealism. However, you may be forgiven for thinking that it was from his Blue period. Actually, *La Mort d'Orphée* is a pen and India ink drawing, on blue paper."

She shivered, and knew it was not from the cold. She felt humiliated. She felt so stupid. All she could say was "Oh!"

Edward leaned towards her and waved away the smoke, their faces were very close. She was acutely aware of his burning eyes; the other details of his face were relegated to a blur. He sat back again, smiling, she wasn't sure if he was trying to put her at ease, or belittle her as he asked, "And how was the audition? Are you up for any parts?"

Feeling the need to be on level ground with him, she tried to emulate his staccato pattern of speech, and answered rapidly, "Well, not actually. Nate doesn't have any immediate work for me. But, I did take the liberty to mention that you had asked if I would be interested in playing a role in your new play, *Escape to Nowhere*."

His eyes narrowed. With a circular motion of his finger, he signalled the waiter to bring another round. She wanted to protest, but she couldn't find the words, so she silently succumbed.

He put his pipe back on the table, and asked unemotionally, "Eleanor, *are* you interested in playing a part in my play?"

Her heart gave a little shudder. Was he actually asking her to play a role? She had to clearly understand what he meant. "Yes, Edward, I am very committed to playing a role in *Escape to Nowhere*. I have read the play twice and I think it is absolutely wonderful." She hoped she was not being too theatrical, at least she didn't tag on, "Darling".

He remained silent for a few moments, just staring at her with those deep, glinting eyes. She inwardly shrivelled in his light.

The drinks arrived, Edward nodded his acceptance, and the waiter reverentially retreated. Edward raised his glass in a silent toast.

She returned the gesture.

After drinking a large draught of beer, he wiped his lips on the back of his hand and continued. "And which part did you picture yourself playing?"

"Ruth," she replied immediately, feeling confident in her knowledge of the character. "I have an uncanny affinity towards her. I feel that Ruth escapes, from nowhere, only to find her self nowhere."

His smile was almost condescending. "I admire your ambition, my Dear, but I think you would be far more suited to the part of Dolly, the photographer's assistant."

Her shoulders momentarily slumped, then almost immediately, they straightened as she realised that he might actually be offering her a part in his play. She didn't want to jeopardise this opportunity, she would be thankful for any role. "That is very interesting, Mr Shafto. Why do you see me as Dolly?"

He silently mouthed the word "Edward" and leaned across the table, almost talking directly into her left ear, he spoke slowly and quietly. "I want you to play the part of Dolly, because I see her in you, and I see you in her. Like you and your relationship with your family and job, Dolly is incarcerated against her will, pleading sanity in an insane environment. And whilst desperately trying to hang on to her sanity, she gradually succumbs to the same environment which has imprisoned her, and eventually becomes the same as everyone else around her, insane."

Eleanor sharply withdrew her head. "Do you think I am insane, Mr Shafto?"

"Edward, please, I abhor formalities."

"Edward," she awkwardly whispered.

"I don't think you are insane in any clinical sense, my Dear, but I suspect that you *do* feel imprisoned by your life, and desperately want to break out, before you settle for the same, safe existence of those around you, who uncomplainingly and inevitably, meld into the commonplace and mundane."

She was overwhelmed by this man. In three short meetings, he had peeled back the guarded layers of her reserve, and now he was exposing her soul. She was afraid that she was on the brink of the breathtaking sublime, and despite her fear, she wanted to take the leap and fly, not caring if there was a safety net. His voice suddenly came into focus, he was saying; "…. after all, it is a personal choice. Nevertheless, to swim in the mainstream and choose run-of-the-mill insanity is the easiest way to go. Wouldn't you agree?"

Eleanor looked into his intense eyes. "Yes, Edward I agree. I didn't see it that way at first"

"I didn't expect you to, my Dear. It is easier for me, because I created the role, now I want you to play it. You are going to speak my words and take my direction. I am the playwright and you, my Dear, are the actress. Do you understand?"

"I understand," she said, not really understanding, or even caring if she would ever understand.

"Good," he said, raising his glass, "then it's settled. Eleanor Martin will play the role of Dolly, in Edward Shafto's production of *Escape to Nowhere*." Clinking his glass against hers, he toasted. "Let us drink to our success. Let us escape to nowhere."

She was flying. She was soaring. Standing and raising her glass, she answered his toast. "To our success! To our escape to nowhere!" She was also feeling a little unsteady, and she leaned forward on the table for support. Their faces were so close she could smell his maleness; he chuckled expectantly. She watched, as he slowly stood and laid his hands on her shoulders, and with gentle pressure, returned her to her seat. She was falling under the spell of this brilliant, man. She would surrender to him, and put herself in his guiding hands; she was losing herself, she was in need of him… The shrill, brittle blast of a passing tug snapped her out of her fantasy.

Looking at his watch, Edward exclaimed, "Tempus Fugit! We haven't even eaten lunch. Forgive me, Eleanor, would you like some lunch?"

"No thank you, Edward, for some reason I don't feel hungry."

They both smiled.

"Very well then," he rapidly concluded. "I'll pay the bill and we'll be off. My car is here, I'll drive you home."

He had made the decision and she was more than willing to abide by his wishes. She felt safe and protected; he was the director and she the actress. However, there were a couple of niggling points that were still irritating her. Gaining courage from the effects of the gin, she enquired, "Edward?"

"Yes, my Dear?" he said, gesturing to the waiter that he wanted the bill.

She was becoming comfortable with these little endearments, and felt secure in her enquiry. "I have one or two questions for you."

"I am not surprised," he chuckled, "but if they are about the play, could they possibly wait until later?"

"They don't exactly pertain to the play, but there are a few points that I would like to clear up."

"By all means," he said expansively, lounging in his chair and extending his arms with upturned palms, "be my guest."

"Well," she said tentatively, "they relate to your secretary."

He frowned and forced a slight smile as he drew a small, sharp intake of breath.

"When I phoned your secretary," Eleanor persisted, "she informed me that you already had my telephone number. I don't remember ever giving it to you."

His eyes widened with faux injury. Pulling a large, white five-pound note from his wallet, he said, "Please, forgive my presumptuousness, Eleanor, when I was in your room, I saw your telephone number on the telephone dial." He gave the money to the waiting waiter and the waiter retreated. "And the next question?"

"It's not exactly a question, but a comment. Maybe it is me being presumptuous, but, I did find your secretary's telephone manner a little unprofessional."

"In what way?"

"Well, she did seem a little too familiar, referring to you, her employer, as Edward, rather than, Mr Shafto."

He chuckled, as he slipped his wallet into the inside pocket of his jacket. "You will have to forgive Dorothy. You see, it wasn't my office you phoned, it was my house."

"She works out of your home?"

"Well, yes. She looks after all my appointments. You see, my Dear, she isn't actually my secretary *per se*, she's my wife."

They simultaneously arose from their seats and bluntly faced each other across the table; the challenge was reflected in their eyes. There was an aching moment of silence, before a sudden sharp, cold wind knifed off the surface of the river and cut between them.

"But you told me to phone your secretary." she said accusingly.

He was very matter-of-fact in his quiet response. "Knowing the attraction we have for each other, if I had asked you to phone my wife, would you have phoned?"

"I'm not sure," she mumbled. Despite his wife's warnings of his seduction, impotence, rejection, and the pathological need to be always right, she reluctantly decided to let the matter drop. However, she did feel cheated; there was a lot she didn't know about this man. But, what right did she have, demanding that he suddenly change his life, just for her? He had enunciated their mutual attraction, and he was right, she was attracted to him, yet he made her feel off balance. Nevertheless, it was the first time in her life that she felt extraordinary, and she liked the feeling.

'"Then I am right," he said, as he came around the table and took her arm, firmly guiding her towards the warm interior of the pub, where he intended to settle the bill and retrieve his change. "Don't worry, Eleanor, things have a way of working out for the better, just leave it to me."

Despite Dorothy's dire warnings, she felt that she had no choice; she was drowning, and he was her life raft.

In the wake of the departing couple, Old Father Thames kept rolling along, the crisp cold wind whipped up stinging spume; the screeching seagulls swooped down on the empty table, and were unrewarded.

*

During the next few months, *Escape to Nowhere* went into rehearsals, with Eleanor in the role of Dolly. In the late summer of 1935, the play opened at the Southampton Empire to an audience of forty-two, it was panned, royally. The local critics were unanimous in their condemnation of the writing, the directing, and the acting. The London papers didn't even bother to attend, nor did Nate Schreiber. It was a monumental, critical, and box-office flop; Edward decided to cut his losses and pay off the cast and crew. Needless to say, this was a bitter disappointment to Eleanor, whose one fleeting chance at fame and fortune was cruelly thwarted. However, Edward, having successfully lured his prey into his web, seemed to take the play's failure with remarkable equanimity, and immediately set to work on his next script. Perhaps, after all, he did not view *Escape to Nowhere* as a failure.

During the rehearsals of the play, Eleanor and Edward's intense attraction to each other became evident; they had fallen deeply in love, it became a symbiotic relationship; they needed each other. After the play had closed, he left his wife, Dorothy. Seeking anonymity, the love-struck couple decided to move away from London to the countryside. They bought a house in Wilmington, Kent, the Garden of England, and decided to raise a family; a decision that was frowned upon, by all who knew them, particularly as Edward was still married to Dorothy.

Eleanor was thirty-five when she lay with Edward for the first time. He was not a good lover; his potency lay in his verbal acumen. When Eleanor did eventually become pregnant, Edward was overjoyed with this minor miracle. He tried to obtain a divorce, but his estranged wife would have none of it. Bobby Shafto was predestined to be born a little bastard.

Chapter Six

THE MAGIC MAN

He arrived at their door, three days after Edward and Eleanor had moved in to 80 Warren Road, Wilmington. The property had been vacant for quite some time and the place was a shambles. The garden was a jungle of overgrown weeds and brambles, and the house was mildewed through neglect.

He was a transcendent creature, of an indeterminate age, with a large and solid frame. His face was craggy and weather-beaten. His head was graced by a shock of wild, flaming, red hair. She was drawn to his enigmatic eyes; each was of a different gem-like colour, like an odd eyed, white oriental cat. His right eye was the colour of lapis lazuli, and his left, the colour of turquoise; they sparkled over his high cheekbones, which hugged a pug nose that looked as though it had, at one time, been on the receiving end of a heavy blow. His well-defined and generous lips formed a ready smile. He wore his cloth cap like a crown, and as Eleanor opened the door, he removed it, swinging it in a wide arc to his side, in one fluid and graceful motion. Bowing his head, infinitesimally, he spoke to her. His voice washed over her like the gentle lapping of an incoming, summer tide on warm sand. "Good morning, Mum, I was wondering if you might have any work for me, in exchange for a meal."

She had heard about these tramps, who wandered the highways and byways of the English countryside. They were the mainstream's disillusioned and disenfranchised, who loved the freedom of life on the open road. They came from all walks of life, some out of economic necessity, and others by choice. They were the Tortoise subculture; everything they owned they carried on their backs, and they seemed to be in no hurry to get anywhere.

Eleanor took note of this romantically grizzled giant, enshrouded in his old naval duffel coat; she also noticed that the bottom toggle-loop was severed and hanging loose. Looking at him, she was reminded of the first stanza of Robert Louis Stevenson's poem, *The Vagabond*.

> *"Give to me the life I love,*
> *Let the lave go by me,*
> *Give the jolly heaven above*
> *And the byway nigh me.*
> *Bed in the bush with stars to see,*
> *Bread I dip in the river —*
> *There's the life for a man like me,*
> *There's the life for ever."*

Wiping her hands on her apron, she smiled politely at him, and hesitantly said, "Well, actually you might have come at an opportune time, as you can see, the house and garden are in a mess. We have just moved in, and it all seems a little overwhelming, I really don't know where to start."

He smiled reassuringly, "Well, Mum, if you give me the opportunity, I am sure we can straighten out this mess. I have a strong back and I enjoy physical work. Don't you worry, between you and me, we can get this garden ship-shape again."

She turned her head and looked back into the house towards the closed door of Edward's study, where she knew he was writing. "We could certainly use the help. Excuse me a moment won't you, whilst I consult with my husband?"

Cap in hand, he bowed slightly, 'Certainly, Mum, my name is Arthur Hobbs."

Eleanor smilingly nodded, "I'm pleased to meet you Mr Hobbs. I am Mrs Shafto." She felt a little twinge of guilt at her deceit, but Edward had insisted that they publicly present themselves as husband and wife… It would be too shameful to present to the community the image of living together out of wedlock, never mind the possibility of producing illegitimate children.

Leaving Arthur Hobbs on the threshold, she knocked on the study door and heard Edward's muffled reply. "Come."

She opened the door ajar, and poked her head inside. "May I come in, Dear; I would like to ask you something."

"Couldn't it wait, Dear, I am in the middle of a very important scene."

"Well, as you wish, Dear, but there's a man at the front door, who is looking for work, and we could certainly use the help."

"What sort of work?" Edward enquired.

"He said he'd be willing to get the garden shipshape, and you know what a mess it's in."

"Well, Dear, I just haven't had the time to work on it."

"I know, Dear, that's why I'm asking you. Mr Hobbs and I will do the work and you can continue writing."

"How much does Mr Hobbs want?"

"He says he is willing to work in exchange for meals."

"He is? Is he a tramp?"

"Yes, I think he might be, Dear. Would you like to meet him?"

"No, I really don't have time now. Why don't you put him to work, and I'll inspect what he's done at the end of the day. Then I'll decide if he continues, or not."

"Very well, Dear," she eagerly agreed, and closed the door firmly and quietly behind her.

*

After a full day's work of attacking the brambles and weeds in the overgrown kitchen garden, and on meeting Edward's approval, Eleanor invited Hobbs into the kitchen, where a pot of nourishing beef stew was simmering on the giant, black, cast-iron, Aga stove. Seating him at the huge scrubbed kitchen table, she served him a big bowl of beef stew, accompanied by doorsteps of freshly baked, warm, white bread, spread with melting, creamy butter. She poured two half-pint glasses of scrumpy, and putting one in front of him, joined him at the table. She silently watched, as he ravenously consumed his supper. He didn't say a word throughout the meal, for his mouth was always full.

After two bowls of stew, he wiped his mouth on his sleeve, and insatiably quaffed the half-pint of farmhouse cider. Emitting a little belch, he sheepishly glanced at her; she smiled and looked up at the ceiling in mock disapproval. She poured him another glass of scrumpy, and he sat back in his chair with a satisfied grin, he looked so relaxed and contented. They didn't speak for a few moments; the restful silence magnified the tiny ticking of the kitchen clock on the Welsh dresser.

He lifted his glass and sipped with satisfaction. "Thank you, Mum, I think that was the finest stew that I've ever tasted."

She could tell he really meant what he said, and she was immediately taken by his ingenuousness, she smiled in appreciation and felt a warm blush rising on her cheeks. Aware of her embarrassment, and needing to regain control of her emotions, she felt the need to distance herself from him. Pushing her chair back, she reached for his empty bowl, taking it to the sink and looking out of the window that faced the vegetable garden, she said, "Why thank you, Mr Hobbs, and you too have done a yeoman's job of clearing the kitchen garden."

"Thank you, Mum," he acknowledged with delicate humility. "Would you be wanting me to continue? I noticed that the rest of the grounds are in a fearful mess."

Her eyes pulled focus to his reflection in the window-pane, transmitting the mellow gold of the early evening light, which was washing over him like the subtle brush strokes of a Renaissance master. His odd-coloured eyes were changing their luminosity and hue as they reflected the ethereal rays of the setting sun. He looked surreal, an untouchable, a godlike figure. She was enchanted by him and knew that she wanted him to stay. "If my husband agrees, you are welcome to stay," she answered, perhaps, a little too eagerly. "I think we have lots of work for you. But, don't you have to move on?"

He sat at the kitchen table with such a childlike air of innocent self-possession. She watched his reflection slowly leaning forward, and she felt the warmth of his voice infusing her spine.

"Not really, Mum, I have no particular place to go, and I am in no particular hurry to get there."

She found Arthur Hobbs to be strangely disquieting; she was not accustomed to such unassuming gentleness. Yet, she must remember her station in life. Assertively folding her arms across her breasts, she turned to face him. Stabilising her buttocks against the edge of the cold ceramic tiles of the sink-surround, she self-importantly stated, "You are welcome to stay, Mr Hobbs, as long as there is work for you to do. Wait here whilst I talk to Mr Shafto," and putting the remains of the cider jug in front of him, she left him sitting at the kitchen table, silently satisfied.

*

Being thoroughly impressed by Hobbs' work, Edward agreed that he was definitely needed to maintain and improve the house and gardens. He offered him a small stipend and accommodation in the gatehouse, which Hobbs gratefully accepted.

After a month of tireless labour, the house and gardens were gradually returning to their former splendour. Hobbs had so endeared himself to Eleanor and Edward that they were reluctant to let him go. After all, they reasoned, they would need continuous help with the upkeep of the house and gardens… And so, the magic man remained.

Chapter Seven

Off Course

Edward, who spent most of his time in his study, writing, or painting, wasn't particularly suited to manual labour. Therefore, it was left to Eleanor and Hobbs to complete the reclamation of the house and garden. During those long, late summer months, they worked side by side, immersing themselves in the Zen of hard physical labour. She grew to love his company; they were totally at ease with each other and developed a close friendship. It was during this time, as is wont with newfound friends; they exchanged their deep and abiding confidences.

September was drawing to a close, the arc of the sun was tilting towards the north-west, a gentle breeze was freshening, puffy cumulus clouds were scudding across the bowl of the evening sky, and desiccated leaves were seesawing down to the warm earth.

Eleanor and Hobbs were seated in the garden, drinking their customary glass of scrumpy; it had become a ritual for them, a reward for a hard day's physical labour. In the soft glow of a late summer's evening, feeling the mellow relaxation of physical weariness, they shared their hopes for the future and their memories of the past. They were sitting on a voluminous car-blanket and lazily leaning against the grey dry-stone garden wall, the scrumpy was working its magic. She sensed that he wanted to unburden his thoughts; that he needed to talk.

Arthur refilled his glass and leaned back against the sun-soaked stone wall, grateful for its warmth penetrating his aching back. Looking into the glimmering gold of the setting sun, reflected off the windows of the house, he embarked on the story of his personal odyssey.

Eleanor stretched herself out on the blanket and closed her eyes, submitting to the caress of his soothing voice. Arthur related to Eleanor the long and winding path that brought him to her door.

"I was at sea for eighteen years. My last ship was the P&O liner RMS *Strathaird,* from which I was dishonourably discharged. It was a simple mistake that ended my career, but I understood the enormity of it."

She lay placidly quiet, listening to his voice and absorbing his words.

"I'd served aboard the *Strathaird* as a Quartermaster since her maiden voyage in nineteen-thirty-two. She was on the Australia run, calling at many ports en route, through the Mediterranean, the Suez Canal, the Red Sea, India, and Ceylon.

"From the very first trip, my shipmates nicknamed me, Archie, I never did quite understand why. I vaguely thought the name Archie was taken from some character in a book, but like a lot of words, the origin had faded with time. Suffice it to say, that on board the *Strathaird,* Arthur Hobbs's nickname, became Archie Hobbs."

She silently rolled the name around in her mouth; "Archie, Archie."

"My primary responsibilities as a Quartermaster were as a helmsman and lookout. On that fateful night that led to my dismissal, the ship was in the Indian Ocean, four and a half days out of Colombo, Ceylon, and bound for Fremantle, Australia, which we were scheduled to reach in two days. We expected to cross the Tropic of Capricorn about an hour into my watch. At eight bells, on the stroke of midnight, I relieved the wheel. I liked the ritual of taking over the helm as the bell was tolling; it was a comforting constant in a rapidly changing world. I received the course from the 8 to 12 helmsman.

"One-two-oh degrees, she's taking a little port helm"

"I repeated the course, "One-two-oh degrees," and then took over the wheel. He reported the course to the officer-of-the-watch in the chart room, and then went below.

"It was a warm night, with overcast skies, the ship was running before following seas, and there was virtually no wind. With the pad of my right thumb, I felt the familiar crisscross notch that was carved into the tip of the amidships spoke. I concentrated on the dim, green glow of the gyrocompass. As the degrees ticked slowly to starboard, I noticed she was yawing a little. I calculated that the sea was on the starboard quarter. With a half a turn of the wheel to port, I soon was able to bring her back on course. This seemed to correct her nicely. The ship's head would veer off to starboard, I'd give the wheel half a turn to port, hold it there until she'd start drifting back, then I'd let the wheel come back to the amidships position. She'd hold her course for a while, then she'd wander off to starboard again and I'd repeat the action. I soon settled into an easy and familiar rhythm.

"The Bridge-Wallah had gone below to make the second officer his tea. My watch-mate, Sid, was keeping lookout on the port wing of the bridge. Sid and I hadn't slept since the previous morning, preferring instead to have a few bevies, do our *dhobeying*, and write letters, in preparation for shore leave in Fremantle. I could see him pacing back and forth, trying to stay awake. He walked six paces, turned, and walked back six paces, maintaining the same repetitive, measured, and synchronized step, at the same monotonous speed.

"In that darkened wheelhouse, bathed in the hypnotic green glow of the gyrocompass, degree by degree, I felt the heaviness of fatigue weighing on my eyes. My thoughts drifted back to Janice in Sydney, the mother of my child; who would have been two years old then."

On hearing this revelation, Eleanor's eyes snapped open, and her stomach involuntary tightened, but she didn't interpose.

"Every three months, when the ship was in Sydney they'd come aboard for a visit. I remember how rejected I felt, when Janice married that sports reporter. She'd told him that she was determined that she didn't want to raise a child whose father was away all the time. She'd had a previous affair with another sailor that because of his continuous absence, ended up on the rocks. So, in a classic defensive manoeuvre, without letting me know that she was pregnant with our child, she broke off with me. The sports reporter, despite knowing that she was pregnant by another man, offered her a secure life in which to bring up her child."

"Oh no," Eleanor sympathetically sighed.

"Suddenly, I felt my knees give way, and I clutched onto the wheel for support; I realised that I had nodded off. I blinked rapidly, trying to refocus on the dull green glow of the gyrocompass. I noticed that the ship's head had drifted off a few degrees. I corrected the course and leaned back against the bulkhead, stiffening my knees for support. However, my thoughts inevitability returned to Janice.

"I was hurt when she told me of her plans to marry, but I wasn't prepared to protest her decision and swallow the anchor, for the sea was still my mistress."

A flicker of a smile played across Eleanor's lips; she was breathing easily.

"I felt the sudden strain on the back of my neck as my chin hit my chest. I instantly snapped my head back, banging it on the steel bulkhead behind me. A jagged pain shot through my head and I saw fierce flashes of burning white light. I stretched my eyes open wider and shook my head. However, in the dark silence of the wheelhouse, it didn't take long before I was floating back to Janice.

"When my daughter, Hope, was born, Janice wrote to me, telling me that I was the father, and would very much like to stay in touch. However, she remained adamant that she would not jeopardise Hope's security. She told me that at no time would I be allowed to meet her husband, or even know his name. This anonymity, she said, was essential. I had no choice but to agree with her terms. I reasoned that at least this arrangement would allow me to see Janice and Hope periodically; I was looking forward to seeing them again."

Eleanor stared up at the cool, pink-tinted clouds, not understanding the red-hot stab of jealousy that pierced her.

"Gradually, I became aware of the rapid ticking of the gyrocompass as the ship's head swung to starboard. Through the open door of the wheelhouse, I could feel the warm tropic wind on my cheek; the sea was now on the starboard beam. I quickly gave her port wheel and brought her back on course. I had barely completed the adjustment, when the Second Officer emerged from the chartroom to check the course. Being satisfied it was correct, he strode out to the starboard wing of the bridge, where he stared into the blind blackness of the night, and then returned to the chartroom and his tea.

"I was becoming mesmerised by the green glow of the compass; I squinted and blinked, trying to focus on the blurred degrees. I shook my head and stretched my unco-operative eyes open even wider; I was exhausted.

"My thoughts drifted back to the time, when Janice and I first met; it was just after New Year, on a warm summer's night. I was on gangway duty, on 'A' deck, and it was close to midnight. I saw her gliding along the upper level of the wharf, towards the gangway; she was floating through the pools of floodlight that washed over her. I was instantly captivated by the fluid way she moved; she looked so allur-ing, I almost shot out of my body. I guessed that she would be about thirty years old; I was fifty at the time."

Eleanor rolled onto her side to face him; the sun's reflec-tion was bouncing off her bedroom window. She became aware of the golden light glinting in his odd-coloured, lu-minous eyes; it was as though they were on fire.

"As Janice climbed the gangway, her simple, loose, white cotton dress played around the contours of her body. Her jet-black hair bounced off her bare shoulders. She smiled, her generous lips revealing strong white teeth. Even in the dim wash of the floodlights, I could see that her skin was tanned and she absolutely glowed with vitality. Her feet were shod in brown leather sandals, and as she walked, with each step, her hips would rhythmically thrust forward. The only adornments gracing her body were a thin silver chain around her neck, complemented by another silver chain encircling her right ankle. All this, I noticed in the short time it took for her to approach the gangway and reach me at the top.

"G'day mate" she drawled. "May I come aboard?"

"She wore no makeup, except on her full lips and around her dark-brown eyes, which at this point were shining right at me, in what I interpreted as appreciation; I felt I had never been appraised quite so candidly before.

"Looking directly into those captivating green-flecked eyes, I felt I was blushing. "Welcome aboard, Miss, do you have a pass?"

"No, mate, I don't," she sighed and looked away. I thought I saw a teasing smile playing around her mouth as she asked, "Do I really need one?"

"Well yes, I'm afraid you do," I mumbled. Not wanting her to walk away, I hurriedly asked, "Who are you visiting? Perhaps I could let them know you are here."

"She leaned back against the wooden top-rail and hooked her left foot on the lowest rail. Her tanned knee disappeared from view beneath the hem of her white, cotton dress, giving the illusion of her only having one leg, and accentuating the silver chain encircling her remaining ankle. Her elbows were propped on the wooden top-rail, which tightened her dress over her full breasts; I was entranced. She tilted her head back, exposing the long, smooth, vulnerable line of her throat, and slowly turned her head to look at me, directly in my eyes. She opened her mouth and silently held it open for a few tantalising seconds, before saying, "I'm not visiting anybody mate, I'd just like to be shown around the ship." Meeting my approving eyes, she asked candidly. "Maybe you could do me the honour?"

Eleanor rolled away from him, onto her other side, and watched a Red Admiral butterfly resting on a long, thick, blade of grass. It delicately and rapidly opened and closed its wings, like the seductive flutter of come-hither eyelashes. .She smiled wanly.

"I was taken aback. Here was this magnificent woman standing before me, calmly asking me to escort her around the ship; how could I resist? "I'd love that," I said, smiling broadly. "I'll be off duty in ten minutes, if you can wait that long, I would be honoured to give you a tour."

"She laughed huskily. "Fair dinkum?" she asked. "That would be bonzer." At that supernatural moment, I was captured, hogtied, and helpless; I felt I would go to the ends of the earth for her. We chatted aimlessly for the next ten minutes, and when I was relieved of the watch at midnight, we embarked on the tour of the vessel.

"As she walked beside me along the deck, I felt her powerful magnetism; the hairs on my arm stood erect, and my loins stirred, I shuddered with erotic pleasure. Even now, I can still recall that feeling."

Eleanor watched the Red Admiral gracefully unfold its wings to reveal the full spectrum of its rich colours.

"We conversed comfortably, but it wasn't until about an hour later, when we were back at the gangway, that we actually introduced ourselves. I took her hand to help her up the step, and I couldn't let go."

"Ta, very much, sailor, what's your name?" she drawled.

"Archie." I announced eagerly. "And yours?"

"Janice" she replied with a radiant smile.

"Janice." I smiled. "Janice." I smiled again. It's difficult not to say Janice without smiling."

Eleanor silently mouthed the name, but her smile was cold.

"Well Archie," Janice said, "I really enjoyed the tour, and I'd like to return the favour sometime. Maybe I could show you around Sydney."

I smiled expectantly. "I'd like that, Janice." I was still holding her hand and beaming like a love-struck fool, which I was.

"She laughed, "Well, how about right now mate?"

"Now?" I exhaled.

"Yeh, now, abso-bloody-lutely, let's go to Bondi Beach, it's really bonzer on a hot night like this." She executed a graceful pirouette; her thin cotton dress billowing out to expose her naked thighs. "Well, do you want to come?" she teased.

"I caught the *double entendre*. Her smile engulfed me. "Of course I do, let's go." Without bothering to change into civvies, I stepped up to join her, and hand in hand, we blissfully strolled down the gangway on our way to Bondi Beach."

Eleanor watched as the Red Admiral cast off its moorings and took to the air; fluttering skyward into nothingness. Where the butterfly had rested, she reached over, slid out the long blade of grass from its slippery sheath, and placed it between her teeth.

"Under the Southern Cross, laying on a blanket, stretched out on the warm sand, the waves gently rolling in, and sublimely entwined; we embraced. We didn't speak a word; all that we could hear was the gentle growling of waves on the soft sand, and the sweet sighing sensualness of our own desire. I became intoxicated with the natural scent of her body."

Eleanor held the long, juicy stem of grass between her teeth, and closing her eyes, she softly sucked its sweetness.

"Under her loose dress, my hand traced the silky contours of her body. I tasted her moist and giving lips, and felt the fullness of her breasts and the hardness of their nipples. I tenderly stroked the insides of her smooth, bare thighs and the two joined fingers of my right hand, gently and firmly entered her; she gasped and inhaled sharply. As our breathing quickened, I felt the uncontrollable surging waves of passion, coursing through me, and I erupted."

Eleanor was becoming perturbed by his unvarnished frankness, she was not used to hearing revelations of such intimate detail, but, at the same time, she wanted him to continue. She spat out the blade of grass and turned again to lie on her back. She closed her eyes tightly, and surrendered to the images of tiny, white, irregular shapes, floating over a dark, velvet-red background. Her breathing deepened.

"My body convulsed, and my eyes quickly refocused to see that the ship was rolling heavily. A storm had erupted, and the seas were pushing in on the port beam. I was leaning heavily on the wheel, and quickly released it; it whirred back to the amidships position. I stared, with wide-eyed panic, into the accusing green eye of the gyrocompass. I saw that the ship had drifted far off course, so I quickly spun the wheel three complete turns to port, to bring the ship's head around to oh-two-oh degrees. I steadied her on that course. The wind had freshened and the seas were now leaning on her port bow. I wondered how long I had been asleep.

"The Second Mate marched out from the chartroom. "The wind is rising, Hobbs. Hold your course."

"Aye aye, sir." I was thankful that I was back in control.

"For the next hour and a half I held the ship's head steady. When Sid came to relieve me, at 0200 hrs, I gave him the course. "Oh-two-oh, Sid. The seas are on the port bow." He thanked me and repeated the compass bearing. I then went in to the chart room to report the course to the officer-of-the-watch. "Course, oh-two-oh, sir." Stirring his tea, whilst scanning an old London newspaper, he replied, "Oh-two-oh. Thank you, Hobbs."

"I went out to the port wing of the bridge to take up my post on lookout duty. I had just stepped out onto the open deck, when I heard an almighty bellow erupting from the chartroom.

"Hobbs, get back here, on the double."

"Yes, sir," I yelled, rapidly retracing my steps. I saw the Second Officer bent over the chart-table with pencil, dividers, and parallel rulers, in hand.

"What course did you say?" he asked, in a quiet and tensely controlled tone.

"Oh-two-oh, sir" I sharply replied.

"You blithering idiot," he roared, his face reddening, the veins standing out on either side of his forehead, "you have put the ship one hundred degrees off course. How bloody long were you steering oh-two-oh?"

"He made a short threatening step towards me, and I started to back away.

"Stand still when I'm fucking talking to you; you worse than useless piece of shit."

Hobbs was suddenly aware of what he had just said. "Excuse the language, Mum, it just slipped out."

Her eyes had snapped open on hearing his salty dialogue. "That's all right Hobbs, I am quite enjoying the story, please go on."

"Very well, Mum. Well, after he swore at me, he thrust his bespittled face into mine, until our moist and nervous noses were almost touching. Then he shouted, "I am asking you a question sailor. How long were you steering that course?"

"I really don't know, sir, I am very sorry," I stammered.

"The Second Officer strode back to the chart table and slammed his fist hard down on the approximate position where he thought the ship should be. "Sorry?" he bellowed, "is that all you can say? I promise you this, Hobbs; I am going to make sure that you bloody well will be sorry." Turning his back on me, he yelled, "Now get the fuck out of my wheelhouse."

Hobbs gave a quick sidelong glance of apology to Eleanor, but she didn't seem to notice, so he continued.

"I was shaking as I slithered out to the wing of the bridge. I heard the Second Mate giving the course to Sid at the wheel. "Starboard easy, to one-two-five, Quartermaster.""

"Aye aye, sir, one-two-five," Sid replied.

"The ship's head swung to starboard. I could hear the steady ticking of the gyrocompass as it described the arc of degrees, until the wind and the sea had died down and the corrected compass bearing had been reached. She was on course, with a following sea, heading for Fremantle.

"It wasn't until two hours later, when the clouds started to dissipate and the heavens were visible, that the First Officer, on the four-to-eight watch, was able to triangulate the stars with the horizon. He then calculated the ship's position on the chart, and found that I had put the ship sixteen miles east, and thirty miles astern of the position she should have been in. We had crossed the Tropic of Capricorn three times in the space of four hours.

"I was brought up in front of the Captain at 0800 hours. As a result, I was banished from the bridge and relegated to day duties; polishing brightwork and splicing ropes. I was told that on the ship's return to London, I would receive a dishonourable discharge. I was well aware of the possible implications of my error, and I felt fortunate that the ship was in the open ocean, with no obstructions in her path. To this day, I shudder to think of the possible consequences, if we had been closer to land.

"We reached Fremantle half a day behind schedule. Arriving in Sydney, I met Janice and Hope. I told Janice the disastrous news, and paid my sorrowful farewell to them. I promised them that one day I would return. As a parting memento, I gave Janice a Siamese-silver locket, with my picture inside, that I'd had crafted for her in Colombo. It was an oblong shape, and on the surface was a delicate engraving of an open hand, with the two middle fingers joined together. Janice gave me a photo of herself and Hope. This, I put into my wallet, vowing to carry it with me to my dying day."

Eleanor was wrenched out of her dream-like state; she sat bolt upright and turned to Hobbs. "What was the meaning of that engraving?"

Hobbs lifted both of his hands and spread his fingers, accentuating the two middle fingers of each hand, which were joined. "Because I have webbed fingers."

She exhaled a long and diminishing sigh. "I see. I have never noticed them before." Her gaze lingered on his webbed hands.

Hobbs continued with his narrative. "At the end of the voyage, at Tilbury docks, I was given a dishonourable discharge. I couldn't go back to sea again; I was too ashamed. I decided to swallow the anchor and seek employment as far inland as I could go. Archie relinquished his shipboard nickname and returned to being Arthur again. That was when I decided to become a tramp and travel the open road; and as the Fates would have it, I arrived on your doorstep."

Despite, or because of, those strange, indefinable stirrings within her, Eleanor had been held spellbound by his narrative. She had, never before, met anyone like him; he was so open, so honest, so ingenuous; he was the total antithesis of Edward. She found Arthur Hobbs to be a very enigmatic man. "Do you still have that photograph, Arthur?" She was conscious that this was the first time she had addressed him by his first name; it seemed to come so naturally to her.

"Yes I do, Mum," he answered, as he reached for his wallet and withdrew a folded photograph, which he silently passed to her.

Looking at the black-and-white picture of Janice and Hope standing hand in hand under a eucalyptus tree, made her catch her breath; they looked so happy together. Janice was exactly as Hobbs had described; she looked strong, vibrant, and very beautiful; she glowed with pride. However, it was the picture of Hope that melted her heart; the little girl in the photograph had wavy black hair, just like her mother's, she wore a light print frock, and was looking up at her mother with a wide, adoring smile, her eyes were shining, and Eleanor could discern the high cheekbones of Hobbs in her face. As Hope held her mother's hand, Eleanor looked for, but couldn't see any webbed fingers. She felt her bottom lip trembling. "Oh! Arthur, Hope is so beautiful, she's such a darling." She passed the photograph back to him and was surprised to see her hand shaking; she couldn't understand her agitation. To control the shaking, she folded her arms across her breasts, and said softly, "I would love to have a child like Hope."

Tenderly putting his arm around her shoulders, Arthur murmured, "Maybe you will, Mum, maybe you will."

She looked up at his gentle face, and blinking rapidly, she felt her eyes moisten.

The late summer sun was setting, the shadows were lengthening, the breeze was freshening and scattering golden leaves about them. In the shadow of the grey, stone wall, she felt the chill of the approaching evening. He moved closer to her and protectively drew the blanket over them. She rested her head on his shoulder and was comforted.

*

Her eyes mist over with the memories of those loving and happy times. Outside her bedroom window, the sun has reached its zenith, and all activity has come to rest. The birds and animals are silent, Hobbs has vacated the garden, Edward has sullenly retreated to his study, and Bobby is sleeping, his wide-open eyes still fixed on the web.

Chapter Eight

A SHIMMERING ANGEL

At the age of three, Bobby has grown to a height of twenty-seven inches, and weighs twenty-two pounds. It is a warm summer's day; Edward and Eleanor are relaxing on the terrace, in their green and white, striped, canvas deck chairs, enjoying their afternoon gin and It. He is reading his newspaper, and she is looking at Hobbs the gardener, who is vigorously cranking the handle of the garden pump. The water is spurting spasmodically into a large rubber wading pool, where Bobby is naked, and gleefully splashing about in the half-filled pool, encouraging Hobbs to pump as hard as he can.

"More, Hobbs, more, faster, faster."

Hobbs is laughing. "I'm going as fast as I can, Master Bobby. My arms are turning to Jelly."

Bobby giggles. "You're funny, Hobbs." As the water level rises, Bobby lifts his feet from the bottom of the pool. Floating freely, he starts to doggy-paddle, whilst yelling, "Fill it all the way up, Hobbs."

Eleanor, who is watching Bobby revelling in the exuberance of the living, is sadly reminded of Bunny, her unbegotten son. She is also afraid that Bobby is out of his depth in the pool, and yet, he is so unafraid. When the water rises to about six inches from the lip of the pool, she intervenes. "That's enough, Hobbs; I think that is quite deep enough."

"Oh no, Mummy, please, I like it deep," shrieks Bobby, as he gleefully doggy-paddles around the pool.

"No Bobby. I said that is deep enough." She looks sternly at Hobbs and rebukes him. "Hobbs!"

Hobbs dutifully stops pumping. "Very well, Mum, I will be in the kitchen garden if you require me."

She watches his familiar rolling sailor's gait as he ambles away.

Bobby shouts. "Thank you, Hobbs." He takes to the water like an aquatic mammal, his webbed hands, propelling him with impressive agility around the pool. Glancing up at his mummy for approval, he sees that she is smiling back at him. Growing tired of swimming, he stands up in the pool, the water coming up to his chin; level with his eyes. He can see his little toy boat that Hobbs has carved for him, bobbing peacefully on the surface of the water. With both hands, he pushes mighty waves towards the tiny craft, which immediately pitches and rolls under the onslaught of the rough seas. Cupping his hands, he scoops up the water to rain heavily down on the beleaguered vessel. He smacks his hands hard on the water's surface, creating loud and sharp thunderclaps. He swirls his arms around the tiny boat, conjuring up a ferocious storm that threatens to sink the little ship, causing it to roll dangerously on its side. For a lingering moment, its funnel dips precariously into the rough waters, before rolling back onto an even keel. Again and again, the little craft heroically defies Neptune's wrath, and no matter how big a storm Bobby creates, the intrepid little boat stays afloat. He shouts with delight and wonder, "Look, Mummy, I made a big storm and the boat didn't even sink."

Reaching for a towel, she smiles, "That's very clever, Darling, now out you get, I think you've been in the water long enough."

"No I haven't, Mummy," he protests.

"You must be getting tired, Darling; I think its time for you to come out."

"No, please, Mummy, just a few more minutes."

"Bobby, if you stay in any longer, you will shrivel up and look like a prune."

"You're funny, Mummy," he laughs.

"Come along, Darling, it's time for your afternoon nap."

"Please, Mummy, I don't feel tired. I promise I won't swim I'll just float. Please! Please!"

She hesitates. "I don't know if your father would approve." Looking towards Edward, she enquires, "What do you think, Daddy, is it all right if he stays in a few more minutes?"

Edward decisively turns the page, and shaking out the paper, he gruffly replies, "I don't see what harm it can do the boy." He then carries on reading his newspaper.

She sighs in resignation and capitulates, "Well, just a few more minutes then, Bobby."

"Thank you, Daddy," shrieks Bobby, in delight. Floating face down in the water, with his long flaxen hair flowing like kelp in a tide pool, he becomes engrossed and fascinated by the appearance of a shimmering angel, surrounded by a circle of liquid light, which, he assumes, is formed by the sun's rays reflecting off the bottom of the pool.

He must have been floating in this position for quite a long time, for eventually; he feels the need for air. He tries to roll over, but is unable to do so; he is finding it difficult to hold his breath. Through the water, he can faintly hear the muffled conversation between his mummy and daddy.

Her voice is rising as she says, "Edward, he has been in that position for too long. Do you think he is all right?"

He hears his father's barely audible reply. "Of course he is all right. He's a born water-baby, look."

Bobby feels the pressure of his father's determined finger pushing on the small of his back, slowly submerging him until he is half floating like a waterlogged log. His chest is tightening, and he starts to panic, anxiously trying to gurgle for help.

With bubbles bursting around his ears, he hears his father's barely audible laughter. "Look, Dear, he is fine. He loves the water. He loves it so much, he won't get out."

He hears his mother pleading. "Please be careful, Dear. I think he has had enough."

Daddy's voice Is expressionless. "Don't worry; he will come up for air when he is good and ready."

Bobby's ears are popping, his head is screaming, and his lungs are exploding; the living light of day is dying. Transcending the element of water, he feels the whole universe turning, and except for a constant, rhythmic pulse, the cosmos becomes quiet and dark. He is a luminescent body suspended in a warm, opalescent liquid mass. As he is floating, he is aware of the powerful, agitated presence of another suspended self. Suddenly, they are being violently pushed through a narrow tunnel. The walls are convulsively expanding and contracting, and propelling them towards a blinding, white light.

He hears the garbled and panicky voices of his mother and Hobbs shouting from a long way away. He feels the tremor of hurriedly approaching footsteps, and the voice of Hobbs anxiously calling,

"Sir, sir, leave him alone, you're drowning him, stand back sir, I said stand back."

Bobby hears his father's distorted laughter. Suddenly his body jerks into volatile spasms, as he is flipped onto his back. Turning his gasping and contorted face towards the blessed light of the heavens, he frantically sucks in the god-given air, and feels the great, strong hands of Hobbs, tenderly lifting him out of the unholy water. He sees his father's unsmiling face, morphing into a primitive mask. Dry eyed, Bobby stares accusingly at his father, a long, cold, hard stare.

Hobbs gently stands him up, engulfing him in a huge towel. Bobby feels the soft grass beneath him; he is relieved to be standing on the firm earth once more. Hobbs towels him off, and briskly massages him, until his skin is tingling and he feels the welcome warmth radiating throughout his tiny body. Wrapping him in the towel, Hobbs pats him firmly on his back. "Come along, Master Bobby, you'll be fine now. You've just swallowed a little water, that's all."

Bobby tastes the bitter bile rising; it is as though a dragon has spat in his throat. His stomach immediately erupts, and he violently vomits, water gushes out, like a torrent through the mouth of a hideous gargoyle. From his rancid mouth pours forth a dark and terrible voice, it comes from time beyond time, those awful, supernatural screams, are streaking skyward.

"Father do not look to do harm to your son, for you will do harm to me. I, your son, exist within your son, and he exists within me, we are identical twins, we are indivisible. Remember that your son, who is within your son, continues to be your son. Remember that there is still life. Be aware."

Bobby is terrified and trembling, "Who are you?" he screams.

"It is all right Bobby. It is I, your identical twin brother, Bunny. I am within you. I am your other self. You are twice born."

Bobby is still shaking; he is alarmed and bewildered. He watches the colour draining from his father's warped face. He hears his mother's frightened whimper. He looks up to Hobbs, who remains strangely impassive. Cradling Bobby in his mighty arms, Hobbs carries him into the house, gently laying him on clean white sheets, and watches over him as he shudders into a wide-eyed sleep.

At the poolside, Eleanor arises and silently follows in the shadow of the departing Hobbs. She was witness to Edward's cruelty. She knows that he feels he was denied his perfect family, two whole and healthy boys, and a loving wife. She knows that as long as Edward is alive, he will never forgive her and this tiny, flawed child, for the strangulation of his stillborn twin brother. Edward's torment is palpable, and she feels it deeply. She cannot trust herself to speak, for she knows that anything she says will be curtly dismissed. He makes her feel guilty, yet her compassion and love for him still remains undaunted. She is unable to give voice to her tangled emotions. For some indefinable reason, she still feels magnetically drawn to this man; she just can't help herself. Her overwhelming need for him cannot be denied. She loves him, unhappily, too much.

Chapter Nine

INFERNOS PLUMMETING OUT OF THE SKY

Four years have passed since that fateful day of Bobby Shafto's emergence into this irrational world. He now stands thirty inches and weighs twenty-six pounds.

It is at the height of the Blitz, in early May, 1941. Every night, massive formations of German planes pass over the house, on their way to bomb the pockmarked face of London. Sometimes, a stray incendiary bomb would fall, let go too soon, like a wayward teen, to wreak minor havoc on the unsuspecting countryside.

In his own little air-raid shelter, under the kitchen sink, Bobby is falling into an unblinking wide-eyed sleep as he listens to the voice of Churchill on the wireless, urging the British people to hold out against the "*Naahhzies.*"

Bobby is rudely awakened by the wailing of the air raid siren, at the Vickers Armament factory on Powder Mill Lane, about half a mile away. He scuttles over to the window, carefully peeling back a corner of the blackout curtain, and peers into the cosmic blackness. He looks in wonder at the bright, stabbing, beams of the searchlights, scouring the night-sky for enemy planes. He hears the droning of the massive bombers passing overhead, and as the sound of their mighty engines disappear into the darkness, he is suddenly blinded by a brilliant burst of flames at the bottom of the driveway. Blinking rapidly he recovers his sight and shouts in alarm, "Daddy, Mummy, the driveway is on fire."

Behind him, he hears his father yelling. "Bobby, get away from that window, at once." His father's hand tightens around his arm and he is spun around forcefully. Both of his arms are held in an iron grip as he is frenziedly shaken, over and over again; his head uncontrollably bobbing back and forth like a rag-doll.

"Don't you ever do that again," his father is yelling. "What did I tell you about looking out of the window at night?"

Bobby, knowing he has broken the rules, doesn't answer, and it takes all of his control to stop his mouth quivering.

The shaking stops. "Well? Well?" his father yells, "Answer me when I ask you a question."

Bobby's arms are hurting from the tightness of his father's grip, he is too afraid to speak.

His father keeps on shouting. "Because the bloody German planes will see you and drop a bomb on you. Can't you ever get that through your thick skull?" He is on his knees, rapping his knuckles painfully on the top of Bobby's head, who is still unable to speak. Their faces are very close, he notices how red his father's face is getting, and he smells whisky on his breath. Then he hears the long steady note of the air-raid siren, signalling the 'all clear'.

His father relaxes his grip and tersely instructs mummy, "Now get the child dressed and help us put out the fire."

Bobby is pushed roughly across the kitchen floor. With quick, jerky little steps, he stumbles forward, and his face crumples.

Mummy puts her arms around him, making shushing sounds, whilst gently patting him on the back. "There,

there, darling, Daddy didn't mean to shout at you, he just wanted you to be safe." Bobby knew he only felt safe in his mummy's arms.

Switching out the light, his father stomps out of the kitchen and through the front door. By the light of a torch, his mummy bends down on one knee, to put on his Wellingtons, he lifts his leg and extends his arms, reaching for her shoulders. "Now put on your dressing gown and we will go and help Daddy put out the fire," she smiles at him and wipes away his tears with the soft pads of her thumbs, "now there's a brave soldier," he smiles bravely. Clad only in his pyjamas, dressing gown and gumboots, and carrying his Mickey Mouse gas mask in its brown cardboard box, he reaches for his mummy's hand, and together they leave the house.

When they arrive at the conflagration, Hobbs is wheel-barrowing sand to the blazing incendiary bomb; luckily, the fire has not spread. Bobby watches as his mummy and daddy heap on the sand. Bobby is transfixed by the fiery spectacle, and giddily running up and down the driveway, he feels a surge of energy generating wild and thunderous whoops of excitement. He senses Bunny's commanding power stirring within him; he is powerless to stop the con-voluted *Bunnybabble*.

"Sand and fire, fire and water, rain the reign of destruction and devastation. Infernos plummeting out of the sky, plunging down to earth. Tiny humans defy-ing the gods, wretched bones and flesh at the mercy of the supreme ironies. Out of the wet, warm wombs of women, emerge frail and vulnerable creatures; maggots , hairless, no scales, no armour, thinking, always thinking, defying instinct, inventing lamenting, struggling to draw

breath, vaingloriously trying to conquer the natural with the unnatural. They are doomed to fearfully crawl back to their cold caves and die as maggots die; reviled and forever forgotten."

The grownups don't seem to notice Bunny's outburst, as they are still concentrating on the daunting task of putting out the flames. Bobby is afraid no longer, he is happy that Bunny is still within him. Although he doesn't understand all that Bunny is saying, he is thankful that his twin brother still exists.

Bobby watches Hobbs transporting the sand and giving encouragement, letting Mummy and Daddy be the heroes. He notices that Hobbs stays in the background throughout the whole performance; being a perfect member of the supporting cast.

After the fire is out, he stands in the newly ruined driveway, watching as Hobbs makes a point of respectfully shaking his father's hand, looking him straight in the eye, and congratulating him on his performance. "Well done, sir," was all Hobbs said.

His father, meeting Hobbs's magnificent gaze, acknowledges his support. "We couldn't have done it without you, Hobbs."

His father's attitude towards Hobbs is distant, yet respectful; there is a slight chill between them, it is not really coldness, but more like air-conditioning on a hot summer's day, a comfort zone.

The sky is beginning to brighten. In the east, Bobby sees the first red glow of dawn creeping over the treetops. He gleefully shouts, "Mummy, it's morning now. May I stay and help Hobbs clear up?"

"No you may not, young man," commands his father, "I want you to come back to bed." He stiffly reaches out for Bobby's hand, and Mummy holds his other hand; he is warmed by her gentle touch.

Smiling lovingly at him, she says, "Yes, darling, a good soldier needs his sleep." Hand in hand, they walk towards the house, congratulating themselves on a good night's work.

*

Bobby's bedroom is situated at the front of the house. For a long time he lies on his bed, staring at the ceiling of the darkened room, listening to the scraping sounds of Hobbs clearing the driveway. He is finding it difficult to fall asleep. After a while, he hears the unmistakable, slow shuffle of his father's footsteps, climbing the stairs and walking down the hall towards his bedroom. Bobby pulls the covers up to his chin. The footsteps stop outside his door and hesitate, and then the door is opened, slowly. His father shines his torch towards the bed into Bobby's wide-open eyes. There is a moment's silence, and then Bobby hears his father whispering.

"Bobby? Are you awake?"

He doesn't reply, he hopes that his father thinks that he is asleep. He lay still, his wide-open eyes staring at the ceiling. His father clicks off the torch, and in the dark, he speaks in a way that Bobby has never heard before; his voice is unusually gentle and soft.

"*Good night, sweet prince.*
And flights of angels sing thee to thy rest!"

Then he quietly closes the door, and softly shuffles back along the hallway and down the stairs.

Bobby lies there, not really knowing if he is asleep or awake. Remembering the warm moments with his father, he blinks. It seems like half a lifetime ago. He was in his pyjamas; Mummy was carrying him in her arms as Daddy came out of the bathroom, holding a straight razor in his hand. He was white bearded with shaving cream, and laughingly he kissed Bobby good night, eliciting from him squeals of delight as he felt his father's bristled stubble through the soapy suds on their cheeks. Exhilarating in the clownish mess of their faces, they both wallowed in that rare and touching moment.

Seared into his sensory recall is the rich aroma of pipe tobacco, the masculine smell of sweat, the cultured, well-modulated voice, the sparsely populated crown, and the gigantic stride that measured his father's emotional distance.

Chapter Ten

A CONSCIENTIOUS OBJECTOR

Breaking glass shatters the silence. Bobby, jumping out of bed and running to the window, cautiously pulls back the long, blackout curtains. Instantly, daylight dances past him and crowds the darkened room. He squints into the bright light and looks down the driveway towards the gatehouse. In the morning sunlight, he sees Hobbs bent over, picking up broken glass. Putting on his sandals and wearing only his shorts and under-vest, Bobby quietly tiptoes downstairs, out of the front door, and into the radiant morning light, as he skips gleefully down the driveway to greet Hobbs. By the time he arrives at the gatehouse, Hobbs is sitting on the bench, opening a bottle of beer.

"Hello, Hobbs," greets Bobby, standing back a respectful distance. "What was that noise?"

"Oh! Hello, Master Bobby, I thought you were having a nap."

"I couldn't sleep, and I heard glass breaking, so I came to see what it was."

"I dropped an empty bottle, I'm sorry if it disturbed you."

"That's all right. I would rather talk to you anyway."

"Well, I like talking to you too, Bobby. Would you like some lemonade?"

"Oh! Yes please, Hobbs."

"Come, sit down here and I'll get a glass."

Bobby sits down on the bench, swinging his legs and humming out of tune. Very soon, Hobbs returns with a glass, into which he pours some clear and fizzy lemonade. Bobby bends his face over the rim of the glass, delighting in the sensation of the bubbles dancing off his cheeks and spurting up his nose. The remainder of the bottle, Hobbs pours into his beer to make a shandy, he then puts the bottle down next to three other empty beer bottles. In the warmth of the morning sun, and each other's company, they sit in silence. In time, Hobbs begins to speak, his words are slightly slurred.

"I think your mummy and daddy did a sterling job in putting out the fire from the incendiary bomb."

"So did you, Hobbs."

"Thank you, Master Bobby."

They fall silent again. Bobby feels very close to Hobbs; he doesn't feel the need to speak, just being together is enough. Sipping his lemonade, he stares over his glass observing the gentle giant.

Hobbs, sensing he is being watched, turns to look at him. "What are you thinking, Bobby?" Hobbs has one of those *outside* voices, a voice that seems to come from a great distance, from the other side of yesterday.

"Oh nothing much, Hobbs," Bobby mumbles, but he *is* thinking. He is thinking of how he loves to listen to those wondrous tales that Hobbs would spin; mighty tales of creation, destruction, devastation, and resurrection, epic tales of the gargantuan creatures of the oceans, of colossal animals, of mighty gods and heroic mortals, universal tales of birth, of life, of death, and rebirth, and astonishing tales of the dark, energetic, and endless universe. Bobby knows that Hobbs is a magic man. He drains the last drop of lemonade from his glass.

"Would you like some more, Bobby?"

"No thank you, Hobbs, but I would like something else."

"What would you like?" asks Hobbs, rising to his feet.

"I would like you to tell me another story."

"All right," agrees Hobbs, sitting down on the bench again. "What kind of story would you like to hear?"

"Ummm, let me see. Oh! I know. Tell me a story about war. Were you ever a soldier? Did you fight in a war?"

The smile drains from Hobbs's face, he releases a long sigh, and putting down his glass, he sits with his hands on either side of him, grasping the edge of the bench, as though he is afraid he might fall. He looks up searchingly into the thick branches of the elm tree, its arms stretching towards the sky. He looks down at the old tree's roots, firmly grasping the earth below. He doesn't speak for a few moments, and then he answers, "No, Bobby, I was never a soldier and I didn't fight in a war."

"But, Daddy did, why didn't you, Hobbs?"

Hobbs turns towards Bobby and cups his tiny face in those great, callused hands; Bobby likes the feel of Hobbs's strong hands on his face. "Because, I thought war was wrong, Bobby. I was a conscientious objector."

"What's a conscious jector?"

Looking into Bobby's wide-open eyes and still holding his tiny head in his massive hands, Hobbs smiles. "A conscientious objector is someone who thinks that violence and killing is wrong." Letting his hands fall into his lap, he bows his head and falls silent.

Moving around in front of the gentle giant, Bobby sits cross-legged on the ground. He puts his elbows on his knees and resting his chin in his tiny webbed hands, he looks up to Hobbs, who doesn't immediately speak; Bobby is settling in for a long story.

Hobbs begins. He speaks softly and clearly, all traces of thickness have disappeared from his voice. "The last war was called The Great War."

"Why was it called that?"

"Because, it was meant to be the war, that would end all wars."

"But it didn't, did it? Because we are in another war now aren't we, Hobbs?"

"Yes, Bobby, I'm sorry to say, we are. The legacy of war is oceanic sadness, the earth groans."

Bobby listens, but hears only the soughing of the morning breeze through the branches of the big elm tree. "How did you become a conscious jector, Hobbs?"

"Well, I'll tell you Bobby. It was a long time ago; so long ago, that you weren't even born."

Bobby wrinkles his brow. "That *was* a long time ago."

Hobbs continues. "Yes it was, Bobby. It was in 1914 when England went to war with Germany. After only two years of fighting, there were 420,000 British soldiers dead. That's more than twice the number of the entire volunteer army that they started with; nearly all the original recruits had been killed. The government needed more men to fight, so, in 1916 they introduced Conscription."

"What's scription?"

"That's when you are called up and ordered to fight."

"Were you called up and ordered to fight, Hobbs?"

"Yes I was, Bobby."

"But, you said you didn't fight in the war."

"I didn't, Bobby, because I refused."

"You refused?" he exclaims, his voice rising in astonishment. "What did they do to you, Hobbs?"

"Well, after I refused to attend the medical board, I registered as a Conscientious Objector. I was ordered to appear in front of a tribunal, to explain my objections." Before Bobby can ask the question, Hobbs answers. "A tribunal is a kind of court, made up of important local people like your daddy, as well as some military people."

"What happened at the tybrunal? Were you scared?"

"No, Bobby, I wasn't scared, because I knew that I wasn't the only one to object to fighting in a war." Sitting up straight, he stares over Bobby's head at the grey, dry-stone wall, his voice becoming stronger. "Throughout history, there have been many people who were convinced that at whatever risk to themselves, their commitment must not involve the use of violence. It took a lot of courage to hold out against violence and killing, when they were accused of being cowards and traitors. They never changed their minds, even when their families and friends were threatened, and may themselves even have turned against them. It took courage to defy the leaders of your society, who were determined that war, not peace, was the right and heroic way forward. You see, Bobby, what gave me strength, was, I knew I wasn't alone, and I knew I was right."

"But how did you really know that, Hobbs?"

"Because, Bobby, I believe that every truth is simple and clear, and when we think simply and clearly, we become enlightened, and when we are enlightened, we see the truth and know what is right."

Bobby thinks that Hobbs is a very wise man. "What did the tybrunal do, Hobbs?"

Hobbs smiles as he relaxes his shoulders. "The tribunal was convinced that I was sincere. They gave me a choice; to work in the war effort in a selected civilian occupation or, if I refused, I would be imprisoned."

Bobby lifts his head from his hands, his eyebrows shooting up as he shouts in amazement, "Did you go to prison?"

Hobbs chuckles and shakes his head. "No, Bobby, I was afraid to go to prison, so I chose to work on a farm."

"What's it like to work on a farm, Hobbs?"

"It was hard work, Bobby, mucking out the cow sheds, and working in the fields, but it was very enjoyable. I think you would have liked it. It was a very healthy life."

"How long were you there?"

"Two years, until the end of the war."

"Two years? That's a long time. Was there anybody to help you?"

"That's a good question, Bobby."

Proudly sitting up straight, Bobby declares, "Thank you, Hobbs,"

Hobbs goes on with his story. "Most of the men were away fighting in the war, so women were required to work on the farms; they were called 'The Land Army'. When it was time to harvest the hay, we also had five German prisoners-of-war to help us."

"Golly! Hobbs." Bobby yells, "Weren't you afraid to work with the Germans?"

"Not at all, Bobby, they were just like you and me. They were honest, hard-working men. They all seemed to enjoy the work, and the funny thing is, none of them even tried to escape."

"Why didn't they try, Hobbs?"

"Because they liked it on the farm, in fact, they were relieved that they were captured and didn't have to fight anymore. And do you know, Bobby?"

"I think I do, Hobbs."

Hobbs smiles and concludes his story. "When the war was over, only one of then returned to Germany to live."

Bobby's mother's voice penetrates his attention. "Bobby! Bobby!" He sees her leaning out of his bedroom window. "Bobby, come up to the house, now, your breakfast is getting cold."

He waves. "Thank you, Mummy, I'm coming."

Standing up, he extends his tiny webbed hand towards Hobbs. "Thank you for the story, Hobbs. I think you are a very brave man."

The gentle giant stands up and looking down at him, he folds Bobby's smooth little hand into his calluses, and they shake manfully. "Thank you, Master Bobby. Before you go, I want you to remember what I am about to tell you."

"What is it Hobbs?"

"As you grow up, you will have many adventures, and you will see many different places and meet many different people, some will be your friends and others will want to harm you, but never be afraid. Remember, wherever you are, whomever you meet, and whatever you do, you must believe in yourself, trust others, and respect the natural world. If you do these three things, you will always be protected. You will live in Hope. Now run along, before your mummy gets cross."

"Thank you, Hobbs. I will, I will." He joyfully skips towards the house and his waiting breakfast.

Hobbs watches the little boy happily running towards his mother; he loves him dearly. His thoughts travel to the other side of the world to his daughter, she would be seven now. He has never told Bobby about her, and he has asked Eleanor not to mention her to anyone.

Chapter Eleven

THE DYING SEASON

As the theatre of war turns to Europe, during the summer of '41, the German invaders fly fewer and fewer sorties over the south of England, and the countryside gradually returns to relative calm. As the winter months approach, the sap retreats, the trees shed their leaves, the brightness of the sun is diminished, the air loses its comforting warmth, the earth hardens, and the Shaftos surrender to the dying season.

Eleanor is in the drawing room, watching the cold, grey rain, lashing relentlessly against the windowpanes. Beyond, she sees the saturated and withered flowers that border the driveway, looking like excommunicated bishops, despondent and dreary in their departed glory. In the distance, she can barely discern the shifting liquid shapes of leafless, lifeless trees. She has lighted a fire in the drawing room, to bring a modicum of cheer into this dark and depressing house. She hears the slow-moving footsteps of Doctor Jessup cautiously descending the stairs; they come to a halt at the open door.

"Please come in, Doctor, and take a seat. Would you like a glass of sherry to warm you up?"

"I don't mind if I do, Mrs Shafto," shouts the doctor, as he closes the door behind him.

This frail, stooped, Victorian man, shuffling towards the big armchair by the fireplace, is the Shafto's family doctor. As a young man, he was the attending physician at Edward's birth. He wears a dark, three-piece, pinstriped suit, which is accessorised by a gold watch-chain across his waistcoat. He sports a blue shirt with a starched, white, winged collar and a thin black tie. His pate is bare, and as he smiles, he displays a staggered set of broken yellow teeth. His upper lip is thatched by a full, grey and yellow, tobacco-stained moustache. On his feet is a pair of old and frayed red-plaid, carpet slippers. As he reaches the fireplace, he inelegantly withdraws from his jacket pocket, a packet of Senior Service cigarettes. He shakily extracts one and raises it to his dry lips. He then produces a box of Swan Vestas wooden matches, and awkwardly strokes one across the wrong side of the box. He promptly throws the impotent stick into the fire, whereupon it ignites in a tiny and short-lived explosion of blue, fizzing flames. The second match he breaks whilst striking, and the third, bursts into hot and flickering life. Having successfully lighted his cigarette, he removes it from his mouth, in the process tearing a piece of skin from his bottom lip, which immediately starts to bleed. Licking his wounded lip, he lowers his creaking body into the chair, and looking into the fire, he carefully draws on his bloodstained cigarette and blows beautiful smoke rings.

At the best of times, Doctor Jessup is a soft-spoken man. For Eleanor, this is not one of the best of times; what he now has to say is delivered in almost a whisper. Eleanor has to strain to even get the gist of his announcement.

"I   a...afra.....   tha....yo....hus....ha....no...lo.... t....liv..."

"I'm awfully sorry Doctor, but I didn't quite understand what you were telling me. You see, I'm a little hard of hearing. Could you please speak a little louder? How is he?"

Doctor Jessup is barely audible as he raises his voice. "I'll get to the point, Mrs Shafto. I'm afraid that he is very weak, and I'm not quite sure of how much time he has left."

This suppressed news doesn't come as a surprise to Eleanor, as it confirms her deepest fears. She knows that he is close to death, because ever since he contracted double pneumonia, she had known, in her heart of hearts, he had reached the point of no return.

"Doctor Jessup?" she enquires, as she hands him his sherry. "How long do you think he has?"

Whilst pondering the question, Doctor Jessup sips his sherry, smudging the rim of the glass with his bloody lip; he then draws deeply on his cigarette. Putting the glass down on the side table, in the process, spilling a few drops, and knocking the ash off his cigarette over his waistcoat, he looks at her with his rheumy eyes and murmurs, "I.. aaa..afraid... tha... he... ha... no... long... t... liv."

Eleanor impatiently raises her voice, "I didn't hear what you said, Doctor. Will you please speak up."

Doctor Jessup shouts, "I said I'm afraid that he has not got long to live."

She turns and walks towards the window, seeking solace from the pouring rain. She is finding it difficult to control her irritation with this ancient practitioner. She enunciates her question in a clear and deliberate voice. "Please, Doctor Jessop, could you please estimate, in your learned opinion, just how long he has to live?"

Doctor Jessup gets up slowly from the chair; his creaky frame forming a question mark. As he is brushing the ash from his waistcoat, he shouts, "I would estimate that he has four hours, at the most, before he meets his Maker."

Eleanor stares out at that cold, wet, and forbidding landscape. She is thinking that it is probably time to call a priest to deliver the Last Rights. However, she has found it difficult to believe in a Supreme Being anymore. Ever since Bobby and Bunny had burst into her world, her previously strong, traditional beliefs had wavered. She senses the cold hand of Death knocking at the door.

There is a slow, deliberate knock on the drawing-room door. It startles her, causing an involuntary shiver to shudder through her. She raises her voice. "Come!"

Bobby enters the room. Seeing Doctor Jessup standing with his back to the fireplace, warming his bum, a halo of cigarette smoke hovering over his balding pate, Bobby greets him. "Hello, Doctor Jessup, and how are you today?"

"Ver...wel...Bob....an...ho...r...u?"

"I am very well, thank you, Doctor."

"Tha.....goo...Bob...I...gla...t...ear...it."

Clenching her fists by her sides, Eleanor hastily interrupts the formal pleasantries between the ancient and the modern. "What do you want, Darling?"

"I want to go and see Daddy, can I?"

"May I," she declares, automatically correcting him.

"Yes you may, Mummy. Can I?"

Bobby's literal reply causes Doctor Jessup to show his broken yellow teeth in a crooked smile. His cigarette has burned down to his nicotine-stained fingers, causing him to wince quietly and throw the offending butt into the fire behind him.

She takes a deep breath. "Yes, Bobby, you may go and see Daddy. Be very quiet and don't be too long. Daddy is very tired and needs his sleep."

"Thank you, Mummy. Goodbye, Doctor Jessup." Without waiting for an answer, he runs through the doorway and scampers up the stairs, yelling, "Daddy, Daddy I'm coming."

She listens to the familiar squeak of Edward's bedroom door opening, but she doesn't hear it close, she is able to faintly hear the murmur of their halting voices. Refilling Doctor Jessup's sherry glass, she announces, "If you'll excuse me for a moment, Doctor, I'll look in on them. Please make yourself comfortable."

Doctor Jessup bares his yellow teeth, as his whole body nods in silent assent.

Ascending the stairs, she is unable to hear their conversation clearly. Arriving at the open door of the room, she can see little Bobby, sitting on the edge of Edward's bed. He is leaning close to his father's face, trying to catch what he is saying. Then she hears Edward's hoarse whispering.

"I'm sorry, Bobby. I am so sorry. Please forgive me. Forgive me, please."

Bobby jumps down from the bed. He stands facing his father and seems to grow a little. Then she hears that dark and terrifying voice.

"You cannot suddenly withdraw the dagger and expect the wound to immediately heal. It is too late for forgiveness, Edward. You cannot draw salvation from your last breath. You are predestined to follow the cycle of birth, life, death, and rebirth. Take comfort in the natural order. You will be reborn, but know of your sentence to repeat your uncaring vices, and of the cyclical anguish that will be revisited upon you."

Moving quickly to the bedside, she stands behind Bobby. Placing her hands firmly on his shoulders, she feels him trembling, and his breathing is rapid and shallow.

Edward Shafto is no match for the wrath of his unbegotten son. Eleanor watches in resignation as he slowly closes his weary eyes in ultimate surrender. She hears the crackling rale of his final breath whispering away until it decays. The serpent has sunk its teeth into his heart.

With his mother's hands on his shoulders, Bobby stands stiffly in wide-eyed silence.

Behind her, she becomes aware of the unmistakable aura of Doctor Jessup as he shuffles towards the deathbed. He has ushered Edward into this world, and now he is here to usher him out.

"I think he's gone, Doctor. Would you please examine him?"

"Of course, Mrs Shafto," the ancient practitioner shouts, "if you would take Bobby downstairs, I'll be there shortly."

"Thank you, Doctor. Come with Mummy, Bobby."

Bobby is silent and dry-eyed. She takes him by the hand and gently closes the door on Edward.

"What has happened, Mummy?" enquires Bobby quietly.

"Daddy is no longer with us, Bobby."

"Yes he is, Mummy, he is in his room."

"He has passed away, Darling."

"No, Mummy, he hasn't gone anywhere, he is still in his room."

"Your daddy is dead, Bobby. I want you to be a brave little man. You are now the head of the household."

As they walk slowly down the stairs, Bobby asks, "Why did Daddy die?"

It isn't until they arrive back in the drawing room when she replies. "Sit down by the fire, Bobby, and I will tell you why Daddy died." She retrieves her sherry glass, and sits in the chair opposite him, reaching for the words that would clearly explain why Edward has left them. She takes a sip of her sherry, and looking into his wide-open eyes, she explains, "Daddy died from double pneumonia, which was brought on by bronchitis, which developed from a bad case of the flu, arising from a common cold, which he caught when his immune system was run down, due to lack of sleep, as a result of excessive alcohol consumption."

She can't believe what she has just said, if she could have run and caught her words, she would have. It had all come pouring out, like a great dam bursting under the enormous pressure that has built up over the last few months... Bobby, Bunny, Bombs, Blackout, Hobbs, Doctor Jessup, and ultimately, Edward. A great tidal wave of sorrow and despair sweeps over her and threatens to drown her. She buckles beneath its onslaught, going as limp as a rag-doll in her chair, and gazes at her stoical son sitting opposite. He is staring silently into the fire, and doesn't seem to notice her. She watches him as he absentmindedly reaches for Doctor Jessup's half-empty glass of sherry and raises it to his lips.

There are just the two of them now. Robert has succeeded Edward as head of the household. She knew that Edward, to his dying day, had failed to comprehend that he actually had identical twin sons, who are inseparable. He refused to believe that Bunny existed within Bobby; this had been the great separator between father and son. A great pall of billowing blackness envelops her.

She looks at her tiny, four-year-old son, sipping sherry and gazing into the fire, and her heart reaches out to him. Crossing the gap between them, to where he sits in the big, upholstered chair, she sits down beside him. Putting a comforting arm around him, she gently speaks his name. "Bobby?"

He keeps silently staring into the fire.

Again, she speaks his name, "Bobby?"

He takes another sip of sherry and turns to look up at her. His wide-open eyes are dry; they reflect his numbness.

Kissing his forehead and smoothing back his hair, she murmurs, "Darling, what did Daddy say to you before he died?"

His pupils refocus a little, as he recognises her. In a tiny voice, he replies. "He said he was sorry, Mummy."

"Yes, I heard him say that, Darling. What was he saying to you before that?"

"I don't know, Mummy, he was whispering so low, it was hard to hear. I could only understand two words."

"And do you remember those words, Bobby?"

"I think so, Mummy."

"What were the two words, Darling?"

"I'm not sure, Mummy."

"Darling, I know it's difficult for you, but please try and remember the two words that you heard Daddy saying?"

Bobby puts down his glass on the side table, without spilling a drop, and turns to look into the fire again. Imitating his father's dying whisper, he says, "Ah-ahh-aa-hh-after and 'ffff-fahhhh-ff-father." Then, Bobby whispers, "I'm sorry, I can't remember any more, Mummy."

Standing up, she picks up her tiny child and folds him into her breasts. His arms encircle her neck, clinging tightly, seeking comfort. Slowly walking back and forth, and gently swaying from side to side, she kisses his ear and whispers, "There, there, Darling, it'll be all right, Mummy loves you very much." Over her shoulder, Bobby stares at the rain-spattered window, and blinks.

Edward is gone. He is buried next to his misbegotten son, Bunny, in the graveyard of the old village church in Wilmington.

*

In the days following Edward's death, Eleanor is sent spinning out of control. Edward's will is contested by his estranged wife, Dorothy. The courts rule in her favour, on the grounds that Edward and Eleanor were not married, as Dorothy is still the legal wife of Edward. Therefore, in the eyes of the law, Eleanor has no legal claim to his inheritance.

Not only had she lost Edward, but also all the material support that he had provided. His royalties went to his publisher, his business assets went to his partner, and his bank accounts went to his estranged wife… Dorothy's prophesy was fulfilled, "*He will ultimately reject you. I know this to be true. You cannot win, Miss Martin.*"

Eleanor is left with the house, little money, and little Bobby. To continue to survive, she will have to sell the house and all its contents, and that will mean terminating Hobbs's employment. What hurts her more than anything is the prospect of being without that gentle man, but she feels that she is left with no other choice.

Eleanor can see that it has hurt Hobbs to be dismissed. She knows that his relationship, with her and Bobby, goes far beyond just being their gardener. She also knows that circumstances dictate that he must leave. She sells the house, auctioning off its contents, and dismisses Arthur Hobbs.

Chapter Twelve

BLACK AND WHITE

Eleanor moves to a cold-water flat in Chelsea. Rental property in 1941 is easy to find, particularly in war-torn London, where thousands have fled the city. She tries to get her life together and concentrates on a new career, pursuing her first love, acting. Edward, having been a published and produced playwright, posthumously opens the doors for her. Remembering her one and only role in the ill-fated *Escape to Nowhere*, she thinks that getting work will be tough. However, she needn't have been too concerned, because war is still raging and the Government is looking for performers to entertain the troops.

Cognizant of her strict Catholic upbringing, and being acutely aware of her lapsed faith, and not being able to bear the insufferable guilt, she decides to send Bobby, at the age of four, away from the terrors of London, to a convent in the market town of Abingdon in Berkshire. It is a Roman Catholic boarding school for boys and girls, administered by the Holy Order of the Sisters of Mercy.

*

On the train journey through the Berkshire countryside, in the Abingdon Bumper, Bobby is able to stand on his seat and put his head out of the compartment window; he loves the feel of the wind in his face. As the train clicks past the farmers' fields, he indulges in his favourite pastime of counting cows. Looking towards the engine, before its dense smoke envelops him, he notices that the train is approaching a tunnel; he waits until the very last second, before he pulls in his head. The shrill wail of the train's whistle echoes through the tunnel, and the magnified clacking of its wheels resonate on the track below. Smoke is billowing into the dimly lit compartment as he hears Mummy's raised voice.

"Bobby, will you please close that window. I can hardly breathe from all that smoke."

He has his back to her as he struggles with the leather strap, trying to raise the heavy window. Suddenly there is daylight again as the train bursts out of the tunnel, and he becomes aware of his mother shouting over the commotion.

"No, leave it open, Bobby, and let the smoke clear."

Turning around to face her, he sees her jaw drop.

"Just look at you. Your face is as black as a minstrel's, and your clean white shirt is covered in soot."

He smiles. "You're funny, Mummy."

"It's not funny, Bobby, I'm very serious. Just look at you."

"I can't see myself, Mummy."

"Come here at once, Bobby." She pulls out her handkerchief, and spitting on it, she wipes his face. "We can't have you turning up at your new school looking like a golliwog, now can we?" He shrugs. Taking off his jacket, tie, and shirt, she pulls down a suitcase from the luggage rack. From it, she takes out a clean shirt, and shaking out his jacket, she redresses him. She wipes his face again and rearranges his hair, smarming it down with her spittle.

"There now, you look like a little gentleman again."

Sitting him down, she redirects her attention to her newspaper. He returns to reading the *Beano*, and soon is absorbed in the adventures of *Jimmy and his Magic Patch*.

*

Bobby is holding his mother's hand tightly as they stand before the big, black, iron gates which are set in a very tall, stone wall that surrounds the convent.

Bending down, she hugs him. "Now, Bobby, I want you to promise Mummy that you'll be a good boy and do whatever the Sisters tell you. Promise?"

He feels his mouth twitching; he is struggling not to cry. "I promise, Mummy."

She looks directly into his wide-open eyes. "And, Darling, please, please, *do* try and control Bunny."

"I'll try, Mummy. I promise I'll pretend to change. I promise I won't get dirty again. Please don't leave me."

"It's not because you were sooty, Darling. I have to go, Bobby. You know that Mummy has to make a living for us; don't worry, you will make new friends here." He attempts a weak smile. "That's my brave little soldier. Mummy will be down to visit you as soon as I can, I promise." With one last inspection, she straightens his tie, pats his hair, and blows his nose in her handkerchief. Standing up, she pushes the brass bell button. For three minutes, they stand holding hands, staring through the bars of the big black gates. Eventually they are presented with an apparition of billowing black-and-white.

Bobby's eyes grow wider. The only recognisably human parts of the spectre are two, small, pale, expressionless faces, with tiny, black, beady eyes. They each wear a broad leather belt that hangs down close to the ground, it reminds him of the leather window strap in the train and he really wants to pull on it, but he resists the urge. Beyond the black-and-white apparitions, he notices a big white building with a black slate roof. All the doors and windows are trimmed in black, and the path leading up to the huge, black, front door, is edged in large whitewashed stones. Bobby watches timidly as one gate, squealing on its hinges, is swung open. Simultaneously he sees one of the pale faces open its thin mouth in a welcoming smile.

"Hello, Bobby Shafto, we have been expecting you. I am Sister Mary Bernadette, and this is Sister Mary Agnes, welcome to Our Lady's Convent." Turning to his mummy the Sister reassuringly says, "Thank you for bringing him here, Mrs Shafto, and don't you be worrying about the luggage, Sister Mary Agnes will be looking after that. Now, if you don't mind, I'll be after taking Bobby and introducing him to the other wee boys and girls."

Mummy tries to release her grip but he hangs on. "Sister, may I come in with him to say goodbye?" she enquires.

Sister Mary Bernadette purses her lips, and with a condescending smile, moves her veiled head slowly from side to side. She extends her white hand, in invitation to Bobby. "I am afraid not, Mrs Shafto. After all, it wouldn't be fair to the other children, now would it?"

Mummy's hand tightens its hold on him. "But Sister, I would like to see where he will be living."

"Now don't you be after fretting, Mrs Shafto. He is in the hands of the Lord now. He will be well and truly looked after."

Mummy's grip loosens. "Very well, Sister, I think I understand." Bending down, she gives him a big hug, and kisses him softly on the forehead. Her voice is trembling, "There now, Darling, you go along with Sister Mary Bernadette, Mummy has to leave. Remember, Mummy loves you."

Sister Mary Bernadette takes him by his left hand; his right hand is still clinging to his mummy. He feels the softening of her grip, and he reluctantly lets go as he is resolutely guided through the big black gate by the apparition in black and white.

"Goodbye, Darling," whispers Mummy, with a small smile.

"Good bye, Mummy," he answers, with a deep frown.

"Come along now, Bobby," commands the Sister, in a firm tone.

By that time, Sister Mary Agnes has removed the luggage from the taxi and carried it to the other side of the gates. She slowly closes the complaining gate and slams the bolt home. Bobby looks back through the bars, to see Mummy waving at him and wiping her eyes with her handkerchief. She then turns and is swallowed up by the waiting taxi. As he watches it drive away, he is left with only the emptiness and cold blackness of the colossal gates. Sister Mary Agnes hurries past him, carrying his suitcase.

Letting go of his hand, and quickening her pace, Sister Mary Bernadette speaks. "The first thing I want you to know, Bobby Shafto, is that we are after having rules at the convent, and we expect each child to implicitly obey them. Of course, the most important rule to remember is strict obedience. If you are obedient, the good Lord will love you and look after you."

He is half walking and running behind the Sister, trying to keep up with her as he casts hurried glances behind him at the daunting, black gates that now separate him from his familiar past.

The Sister, glancing over her shoulder, comes to a halt and turns to face him. "Will you be coming along now, Bobby Shafto; we're not after having all day?"

His breathing is becoming laboured, and feeling the excruciating pain of the stitch developing in his right side, he stops in his tracks.

The ominous nun speaks loudly and sharply. "Bobby Shafto, I said hurry up. You must learn to do as you are told; I'll not be after telling you again."

He watches apprehensively as she determinedly moves towards him.

He stands, breathing heavily, his wide eyes staring.

"Come, boy, give me your hand now. You'll have to learn to keep up, even if you are so very wee and weak."

He can't understand why Mummy has left him in this strange black-and-white place. He wants her to take him away. He can feel the pain in his side increasing. Staring at the strange black-and-white apparition, who, through his misty eyes, seems to be melding into grey, he stands his ground as he feels Bunny erupting.

"I may be wee and weak, but my weaknesses and strengths are my own, I alone own them. If I share these attributes with others to scrutinize, dissect, and return to me in a compromised editorial of watered-down advice, I can only receive the diluted essence of many, as opposed to the concentrate of I, for it is only I that can fully understand the full spectrum of I. Black-and-white is grey."

This outburst brings Sister Mary Bernadette to a sudden stop. Her white face is turning red, her beady, black eyes are shining with a strange light, her mouth opens wide, and her voice crescendos. "Young man, don't you ever again be after speaking to me in that tone of voice. Don't you ever again be shouting at your superiors. Don't you ever again be disobeying a holy order. Moreover, never, ever again use words that you cannot possibly understand. Do you understand?"

Bunny has spoken. Bobby stands motionless and mute.

"Do you understand?" the Sister roars. "Answer me, you wicked wee boy."

With eyes wide open, he stares in despair, and promptly pees his pants.

*

Living in this black-and-white world, under the tutelage of the Sisters of Mercy, Bobby learns strict obedience, respect for the Lord, and a strange, submissive strain of love. He learns that the reward for obedience to the Lord and His administrators, is rewarded by a feeling of untainted innocence, which gives him a euphoric sensation of rarefied, out-of-body soaring and mystical purity; an impression of truly being in the light of the Lord. On the darker side, he learns that the consequence for wandering from the path of virtue, engenders within him an unfathomable guilt, which produces an effect of being a soiled, wretched, and unwanted sinner.

Over the ensuing months, Bobby comes to realise that he is poles apart from other mortals. He feels he is very different from everybody else around him. A visceral frustration haunts him, because no one at the convent can understand his relationship with his twin brother, Bunny. His mummy and Hobbs are the only ones who can appreciate the symbiotic life that he shares with his brother; he feels a deep longing for them. For the first time in his life, he is truly alone, and he withdraws deep within his own universe. His only form of communication, with the other kids and the Sisters, expresses itself in sullenness, distrust, and the occasional outburst of *Bunnybabble.* The Sisters diagnose this desperate retreat as lack of faith. They pray for him; but their prayers go unanswered; they are powerless to change what essentially is.

Chapter Thirteen

ACID GENEROSITY

The boys and girls of the convent sleep in large dormitories, which are situated in separate wings of the building, Bobby's dormitory is on the third floor. It is a long room with windows on two sides; forty boys sleep in two long rows of iron beds. One Sister is in charge of each dormitory, her cell being at one end of the room, next to the washing room that holds twelve sinks and five bathtubs. The floor of the dormitory is polished hardwood; the sparkling finish, reflecting the hard penance of the boys who are deemed to be sinners.

One evening, about a year after his arrival at the convent, Sister Mary Bede, who is in charge of Bobby's dormitory, introduces a strange boy to his bed; she tells Bobby that the intimacy will open him to the chance of being more sociable. In consolation, she gives Bobby an orange, a rare treat in this time of war and deprivation. He is told to share the orange with his uninvited bedmate. However, Bobby deeply resents the intrusion on his personal space, and is not inclined to be charitable to a stranger. Peeling the orange, he delights in the touch and aroma of the naked fruit. He then carefully segments it and tastes its delectable flesh. After he has devoured three quarters of the orange, his unwanted guest, lying beside him, asks him if he might have a piece. Bobby's answer is to pass the discarded orange peel to the boy, whilst continuing to devour the remaining sections of the succulent fruit. The unfortunate boy, realising his imposed intrusion on Bobby's space, dutifully eats the peel.

This acidic generosity from the Sisters of Mercy doesn't assuage Bobby's deep feeling of resentment. The womb-like confinement of the two boys, bound together in one tight space, brings back panicky sensations of claustrophobia; he doesn't want to share his bed, or his orange, and neither does Bunny.

"Out, out white maggot, do not soil our bed. This is our private space, it is our individual universe. There shall be no trespassers, no hawkers, no beggars, and no thieves. This space is out of bounds to all and sundry. It is null and void. It is ultimate privacy. Anyone intruding does so at their peril. Out, out, damned spot. Out I say."

Bunny and Bobby unmercifully harangue their hapless guest. They are shouting, kicking, punching, and screaming. The bed sheets become ripped and soaked in sweat. They manage to wrap the torn and soaking sheet around the neck of the unfortunate boy, who promptly soils his pyjamas, and emits a piercing, Bunny-like scream. He is violently tossed out of the bed onto the cold, hard floor, the sheet still clinging around his throat, like a pair of wet and wrinkled, white hands, relentlessly tightening their deathly grip. Whilst the wretched boy lies writhing on the floor, Bobby heaves sharply on the sheet, as his victim is choking and clutching at his intended shroud that is tightly entwined around his throat; he is gurgling and gasping for breath.

The commotion awakens the whole dormitory and the lights are slammed on. Bobby sees thirty-nine other boys standing on their beds, gleefully shouting, "Fight, fight." Jumping up and down, they soar on their trampolines, high in the air they rise, twisting and somersaulting, and yelling, "Fight, fight, fight."

Her prayers being interrupted by the unholy ruckus, Sister Mary Bede comes storming from her cell at the far end of the dorm, shrieking at the top of her voice, "Boys, boys, stop this at once. Silence I say. All of you lie down on your beds, at once."

The bedsprings gradually stop creaking, and the chanting of the boys fade away to a restrained murmur as the last celebrant quietly offers his final but defiant sigh and lies silently prone. Bobby is made all too aware of the sharp, authoritative voice of Sister Mary Bede cutting through the silence. She demands, in a firm and controlling tone, "Now, I want to know, who is responsible for this disgraceful commotion?"

Thirty-nine boys lay still and silent, the only exception being Bobby's unfortunate guest under his bed, who after his near-death experience, is mired in his own filth, all the while, sobbing and slobbering. The poor boy is sprawled on the floor, clutching at the soaking sheet, which is still clinging tightly around his throat, threatening to choke him.

Sister Mary Bede, on inspecting this unfortunate scene, unbuckles her leather belt of righteousness. "Bobby Shafto, how dare you behave like this? Look at what you've done to that poor boy. How dare you? What were you trying to do, kill him?"

"Yes," shouts Bunny. **"Authority can only exist when we agree to obey it. Some times we become disagreeable."**

"Shut up! Shut up! Shut up!" the fearful penguin screeches, her foot stomping wildly on the polished hardwood floor.

"When you have to explain yourself, you loose the poetry."

"Shut up! Shut up!" Tiny bubbles of spittle are forming on her agitated lips. "Shut up!" Sister Mary Bede repeats, struggling to control herself. With one final stomp, she hisses, "Bobby Shafto, I warn you, let that boy go this instant."

Bobby reluctantly releases his stranglehold, and his terrified victim slithers and snivels to safety.

"A uniform only rules the one who wears it."

The Sister is becoming increasingly apoplectic. "Bobby Shafto, I am warning you. Do not say another word. Be quiet and lie still."

With that admonition, Bobby capitulates. However, he thinks that it might have been better if he hadn't let go of the sheet and instead, just carried on yelling and thrashing. For, as soon as he becomes quiet and still, Sister Mary Bede grabs hold of his right arm and yanks him over, face down, on the soaking bed. She then pulls down his pyjama bottom and proclaims.

"Bobby Shafto, you are a disgrace to this dormitory, you are a disgrace to this convent, and you are a disgrace to our almighty and merciful Lord God Jesus Christ. You are most definitely a grievous sinner in the eyes of Our Lord, and for your sins, God is going to punish you."

Turning his head, he notices that all the other boys have come to a kneeling position on their beds, to witness the pitiless discipline.

Sister Mary Bede pronounces the sentence. "The Lord God Almighty, in all His goodness and mercy, has selected me to be the ordained instrument of His holy will, and from my hands you are about to receive His just retribution."

With the holy will pronounced, the Sister of Mercy enthusiastically lays into Bobby with her leather belt. Bobby buries his face in the soaking pillow, clutching it tightly and squeezing his eyes closed as he tenses his buttocks against the sharp and painful sting of the holy flail. During the beating, thirty-nine boys loudly count in unison with each stroke of the strap, "One, Two, Three, Four, Five, aaand Six."

"Shut up! Shut up" yells Sister Mary Bede, whilst re-buckling her instrument of torture around her habit. Gathering her prayers around her, she then commands every boy to kneel beside his bed, with his head bowed and his hands held together in supplication.

"Let us pray," she intones loudly. "Dear gentle Father in Heaven, in Thine infinite mercy, grant us the patience and understanding to forgive this miserable sinner, Bobby Shafto, and set him on the true path of righteousness. Look down with compassion on Your lost lamb, and bring him back to the fold, so that he may always remain Thy humble and obedient servant, for ever and ever, Amen."

The boys murmur a ragged and unenthusiastic, "Amen." Bobby remains silent, whilst his simpering, uninvited guest, who by now has slithered to the end of the dormitory, is separated from the choking, soaking sheet and hurriedly ushered into the washing room.

*

This incident becomes the seminal turning point in Bobby's young life. He doesn't understand the reason for the cruelty that is inflicted upon him. He doesn't understand what is expected of him. He doesn't understand what, or who, he is asked to believe in. He doesn't understand the need for blind obedience. He doesn't understand the whole meaning of religion, and most of all, he has no comprehension whatsoever, of the concept of a Supreme Being. The only thing he does understand is that belief is beyond reason. He is forced to exist in a completely alien space. He becomes profoundly unhappy and withdraws into the protection of his personal shell, where he implodes.

Chapter Fourteen

ONE CHRIST DIVISIBLE

Wearing an embroidered, white sash across the little shoulder of his white shirt, and holding his brand new prayer book, Bobby is in the convent chapel, kneeling at the altar rail, participating in his first Holy Communion.

The priest, holding the jewel-encrusted, silver chalice, passes along the row of tiny, shiny faces, their uneasy eyes squinched shut, their anxious mouths agape, their tentative tongues protruding; like young, hungry chicks in the nest, begging for the worm. As the priest pulls the wafer-host from the chalice, he intones a secret incantation in the dead language.

"Corpus Domini nostri Jesu Christi custodiat animam tuam in vitam aeternam."

With each host, he makes a barely discernable sign of the cross, and then places the single body of Christ on the timid tongue of each anxiously kneeling child. The heavy, and richly brocaded, vestments waft the holy incensed smoke from the thurible, into Bobby's weeping eyes and nostrils. The exalting choir is chanting.

"Agnus Dei, qui tollis peccata mundi, miserere nobis.
Agnus Dei, qui tollis peccata mundi, miserere nobis.

Agnus Dei, qui tollis peccata mundi, dona nobis pacem."

Bobby feels unbearably clean; the priest is now in front of him, placing the soft, white wafer on his outstretched tongue.

"Corpus Domini nostri Jesu Christi custodiat animam tuam in vitam aeternam," he chants.

Jesus Christ is in his mouth, he finds Him hard to swallow. With the tip of his tongue, he scrapes Him from his palate, and as he swallows the soft pieces of His flesh. Bunny bellows. His words are in the air and Bobby can taste them.

"One Christ is divisible. To believe in the existence of one god, confirms the existence of many. Fundamental belief makes one brave and foolish. If we only beat on one drum, we will always hear the same sound. Beware of perfection; the only possible change is for the worse. Do not fully submerge yourself, for you are sure to drown. Withdraw your feet from the sucking mud, leave your boots behind, and be free."

Bunny's ranting reverberates throughout the chapel. To Bobby, what he is saying makes more sense than the reverential intonations of the dead language of the Mass.

The priest immediately puts down the chalice and raises his crucifix. With the aspersorium, he hastily sprinkles holy water on Bobby's head, whilst chanting. *"Asperges me."*

The choir answers, *"Domine hyssopo, et mundabor lavabis me, et super nivem dealbabor."*

The priest then places the crucifix on Bobby's bowed and soaking head, and mumbles, *"Miserere mei Deus, secundrum magnam misericordiam tuam. Gloria Patri, et Filio, et Spirtui Sancto."*

After many incantations, and sprinklings of holy water, and multiple signs of the cross, Bunny refuses to be exorcised.

"All that you can do is to speak your own language. The truth is what you believe it to be, nothing more. The message sent is not the message received."

The Sisters immediately bow their heads in frantic prayer, for they are afraid of that terrible voice, they believe it to be the Devil himself, and Bobby, the Devil's instrument; the evil host incarnate

*

Feeling very unhappy in the uniform and strictly disciplined environment of the convent, Bobby seeks comfort and pleasure outside the dark habits of the nuns. There is a W.C., on every landing of the dormitory building; his favourite is on the third floor. Pleading the need to pee, he often repairs to his inner sanctum.

The tiny windowless room, with dull, institutional-green paint peeling from its walls, a dusty bare bulb hanging from the ceiling, and worn, dirty-white linoleum on the floor, is only large enough to accommodate one toilet-bowl, with just enough room for him to turn around. To Bobby, this tiny room is very special, for it can transform itself entirely into another space and time. Sitting on the toilet-bowl, he imagines it to be an ornately carved wooden throne, the peeling paint on the walls is metamorphosed into elaborate tapestries, the worn linoleum on the floor, is changed into a luxurious and intricately woven Persian carpet and the dusty, bare bulb, becomes a delicately dancing torch flame. The room is entirely transformed into another world.

The whole wall facing him is magically changed into a massive, ornately carved, secret door that when opened, by reciting the secret password, "*Open Sesame,*" reveals a scene from the Arabian Nights. In the light of many flickering torches, he sees, spread around the lush carpeted floor of the damask-draped room, enormously plump, silk cushions, on which recline dark, swarthy warriors. They wear turbans that are clasped with massive, deeply coloured, dazzling jewels. They are dressed in costumes of finely embroidered silk, their bejewelled scimitars are lying by their sides, and the smoke from their hookahs smells sweet and intoxicating.

These potentates are being served rich meats, fish, and fruits, by beautiful, dark-haired, olive-skinned, harem girls, who wear multicoloured, diaphanous veils, which reveal tantalizing glimpses of their near-nakedness; they are erotically dancing to the strains of sensuously crying instruments.

The most beautiful girl of all approaches Bobby on his throne, and kneeling at his feet, she serves him delectable, juicy orange sections; he sits on his throne until his bum is numb. Then, the beautiful harem girl inevitably retreats into the inner sanctum, and the massive door slowly swings closed behind her. At this point, the tiny windowless room, the dull, institutional-green, peeling paint, the dusty, bare bulb, and the worn, dirty-white linoleum, re-appear; it is time for him to return to grim reality.

Chapter Fifteen

The demon at the gate

On Sundays, after morning Mass, the convent kids are taken to Barton Field to play. This three-acre field is owned by Our Lady's Convent, it is situated about half a mile down the public road.

This particular Sunday, they are walking in a long crocodile line, chaperoned by a Sister at the head and a Sister at the tail. A convoy of American soldiers, riding their impressive lorries, tanks, and gun carriers, are overtaking them. The scrawny, short-trousered kids look up to these robust, noble, and godlike liberators, and repeatedly yell in unison, "Got any gum chum? Got any gum?" In reply to these exhortations, the air is filled with joyful laughter as packages of spearmint gum rain down on them; it rains Wrigleys. As the convoy passes by, many eager hands reach for the manna that is falling from above, and the little crocodile rapidly disintegrates.

"Back in line now, back in line," command the nuns at the head and tail of the crocodile, and the obedient boys and girls dutifully regroup, except Bobby, who continues to pick up the gum. "Bobby Shafto," scream the black-and-white duo. "This is the last time we are going to tell you. Get back in line, at once." The crocodile giggles.

On arriving at Barton Field, the eager kids are let loose to play. Bobby, and a few of the boys, head for the excitement of the woods. On the other side of the woods, by the roadside fence, in a clump of large rhododendron bushes, the boys have fashioned a camp, its floor is lined with a thick bed of fir branches and dried leaves.

From this camp, they sally forth, stealing back through the woods and out onto the playing field. Where, away from the watchful eyes of the penguins, they skilfully cull a giggling, and all too willing, girl from the perimeter of the crèche, and hustle her back through the woods to their camp. There, they tie her ankles and wrists together, with their black-and-white school ties, and feed her chewing gum and lemonade powder. Then, each eager boy awkwardly kisses her on the cheek, and she is set free. There is a code of silence between captor and victim, that ensures that the penguins are never aware that one of their huddle has been willingly caught, kissed, and released.

Gathering more fallen branches for the sacrificial bed, Bobby notices a deflated, slimy, white balloon hanging limply on the end of the lower branch of a fir tree. He plucks it off, and putting it to his lips, he blows into it, until it inflates to a large, white, rubber bubble. Tying it off, he runs out onto the field to show all the other kids, he is shouting excitedly, "I've got an American balloon. I've got an American balloon."

To his utter dismay, Sister Mary Anthony yells at him. "Ahh, ya notty boy ya, ahh, ya notty boy. Put that filthy thing down, at once."

He meekly lets the slimy white balloon sink sluggishly to the grass.

Whilst stomping on the wobbly, rubber receptacle, the outraged penguin is shouting in righteous rage, "Disgustin', disgustin' disgustin'. Ah, ya notty boy ya. Ah, ya notty boy." The inflated balloon finally surrenders to her virtuous heel, and anti-climatically spews out its impotent contents over the infertile soil.

Sister Mary Anthony glowers darkly at Bobby and growls, "Bobby Shafto, you are an evil child. May the good Lord have mercy on your soul." Pointing towards the gate, at the entrance to Barton field, she commands, "Now go and stand by the gate, and pray for forgiveness, until we are all ready to leave."

He is confused, deflated, and embittered. Starting to pray, and not understanding why, he mumbles his ingrained mantra. "Oh Lord, I ask for Thy forgiveness. Please take this punishment from me. But if it be Thy will, then Thy will be done."

In answer, Bunny's dark voice comes from within, and sweeps across the open field like a strong, cold wind, bringing with it a frozen silence; all movement shivers to a halt.

"You unmerciful penguin, look into your own soul to see the murky stain of sin. Stomp not on virtue, but upon your own hypocrisy. Rant and rail, not against the symbols of love, but against your own revulsion. Do not transfer your own guilt to the innocents, for they see no evil; what is to one is not to another. Walk carefully, penguin, for the ice is thin, and hell is cold."

In the dying wind, their habits in disarray, their eyes turned upward towards heaven, and repeatedly crossing themselves, the good Sisters kneel in prayer and supplication. The children start skipping apprehensively, and humming dissonantly as they cast sidelong glances towards the demon at the gate.

*

Bobby has become a lost soul. He is rebelling against all religious orders as he rants and rails against the existence of one omnipotent and omniscient god. Not even the passionate discipline of the Sisters of Mercy will re-instil in him that vital belief in the Lord, for the Sisters of Mercy are without.

At the age of seven, the age of reason, fearful that he might infect the rest of their flock with his malevolent, agnostic, and contagious disease, Bobby Shafto is summarily culled, isolated, and expelled from Our Lady's Convent.

Chapter Sixteen

THE SONG OF THE SIRENS

London in 1944 is a perilous place to send a little seven-year-old boy. Cradled in his mother's arms, Bobby is dreaming of his mythical hero, Odysseus, bound to the mast of the *Argo*, gazing towards land, as the crew, with wax-plugged ears, row vigorously. They are deaf to the Sirens' seductive overtures, which are relentlessly beckoning them closer to their promising embrace. Despite his repeated entreaties to be released, his faithful crew heeds him not. He looks longingly towards the inviting shore, wanting to be with the sweetly singing Sirens. In vain, he struggles to free himself. Looking achingly towards his shipmates, he pleads to be untied; his cries go unheeded. The song of the seductive Sirens envelops him. He squinches his eyes in frustration, and on reopening them, he sees the angelic face of his mother, smiling sweetly down at him. She is softly singing,

"Bobby Shafto went to sea-ee
Silver buckles on his knee-ee
He'll come back and marry me-ee

The high pierced wailing of the sirens continue; his mother remains steadfastly singing,

Bonnie Bobby Shafto."

Over her soothing voice, and the shrieking of the air-raid sirens, he hears the unmistakable drone of a Doodlebug, and the repeated, short, hacking cough of a nearby anti-aircraft battery. Through the blackout curtains, he imagines the bright, white stabbing beams of the searchlights as they puncture the night sky, probing for the buzz bomb. The "rumph- rumph" sound, of the flying bomb comes to an abrupt halt. Suddenly all sounds cease. The shrieking sirens wail into stillness, and his mother's song is transformed into the sharp sucking sound of silence.

The Doodlebug's engine has cut out, it has reached its designated target range, and it begins its eerily, silent and swift descent from an altitude of 4,000 feet, at a rate of 33 feet per second per second; no one knows where it will land.

In that awe-full, timeless hiatus, his mother quickly wraps him in his dressing gown, and puts on his gumboots. Grasping her torch, and donning her air-raid warden's helmet, she carries him quickly towards the front door of their 4th floor flat; within fifteen seconds, they are there. Abruptly, the deathly silence is cruelly terminated as the one-ton warhead finds its target at the far end of the block of flats. As he clings to his mother for protection, the sonic shock, and hot blast of the massive explosion shatters the glass in the transom above them, which splinters on impact with her helmet, and glances off to shower harmlessly around them in the shape of a tinkling, crystal umbrella.

By the time they have descended the four flights of stone steps to the ground floor and emerged onto the street, the building at the far end of the block of flats is engulfed in flames. He hears multiple explosions as gas lines are detonating; the stench of rotten eggs, mixing with the acrid smell of burning, makes him feel sick. A dreadful shower of bricks and glass rains down. In the intense heat, red-hot iron railings are twisting like plasticine. Panicking people are pouring helplessly from the ground-floor doors and windows. Some others are jumping from fateful heights, only to be dashed against, and become part of, the melting blacktopped surface of the street.

He hears implosions within explosions. One complete wall of the building folds in on itself, brick upon tumbling brick, spewing out clouds of smoke and dancing sparks, accompanied by the deafening reverberation of titanic tearing and ripping as the building is disembowelled. Up the complete line of the chimney, the gaping wound exposes the dying building's spinal column, showing each naked vertebra, fireplace over fireplace over fireplace. Over the fourth-floor fireplace, pinned to the mantle, a pair of tattered navy-blue knickers is moving vulnerably in the rapacious currents of the hot and angry air.

Lying at his feet are two dead boys, about his own age, their naked bodies miraculously unmarked. The concussion from the blast has blown all their clothes off, including their socks. They must have been frantically running from the building, only to be pursued, captured, stripped, and raped by the massive shockwave.

Seeking solace, he averts his eyes, and looking up into the flickering darkness of the charred and leafless plane trees, he sees the Dali-esque images of limbs hanging from limbs, and the smouldering and peeling bark is dripping blood. Lodged in the fork of two twisted and splintered branches, he sees a scorched and hairless head, with empty eye sockets, staring blindly down at him.

A sparrow lands at his feet, unmoving, yet strangely unchanged. Kneeling, he cups this perfect dying form in his little hands. He feels the final warm throb of its life force leaving its tiny body; an eloquent testament to the monumental madness of war.

Deep within him, membranes are colliding and bouncing off each other. A surge of dark energy stirs within his gut. He feels the need to spew out an endless torrent of words. In that dreadful and commanding voice, comes the convoluted *Bunnybabble*.

"This is not the first time. This is not the last time. This enormous conflagration, this all-consuming monster, this vast depository of living and material essence is the crucible that generates the dark energy which continually drives new life forces. Just as the cosmos undergoes its cycles of expansion and contraction, events and lives on earth are destined to endlessly repeat. Time does not begin or end; it moves in a never-ending cycle. This epic dilution of energy will again be reborn, and like a Phoenix, out of its ashes, it will rise again; Creation always walks in the footprints of Destruction."

To stem the advance of the hungry flames, his mother is galvanised into action. It is her responsibility, as an air-raid-warden, to marshal all the other tenants of the block of flats into a water brigade. The young and able-bodied men and women have already left home for the battlefields, the munitions factories, the farms, the airplanes and the ships. It is now up to the elders to defend their homes and protect their young, and it is left to Bobby's mother to direct these ancient warriors in their futile task. They are a puny band of brave but powerless souls, pitted against the colossal devastation wreaked by 2,000 lbs of high explosives.

Being trained by his mother for such an eventuality, he climbs up to the slimy reservoir tank, and dipping through the green scum that is spread over its black and motionless surface, he fills the little red buckets of the courageous brigade with its fetid water. The scrawny warriors, old men, women and children, numbering three score and one, encouraged by their grotesquely dancing shadows, ferociously plunge their tiny stirrup pumps, impotently squirting their feeble spurts of water against the almighty inferno, which is howling back at them in disdain.

Looking upon this vivid scene of magnificent carnage, Bobby is seduced by the vibrant beauty of destruction. The brilliant leaping flames are licking the night sky, reflecting off the low clouds and the shiny, silvery surfaces of the chubby barrage balloons. Kaleidoscopic images of contorted and prismatic representations of that dreadful conflagration are exquisitely reflected in the wasted sheets of water on the road's surface. Fragments of sparkling, splintered glass are scattered over the dark, accepting face of the street, like precious gems, narcissistically lounging on a shimmering cloth of black velvet.

Through the acrid smoke, Bobby can faintly see his mother conducting the death-count. She is determinedly tagging the bodies of every dead person she comes across; some naked, some limbless, and some headless. He notices that she is even putting tags on the mannequins that were blown out of the ground-floor windows of the dress shop. It is difficult to differentiate life from death, reality from surreality.

In time, the sirens sound the long note of the 'all clear' and fade away. Nevertheless, the building continues to burn unabated, and the gallant crew continue their efforts to, valiantly but ineffectually, vanquish their terrible foe.

Later that night, after the Civil Defence Unit has taken control, Bobby's mother, grim and grimy, takes down her exhausted little son from the lip of the rusty reservoir tank. He slumps wearily into her arms and she gently folds him into her breasts. He senses his vision blurring, and with the sting of salt in his wide-open eyes, he falls back to dreaming of sea nymphs.

*

Bobby is eight years of age on April eighteenth 1945. On the seventh of May, the Germans surrender and the war is over.

With the advent of peace, Bobby feels a sense of personal bereavement. *"With this thin, piping time of peace"*, comes the great lethargy, a loss of principle, a loss of belief, and a loss of direction. In the place of daily turmoil, urgency, excitement, intense camaraderie in the face of danger, and a deep loyalty to King and Country, comes a time of aimless frustration. There is no sense of purpose or direction, no cause to believe in, no one to vilify, no more enemies, and far fewer friends. The war was his life; it was all he had ever really known. He has lost his father, his home, his faith, and he has nearly lost his soul. All that he has gained is growing to a height of forty inches and a weight of fifty pounds; he is left with very little.

Chapter Seventeen

I'll be seeing you

During the latter years of the war, Eleanor Shafto was still pursuing her career as an actress and had joined ENSA; Entertainments National Service Association, or, as the wags liked to refer to it, "Every Night Something Awful." They toured the armed forces bases around Britain, entertaining the troops.

When the war ended, she continued touring the resort towns with various repertory companies; every two weeks they were in a different town. Bobby, having received a dishonourable discharge from the convent, travelled with his mother. In between rehearsals and performances, she did her best to educate him.

*

In Cheltenham, Gloucestershire, their digs are above a pub. During the evening, whilst his mother is at the theatre, Bobby helps Mr and Mrs Proctor, the owners of the estab-lishment, by taking out the empty bottles from behind the bar to the shed at the back. As he hefts the wooden crates of empties, he becomes a familiar sight to the regular patrons of the pub. He loves to be part of this happy crowd, whose level of joviality seems to increase with each passing pint.

Bobby remembers his father's excessive drinking, and its fatal effect on his health. Yet, these people seem healthy and happy and above all, good-natured; he wants to be like them. He reasons, if beer makes them happy, then it follows that beer will also make him happy. As he takes the crates of empty bottles to the back shed, he notices that the bottles are not always completely empty, so he swallows the dregs from the odd one, it doesn't take long for him to acquire the taste. Bobby Shafto first tastes beer when he is eleven years old, forty-seven inches tall and weighs seventy-eight pounds.

When his mother comes home from the theatre each night, she stops at the bar for a nightcap before going up-stairs to look in on her son; he is always fast asleep, with his eyes wide open. She never smells beer on his breath, as he makes sure to brush his teeth thoroughly. She has no reason to suspect that he has been drinking.

It is the closing night performance in Cheltenham, and his mother will be back later than usual. Little Bobby has become a favourite with the customers in the pub, and they don't want to see him go. Over the fortnight that he has been here, his intake of beer has increased from, tentatively draining the dregs of three bottles a day, to at least eight. His beer consumption, being such a tiny boy, is having a deleterious effect on his equilibrium.

Tonight he feels sad, for this is the last time that he will be amongst these happy people, and he knows that he will miss them all desperately. He is behind the bar, taking out another crate of empties and trying to drown his melan-choly. He has consumed considerably more beer than is usual, when he is confronted with the thought of leaving this happy place, and he suddenly bursts out into uncontrol-lable tears. The laughter around him gradually dies, and a hush falls on the whole bar. They are all looking at him in sympathy and are commiserating.

"What's the matter, Bobby? Are you all right?"

"Don't cry, son."

"Is it because this is your last night?"

"We'll miss you too, Bobby."

"Never mind, Bobby you'll soon get over it."

"Yeah, Bobby, you've got your whole life ahead of you, not like us old geezers."

"Yeah, Bobby, you've got places to go and people to see, and we are stuck here. And who knows?, we'll probably be seeing you again."

This last remark brings a trace of a smile to his lips. Then, without warning, the inebriated Bunny, with the pure and vibrant voice of an angel, bursts out singing,

"I'll be seeing you;
In all the old familiar places;
That this heart of mine embraces;
All day through."

The crowd is hushed into awed silence. Mr. Proctor stands Bobby on the bar, so that all may have a better view of this tiny boy with the voice of an angel. Bobby is a little wobbly, but Mr Proctor holds onto him firmly.

"In that small café;
The park across the way;
The children's carousel;
The chestnut tree;
The wishing well."

Under the influence, with tears in their eyes, the slightly inebriated and sentimental crowd begins swaying gently with the rhythm of that angelic voice. The tenor of the whole bar is transformed by the bitter-sweetness of the moment. First one, then another, they softly join in, a corporeal chorus harmonizing with an angel.

"I'll be seeing you;
In every lovely, summer's day
And everything that's bright and gay;
I'll always think of you that way."

At this juncture, Bobby's mother opens the pub door from the street; the lights of the passing cars, streaking behind her. She stands there and smiles at him, encouraging him to continue.

"I'll find you in the morning sun;
And when the night is new;
I'll be looking at the moon;
But I'll be seeing you."

The crowd erupts with spontaneous applause and laughter at the wonder of this tiny boy. Lifting him onto his shoulders, Mr Proctor triumphantly carries him into the midst of the multitude. They gather around him, patting him on the back, and cheering in admiration. Bobby has never felt happier in the whole of his little life.

He knows that Mummy knows, only too well, who was really singing. She carries him up to his bed, and watches over him as he slips contentedly into the gentle arms of Morpheus.

*

One year later, in Eastbourne, Sussex, Bobby experiences his first sexual awakening. He has to share a room with the landlady's daughter, Colleen, who is about the same age as him. Her mother has said goodnight to them and has switched out the light. After the door is closed, they lie silently in their separate beds, fitfully trying to get to sleep. He becomes aware of a strange stirring within him that is unlike any feeling he has experienced before. After much tossing and turning, he hears Colleen whisper.

"Bobby, are you asleep?"

"No, Colleen," he whispers loudly in return, "Are you?"

"Not so loud," she whispers back, "Mummy will hear us."

"Sorry."

"Bobby?" she softly whispers again, "do you want to cuddle?"

This is a new direction for him; he finds the thought both comforting and bothersome. "Yes, Colleen, I think I would."

She has already crossed the narrow gap between their beds, and is crawling in beside him. He realises that this is the first time that he has shared his bed with a girl. For a while, they silently hold each other, breathing softly onto each other's necks. With puckered lips, they awkwardly kiss, and whisper sweet nothings into each other's ears. She shows him hers and he shows her his, and feeling the fuzzy warmth of puppy love, they tenderly fall asleep in each others' arms.

The next morning, Colleen's mother discovers the sleeping innocents sublimely entwined; she is not amused. Bobby's mother decides that from now on, it would be better to take him to the theatre with her, so that she can keep an eye on him.

*

Night after night, for most performances, he is in the audience, watching the same play. He eventually becomes very familiar with the dialogue, and if an actor is miscued or dries up, Bobby, in a loud voice, will subconsciously prompt them; this is quite disconcerting for the actors and audience alike. His mother asks him to stop, and he makes a valiant effort to restrain himself. For a few nights, everything is going well; whenever an actor stumbles over their lines, Bobby, with great restraint, makes a conscious effort to suppress his voice. Until, one repetitive matinee performance of Charles Dickens's 'Oliver Twist', Bobby has drifted off to sleep, when he is rudely awakened by a very loud voice, which he immediately knows is emanating from within. It is during the scene near the beginning of the play, where Oliver pleads, "Please sir, I want some more."

The stupefied Mr Bumble then whacks Oliver over the head with a ladle, and reports the incident to Mr Limbkins, who retorts, "That boy will be hung…"

It is at this moment that Bunny, with his unearthly voice, takes it upon himself to continue the dialogue.

"That boy will be hung; I know that boy will be hung. I never was more convinced of anything in my life than I am that that boy will come to be hung."

Bobby is awake by this point, but not quite able to grasp what is happening. The actors, on the stage, are frozen in an awkward, silent tableau. The audience around him are muttering and mumbling. He can sense that all eyes are focusing their hot disapproval upon him.

Yet, Bunny continues babbling on in a monologue that is definitely not from the script.

"And he will be hung; he will be hung from the highest gibbet. What conceit, what demonstrable effrontery to dare ask for more food, when the assembled and august board of this paupers' workhouse has provided much needed sustenance to these ungrateful snivelling near-do-wells. Oliver! Get to work."

Eleanor, who is playing the role of Mrs Sikes, hurries down from the stage, grasps Bobby firmly by the hand, and escorts him backstage to her dressing room; where she locks him in for the remainder of the performance.

This incident heralds the end of his touring days with his mother and the theatre. At the age of thirteen, Bobby Shafto is packed off to the Actors Orphanage.

Chapter Eighteen

A BOY POSSESSED

It is 1950, four years after the end of the War. Little Bobby Shafto, at the age of thirteen, has reached the height of fifty-two inches and weighs one hundred pounds. His mother is taking him to the Actors Orphanage.

The Actors Orphanage is a charitable foundation, administered by the theatrical profession. Its mandate is to house and educate the children of destitute actors and actresses, who have lost one or both parents. Residing at the orphanage are about thirty rambunctious boys and girls, ranging in age from four to seventeen.

The Shaftos' taxi draws up in front of two imposing stone gateposts, which mark the main entrance. On top of each post perches a stone lion, in the rampant position. The gateposts support two, tall, black wrought-iron gates. Set into the right hand post, there is a large bell button, which when pushed, summons Bert the groundskeeper from his cottage, adjacent to the gates. Bert has a burning cigarette, constantly dangling from his cancerous bottom lip. He shuffles, wheezing, coughing, and hunched over, towards the gate. The taxi driver almost feels guilty for ringing the bell, for it looks as though it could very well be Bert's death knell.

On gaining access to the grounds, they are confronted by a long, winding, gravel driveway, stretching roughly a third of a mile, which snakes through grassy fields that are dotted with massive, multicoloured rhododendron bushes. Halfway down, are the playing fields, a necessary part of any English schoolboy's education. The driveway then meanders up to the imposing stone-pillared main entrance of the mansion, then wanders away again, past the tennis courts, more grassy fields, the pigsty, the chicken coops, finally to meet the road again, at the, less than grand, tradesmen's entrance.

The building is an Edwardian mansion, set in forty acres of rolling English countryside, near the town of Chertsey, in the county of Surrey. On three sides, deep woodlands surround the grounds; a rural road embraces the fourth.

The interior of the building is Baroque, with an ornately carved winding oak staircase, leading down to an oak-panelled front hall, the centrepiece of which is a massive, stone, walk-in fireplace. Fluted columns grace the grand assembly rooms. There are wood-panelled libraries, and studies with leaded windows. French doors open onto expansive loggias, and ivy-covered walls look austerely down on manicured lawns.

In the central tower of the building, there is a wrought-iron electric lift that travels up three floors. It ascends from the basement, where the kitchens, pantries, storerooms and cooks' accommodations are located, then up to the ground floor, where the assembly room, dining room, billiard room, library and various studies are situated, then up to the first floor, on which is located numerous bedrooms and bathrooms. It then terminates on the second floor, where the staff's quarters are to be found. Beyond this point, one has to climb a set of rickety wooden stairs that spiral up to the roof of the tower, where fifty feet above the courtyard, a large clapper-less bell hangs; its voice silenced many moons ago by an irate listener.

The first Sunday of the month is Parents Visiting Day. The orphans are made to wear their hated Sunday best. The boys are dressed in grey, scratchy, woollen shirts and shorts, which leave an itchy rash on those with sensitive skin. The rest of the uniform consists of a silver and black, striped necktie, and a grey jacket with the school crest emblazoned on the breast pocket. The crest depicts two lions rampant, under which is inscribed the school motto, *Nil Desperandum* (Never Despair). The girls wear white blouses, short, navy-blue pinafores that also display the school crest on their breast pocket. On the more mature girls, the school motto takes on a more inviting meaning.

On this particular Sunday, Polly Plowright and Gary Roman, whose parents seldom visit, are hiding under the front hall staircase, where they are eagerly inspecting the new arrivals. Thirteen-year-old Gary, a nervous but darkly handsome young man, is crouching next to the loin-stirring, pretty pouting Polly, a lithe and sensuous girl, who looks to be older than Gary is, but in fact is one year his junior. Garry is secretly, and at times overtly, in love with Polly; she has a visceral animal scent that reduces him to a slave in her presence. He feels that he is condemned to be accepted and rejected by Polly Plowright for the rest of his existence.

They watch, as through the front door steps a strikingly, graceful looking woman, whom Polly guesses to be in her mid-forties. By the looks of her clothes, she obviously has fallen on hard times, but she wears her second-hand, fur coat with the dignity and elegance of royalty.

Gary is looking with interest at her son, who he estimates to be a little younger than himself. The boy is tiny and handsome, with blond middle-length hair, clear blue eyes, a slight pug nose, full lips, and the supple sinewy body of a swimmer. His mother is trying to disengage the desperately clinging boy from her fur coat. His big, blue eyes are fixed wide open, like a frightened rabbit, frozen in the headlights of a car. Tears are streaming down his cheeks, splashing off his newly polished second-hand shoes. He is plaintively crying, "No, Mummy, please don't go, please don't leave me, please, please, please."

Her bottom lip is trembling, her eyes are moist, and she is fighting for control. "It's all right Bobby, Mummy will come back and visit soon, I promise." Her voice is quavering. "Please, Matron, would you take him now," she pleads.

"Of course, Mrs Shafto," offers Matron, affectionately known as Matey by the orphans. She is a robust, sensible, and firmly kind woman in her middle years, who wears a ginger wig. Matey's wig is the subject of some conjecture by the children. "Maybe her hair was set on fire on Guy Fawkes day," ventures Daniel Hall, an anaemic, asthmatic seven year old. "Or maybe she had head lice and they ate all her hair off," offers the pockmarked and alarmingly ugly Timmy Grossman.

Gary has noticed that despite Timmy's obvious physical repulsiveness, girls are oddly attracted to him. He thinks it bizarre that good-looking girls seem to be attracted to ugly boys. He coyly brushes his bare arm against the silky skin of Polly's arm, hoping for some response, there is none. His attention is redirected back to the strange little new boy.

"Come along, Bobby, I'll show you where you will sleep," invites Matey cheerily, "and then we can get to know the rest of the family."

Bobby is screaming incoherently, pumping his feet at a rapid pace. His hands are pulling tufts of moulting rabbit fur from his mother's increasingly undignified coat. Matey's strong hand is clamped firmly around Bobby's wrist. She is pulling him towards her, whilst his feet are still pumping in desperation. It is then that Gary and Polly nudge each other as they notice that the two middle fingers on each of his hands are joined together.

Mrs Shafto, wrestling to remain in control, tries to retain her equilibrium. In a poor attempt at acting, she smiles reassuringly at her distraught son, but the effort proves too much for her.

Gary and Polly watch, in utter fascination, as Mrs Shafto slowly wilts; her face crumples, her lips quiver, her slender shoulders slump, her knees, and ankles visibly weaken. For a moment, they expect her to collapse on the floor like a big brown rabbit with myxomatosis.

On seeing this distracting display, Commander Thistleton-Smith, with much puffery, comes steaming to her rescue. The Commander is a retired Naval Reserve Officer, who runs the orphanage like a tight ship, and brooks no sloppy sentiment. "Showing your feelings is a sign of weakness," he is fond of growling. He wears a black patch over his right eye. The rumour has it that he lost the sight in this eye when, as a midshipman, a telescope was rammed into it by an irate senior officer, on being told that he was blocking the midshipman's view, the Commander's version of this incident is decidedly more heroic. He draws alongside the sinking Mrs Shafto, and firmly supporting her under her arm, takes her in tow He turns her stern towards her wallowing son, and steers her, full speed ahead, towards the front door and out to the waiting taxi. Not a word is spoken, at least none that can be understood.

Bobby is gaping at his mother's departing back, the uprooted tufts of rabbit fur still sticking to his sweaty palms. He is reduced to a snotty, snivelling, twittering heap, his legs are no longer pumping; they just wobble weakly. He stares intently at the Commander and the, defeated, and rapidly balding rabbit that was his mother. His face betrays a warp of deep-seated agitation. His lips move silently and slowly. Then a dark and dreadful sound discharges from deep within him. Out of that sweet, angelic mouth, pours forth a terrible and deafening torrent of almost incomprehensible babble. He becomes a boy possessed.

"Run rabbit, run, run, run. Scamper back to your hole. They will still catch you, they will ferret you out, and you will be bagged, skinned, boiled, and consumed. You will be digested, excreted, and metamorphosed into yet another crawling creature. There is no escape. Bunny is in the bag, Bunny is in the bag, pull the cord tightly."

Matey tightens her grip on Bobby, the Commander's back stiffens, and Mrs Shafto collapses on the threshold. Under the staircase, Polly grasps Gary's hand, Gary's stomach quivers, and the taxi purrs softly.

Chapter Nineteen

THE HEADLESS HORSEMAN

The driveway up to the main house of the orphanage holds a special significance for the inmates. At times, it is a path of punishment, as wayward orphans are forced to hand-weed its full length. Sometimes, it is a path to freedom, as they carelessly jump, skip, and hop, on their way to school in Chertsey. However, on the night of the full moon, it is transformed into a path of imaginative terror; for that is when the haunting happens.

They creep from their beds, their noses smudging the windowpanes, their breath coming in short and nervous gasps. With their pyjama sleeves, they wipe the mist from the cold glass, and watch with saucer eyes as the Headless Horseman rides slowly and tauntingly past their pale and frightened, moonlit faces. The legend is that he was a Royalist in the reign of Charles 1. One night, whilst riding through the moonlit woods that once populated these grounds, the hapless horseman was attacked, robbed and beheaded by a gang of Oliver Cromwell's puritanical Roundheads.

He is a nobleman of very noble bearing. Around his neck, he wears a white, bloodstained, ruffled collar, and over his shoulders is draped a flowing black cape, which cascades across the swaying rump of his snorting black steed, whose hot breath condenses immediately in the cold moonlit night-air, like the vaporous smoke from a dragon's fiery nostrils. He carries his sword on his left hip, stylishly swaying to the rhythm of his splendid mount, and under his right arm, he holds his gory, decapitated head.

They have never actually seen the head as his cloak always hides it from view, but they are all convinced it is there. It is a terrible and bloody sight, which repeatedly chills them to the very marrow, except for Kurt Clearwater, one of the older boys, who isn't scared of anything. He tells them, that on one bright moonlit night, he had hidden behind a tree, and had actually seen the Headless Horseman's hideous head. As proof of his daring, in the brave light of day, he will proudly point out to them a trail of darkened stains on the gravelled surface of the driveway. Those stains, according to Kurt, are from the blood of the head of the Headless Horseman, and they will never, ever, wash away. To this very day, those bloody stains, from that gory, dripping, decapitated head, still permeate that dreadful driveway.

On the night of the full moon, the Commander, like a hungry, old, one-eyed lion, ready to pounce on his helpless prey, stalks the corridors of the dormitories, listening for the tiniest sound that will indicate one of his charges is awake. Bobby, on first seeing the ghastly apparition of the Headless Horseman, lets out a terrified scream, which brings a triumphant, smug smile to the old lion's fleshy face. On hearing Bobby scream, all the other boys, immediately realising the impending danger, hastily leap into their cold beds, becoming as stiffly silent as the dead.

The Commander, forcefully throws open the door, and snapping on the lights, bellows, "Did I hear someone shouting, when they should be asleep?" It is not so much a question, as a declaration.

Bobby, lying in his bed, his wide-open eyes staring at the ceiling, tries, unsuccessfully, to stifle his fearful whimper.

The old lion, ever-so-slightly, smirks, then zeroing in on Bobby, he roars, "Shafto, wait outside my office, immediately." Bobby reluctantly throws back the covers and sits on the edge of his bed, searching with his feet for his slippers. The Commander shouts, "Never mind your slippers and dressing gown, go now, on the double." Not a peep is heard from Bobby's dorm-mates.

It is a cold, clear, October night and barefooted Bobby, clad only in his pyjamas, waits alone outside the one-eyed lion's den. In the ethereal light of the full moon, he is shivering with the chilly apprehension of his approaching punishment.

After a trembling hour of unbearable imagery, the Commander comes slowly swaying down the moonlit hall towards him, a round, hulking, brute of a man. He walks with his head turned a little to the right, keeping his good eye looking ahead. Bobby watches nervously as the Commander throws open the study door; he always seems to use this violent gesture to open doors. Pointing imperiously into the study, he thunders, "Inside." Bobby catches the tang of whisky on his breath.

The Commander slams the door behind him. "Take down your pyjama bottom and lean over that chair."

Bobby pulls the cord and releases his pyjama pants. He feels the cold contact of the dark-green leather on his bare and fluttering stomach. He hears a whistling swish, slicing through the air. Looking over his shoulder, he sees the Commander, attentively selecting his instrument of torture from a rack of bamboo canes, thinnest to the left, thickest to the right.

"Eyes front," the Commander roars.

As the canes cut through the air, Bobby listens to the whistling of the diminishing bamboo scale. Then, there is silence, punctuated only by the old one-eyed lion tightly clearing his throat in a low growl.

Having finally selected his weapon of punishment, the Commander bellows, "Shafto, do you know why you are being punished?"

"No sir." Bobby blurts out.

"For disobeying my orders, which are?"

"I don't know sir."

"No talking after lights-out. Do you understand?'

"Yes sir, I promise I won't do it again.'

"No Shafto, I don't think you will."

With a tight rasping bark, followed by an impulsive intake of breath, the Commander brings the full force of the whistling sapling down across the bare and innocent, white buttocks of Bobby Shafto, who squeezes his eyes closed, trying to shut out the pain. Five more times that merciless sapling slices through the air, five more times he hears the Commander's low guttural growl, and five more times Bobby squeezes his eyes closed as he feels the sharp, cutting pain. When it is over, there are six, red, raw, bleeding wheals on his pale, pulsating and tender cheeks. The pain is excruciating, but he doesn't cry out; he is determined not to give this beast the satisfaction of his pitiless victory.

The Commander snarls, "Pull your pyjamas up, go back to bed, and see Matron in the morning about those marks on your backside." The old lion, his voracious appetite being satiated, pokes his finger under his eye-patch, rubbing his rapidly blinking blind eye.

It is only when he is back in the dormitory that Bobby breaks down; they all hear his muffled sobs. He is afraid. He retreats into a dark and dreadful silence. He is scarred for life. He wishes he'd never been born, but he knows it is too much to ask for.

Chapter Twenty

THE INITIATION RITES

Polly Plowright is given to wearing torn dresses that show tantalizing glimpses of her developing, pubescent breasts, and thighs. Much to the chagrin of Gary, she seems strangely attracted to Bobby. This suspicion is confirmed when she tearfully tells Gary that she has pleaded with the older boys to spare Bobby the initiation rites. Gary is aware that it is customary for every new boy, who arrives at the Actors Orphanage, to be subjected to these initiation rights.

A bargain was struck with the older boys that Bobby would be spared, if Polly allowed David and Kurt, the two sixteen-year-old leaders of the gang, to fondle her body and return the favour to both of them simultaneously. David and Kurt, after eagerly agreeing to the bargain, and receiving Polly's pleasurable favours, decided to renege on the deal. They decreed that, after all, tradition must to be upheld. Ergo, Bobby would have to undergo the initiation rites.

Gary is devastated and bewildered. Here is Polly, the love of his life, crying on his shoulder, and confessing to her cruel deception. How could she agree to sacrifice herself in such a wanton way? How could she betray him like that? And all for the sake of a new boy. What is so special about

Bobby Shafto? Gary is seething with jealousy. At that moment, he hates Polly, and Bobby too. He doesn't even question the culpability of the two gang leaders, David and Kurt. He sullenly keeps his silence, being too ashamed to confront them, and too afraid of being ostracized by the whole gang, to walk forever alone.

Bobby is ceremoniously tied face down, to a wooden bench in the football changing room. Paul Havers, a thin, pale, and exceptionally energetic fourteen year old, who is the goalkeeper of the Orphanage football team, is the Chief Torturer. This honour he relishes, perhaps because during almost every football game, Paul suffers unendurable humiliation as the opposing teams are constantly breaking through the Orphanage's weak defence, and mercilessly hammering the football at him, through him, and past him. At the end of every game, he inevitably hobbles ignobly off the field, his pride and body bruised and battered. However, in the role of the Chief Torturer, Paul knows, that this is one time he can inflict the pain and humiliation, instead of being on the receiving end.

Bobby lies stoically and silently on the bench, his mind far away, exploring the possibility of wingless flight.

Kurt and David simultaneously and solemnly intone, "Bobby Shafto…" They wait for a reply, but none is forthcoming. Nevertheless, they continue, "To be a member of the Orphanage gang, you must undergo three sacred initiation rites." There is still no response from the prospective initiate. They go on, "If you succeed in passing these rites, you will become a full-fledged member of the gang. If you show weakness and beg for mercy, you will be doomed to walk forever alone."

There is not the slightest expression of interest from the condemned victim. The rest of the boys murmur a ragged, "Amen," all of them that is, except Gary, who voices his spiteful "Amen" rather forcibly. Then, the two leaders authoritatively shout in unison, "Let the torture begin."

Paul, the Chief Torturer, eagerly slides his instrument of torment from the belt of his trousers; it is an old, ink-stained, twelve-inch wooden ruler. He kneels on the floor and starts to tap lightly, with the flat of the ruler, on the calves of Bobby's bare legs. First one leg then the other, tap-tap-tap, very lightly in quick succession. Gradually there appears a red welt on each of his victim's legs.

From Bobby, comes an echo of the strange, guttural growl of the old one-eyed lion.

Paul, the Chief Torturer, with his eyebrows nearing the top of his forehead in anticipation, his tongue sticking out of the left side of his smirking mouth, causing a string of drool to swing in synch with his tapping rhythm, painsgivingly continues the torment; tap-tap-tap. Before long, tiny droplets of blood rise to the surface of the skin of his victim's sacrificial calves, smearing the calculated surface of the ruler. Paul exhales in satisfaction and looks to his leaders for approbation.

Bobby lies silent and still and dry-eyed.

In unison, the leaders exclaim, "Enough!"

It strikes Bobby as peculiar, that there are two leaders. This would seem to represent, either a perfect democracy, or an uneasy truce.

"Bobby Shafto, you have passed the first test," they intone.

There is no acknowledgment from Bobby; he lies motionless and quiet.

The gang is frozen in an uneasy tableau. Paul, the Chief Torturer, stares anxiously at the prone and silent Bobby Shafto. Has he gone too far this time? As the gang nervously coughs and shuffles, there is gathering apprehension concerning the welfare of their prey. Then, they hear the deep controlled breathing from their tortured victim; he has fallen fast asleep, with his eyes wide open.

The second rite of passage begins. Bobby's webbed hands are tied firmly in front of him, with a long piece of cord. Paul, the Chief Torturer, ceremoniously pilots him out from the changing rooms, through the courtyard of curious onlookers, down the driveway, towards the playing field, with the jeering and cheering rabble running alongside the procession. It stops, long enough, to allow Polly, with a few younger girls in tow, to catch up. With the hem of her torn dress, Polly tries to daub the blood from Bobby's sacrificial calves. The girls weep. Gary, noticing her tender administrations, follows behind the procession with bowed head, sulkily kicking stones.

At the far end of the playing field, lie the woods. On the verge of the woods, is a large patch of wild stinging nettles. It is there, at the top of a steep slope, that the procession comes to a halt, and Bobby is untied and ritually stripped of all his clothes. "Cor Blimey! Will you look at the size of that," cackles Paul Havers, pointing to Bobby's cock. This remark draws guffaws of lewd laughter from Dickie Janey, a particularly obnoxious and loudmouthed eight year old, whose mother, when she visits, is seldom seen without a cigarette, a drink, or a man's tongue in her mouth.

The two leaders intone in unison, "Bobby Shafto, submit your body to the earth," to which he compliantly acquiesces and lies prone. Havers and Janey are told to prepare to roll Bobby down the slope and into the waiting bed of stinging nettles. However, before they can lay a hand on him, with a sudden triumphant shout of ...

 "Lay on MacDuff."

Bobby propels himself down towards, and right through, the patch of stinging nettles, enduring innumerable sharp, scorpion-like attacks on his naked body, until he rolls to a stop at the edge of the woods. Slowly and silently he stands up, and to the amazement of the gathered gang, walks defiantly back through the patch of torturous nettles, staring implacably into the faces of his admiring initiators. Almost immediately, a multitude of small, white blisters swell up all over his naked body.

At which point, Polly, who has witnessed many initiations, but somehow instinctually feels she has to rescue Bobby, comes running on to the field, carrying a bottle of pink calamine lotion. The rabble parts to let her through. Polly is screaming at them, "What are you bullies looking at? Go! Leave, right now, to hell with your stupid initiation rights. Haven't you done enough damage for one day?" Gary bows his head in shame.

She gathers some dock leaves from the edge of the woods and gently rubs them over Bobby's painful blisters. She then removes the cork from the bottle of Calamine lotion, and pouring a liberal portion of the healing pink, creamy liquid into the palm of her merciful hand, proceeds to delicately rub the cooling lotion all over his naked and burning body; the drying salve, making him look like a primitive pigmy in war paint. As the gentle angel of mercy spreads the soothing balm over his upper thighs and buttocks, he becomes aroused, and gradually stands erect, and looking straight at Gary, Bobby beams. Gary can't bear to face him; he turns away, his whole being blindly aching with hate and jealousy. At the sight of Bobby's engorged cock, an embarrassed titter runs through the rabble as they uneasily shift their weight from one foot to the other, in self-conscious synchronization.

But no, they have not done enough damage for one day; the third and final rite has yet to be performed. The girls are ordered to remain on the field, and on the field, they remain. Polly knows that the last rite is not about physical pain, but humiliation, and she doesn't want to be there. Bobby's naked and tortured body is draped with a bed sheet, his hands are retied in front of him with the cord, and he is led by Paul, the Chief Torturer, in slow procession back to the main house.

In the centre of this splendid mansion, at the foot of the tower, fifty feet below the clapper-less bell, lies an open, cobblestone courtyard, measuring forty by forty feet,. In the exact centre of this courtyard, to facilitate drainage, there is a two-foot diameter, cast-iron manhole cover, which is perforated by many holes. Underneath this manhole cover is 'The Den of Death', a circular stone room, measuring about seven feet in diameter and seven feet in height. To access this subterranean chamber of horrors from the surface, requires entrance at the edge of the courtyard, through a three-inch thick, solid wood door, down twelve slippery stone steps, and along a seventeen-foot dank, dark, and narrow, sloping passageway.

Paul relinquishes his prisoner to Gary, who determinedly leads Bobby through the heavy wooden doorway, callously pulling him down the steps, along the slippery, sloping passageway and into the circular, stone chamber of 'The Den of Death', in the centre of which is placed a solitary wooden chair. Gary sadistically rips the sheet from Bobby's wounded body, painfully tearing at his flesh; Bobby doesn't flinch. Having tied his victim securely to the chair, Gary hisses at him. "Stay away from my girlfriend, Shafto. Stay away from Polly." Bobby just stares placidly into his tormentor's hostile eyes, and remains impassively silent. Gary, not receiving any satisfaction, angrily retreats up the sloping passageway, screaming hysterically, "I warn you, Shafto, just stay away from her... or else." Not expecting, or even wanting, a retort from Bobby, he scurries up the slippery steps, and slamming the heavy wooden door behind him, forcefully rams the bolt home.

Directly above him, seven feet from the damp, dirt floor, Bobby sees the perforated manhole cover. The holes are shedding thin, sharp, shafts of light, which highlight his painful, nettle-stung face and body. He is left naked and alone, shivering in the cold, dank semi-darkness. He uncomplainingly awaits his ordeal.

Above him, on the surface of the cobblestone courtyard, the rabble is gathering; they form a crude circle around the manhole cover. Each one of them has consumed two large Tizer bottles of cold water. The leaders, Kurt and David, standing at attention like rigid sergeant majors, shout in unison, "Pre...sent... arms." The rabble proudly displays their members. At this point, they are bursting for a piss, and feeling the cool air on their cocks, with difficulty, restrain themselves. Not a nanosecond too soon, the command from their exalted leaders comes, "Fire!"

With a burst of relief, the floodgates are opened. Generous streams of urine gleefully gush from twelve bloated bladders, splashing onto the surface of the perforated manhole cover, piercing the holes, and replacing the pristine shafts of nature's pure light, with potent streams of warm, testosterone-fuelled piss. It rains down on the head and body of the helpless and naked Bobby. He remains stoic and silent in his saturation; the urine even seems to have a soothing effect on his itching, stinging-nettled body.

Then, up through those perforated holes, from the dark, dank depths of that dreadful 'Den of Death', shrilly issues forth that black and thunderous voice. It reverberates around and around the stone courtyard, ringing through the wrought-iron fire escapes, spiralling skyward, and resonating in a strange and wondrous vibrato from the tower's clapper-less bell fifty feet above.

"This is the last time that I will allow you to desecrate this body. This is the ultimate time that you will violate this sanctum. You have drawn my blood, scarred my body, and baptized me with your unholy water. You degenerate pack of senseless fools. You have no comprehension of who you have so shamefully abused. You cannot hurt me with your feeble ceremonies. You cannot conquer me, because you cannot see me, touch me, taste me, or smell me. You can only hear me. Now hear this: Any one of you, who has acted in malice, is doomed to be punished. You will become a white crow, and will forever walk alone."

Fleeing with open flies, inelegantly splashing their final squirts over each other, the frightened rabble scatters over the surface of the cobblestone courtyard, like desiccated leaves before a wild winter wind.

For his uncomplaining courage, Bobby is enthusiastically accepted into the Orphanage gang, by a near unanimous vote, only one of them has failed to extend his hand. Bobby Shafto will not be doomed to walk forever alone.

Chapter Twenty-One

SEARCHING FOR CLARITY, HOPING FOR SANITY

Sunday is a day of worship. All the orphans have to wear their dreaded Sunday best, and attend the church of their particular religion. The majority of the kids belong to the Church of England, and a few are Roman Catholic.

Amongst those attending the Catholic service, are Gary Roman, Bobby Shafto and the Grossman brothers. The brothers aren't actually Roman Catholic, nor are they Church of England, so they have a choice of which service to attend; they prefer the Catholic one, because it is unsupervised.

The Church of England kids, supervised by the old one-eyed lion, walk in a crocodile line to Lyne Village Church. The nearest Catholic service is held across the road from the orphanage, at Botley's Hospital for the Mentally Retarded, an all-male institution. The orphans often see the inmates of Botley's, being taken for a walk along Holloway Hill. They are always under strict supervision, holding hands in pairs and walking in a crocodile line. This symbolic amphibious synchronicity appeals to Bobby's Catholic sense of humour.

The Communion Service they attend every Sunday, at 'Botley's Hospital for the Mentally Retarded', is a noisy affair. There is none of the quiet reverence associated with the normal Catholic Mass; the boys of Botley's hold nothing back. During the service, there is a continual cacophony of constant talking, shouting, laughing, shuffling, and the occasional enormous grunt. The visiting priest has learned, long ago, to ignore the congregation. He keeps his back to his flock, and continually mumbling the dead language, he quietly fortifies himself with altar wine.

When the Communion bell rings, all heaven breaks loose. The crazy Botley Boys push and shove each other, in their eagerness to be first to queue up at the altar rail, to receive the Holy Body of Christ. Strangely, this turmoil is conducted without a word being spoken, just lots of subdued grunting and shuffling; the Botley boys obviously recognise the sacredness of the sacrament.

This particular Sunday, as he kneels at the Communion rail, Bobby is sorely reminded of the convent, and Bunny's chanting. No matter how hard Bobby tries to suppress his altar ego, Bunny bubbles forth. His voice has the power of a hundred monks droning a Gregorian chant.

 "Insanity is to be within sanity; it allows us to think with clarity."

On hearing this bold declaration, a hush descends on the congregation. The priest nervously continues with his '*Corpus Dominoes*'. Bunny also continues chanting.

 "Wise fools are foolishly wise, for the fool wisely agrees to be foolish."

The Botley boys start to rhythmically shuffle. The priest is silent.

 "You can be sane and still make no sense."

The Botley boys cry in answer, "Amen, Brother." The priest stands transfixed.

"What bothers me is that you believe what you are saying."

The Botley boys slowly sway down the nave, humming in unison. The priest turns his back on the mob and looks to the tabernacle for divine guidance.

"We are no longer the Ringmaster, but the animals and freaks of the sideshow."

The Botley boys increase the intensity of their swaying and respond with a melodious "Ahhh...menn." The priest approaches the altar boy and requests more wine.

"You are you and I am I, and so we remain."

With their arms reaching towards the heavens and their fingers shaking in delight, the Botley boys are approaching rapture. The priest drinks deep draughts of altar wine from the Chalice.

"Don't impose your morals on us; we enjoy jousting with the Devil."

The Botley boys chant a resounding "Ahh...menn, Ohhhh yeahhh." Then, without a murmur, or even the slightest grunt, they lower their arms and shuffle silently back to their pews, reverently re-seating themselves. The priest, not having performed the sacrament of Holy Communion, and having received no divine guidance, gives a hasty blessing, and hurriedly leaves the altar.

Bobby remains, stoically kneeling at the Communion rail. Gary, who by this time is totally discombobulated, turns his back on God and His crazy congregation, and walks down the nave and out into the fresh spring air, searching for clarity and hoping for sanity.

*

It is a mild spring Sunday afternoon; wispy, cumulus clouds are scudding across the sapphire sky, the earth beneath is seething with life, daffodils gather in bunches across the fields and nod in pleasant conversation, the undergrowth is alive with tiny creatures, frisky squirrels and bouncing bunny-rabbits skitter through their tiny jungles, swallows and starlings soar through the sap-rising branches, and a chorus of songbirds are singing the praises of the worm.

Bobby and the gang are hanging around under the big yew tree near the front door, revelling in their braggadocio. The rest of the kids, encouraged by the welcome warmth of the sun, are springing out of the main building, screaming with delight and eager to play.

Five girls, led by Polly, skip over to Bobby. She smiles invitingly, "Do you want to play tag with us, Bobby?"

"I would love to," he coos.

Polly bends down and plants a flirtatious kiss on his cheek. "OK, you are *It*," she sighs, and runs away giggling.

All of the other girls, screeching with excitement, scatter in all directions. Bobby casts a taunting smile at Gary, then swiftly runs to intercept Polly who is laughing teasingly and shouting, "You can't catch me, you can't catch me." And of course he does, right at the edge of the woods, where they eagerly entwine and wrestle each other down into the long and welcoming, wet grass.

The boys are lustily cheering encouragement, and the girls are shrieking in vicarious delight. Gary remains sullenly silent; he feels so small and insignificant, so utterly miserable.   He drifts from the perimeter of the cheering and yelling throng, and shuffles despondently towards the refuge of the sunken gardens to wallow in his agony.   He is a white crow.

Chapter Twenty-Two

WHITE SMOKE RISING

Bobby has now been at the orphanage for two years. He is fifteen years of age, with a height of fifty-seven inches and weighs one hundred and fifteen pounds.

Seven of the gang are gathered in one of the bomb shelters. They sit in a circle on the earthen floor, telling war stories. It is dark and cold in the concrete shelter, it always is, and even the powerful heat of summer's sun fails to infiltrate those thick, impenetrable walls. Bobby is in the centre of the circle, lying on his stomach, laying a fire. He has lit a candle in front of him, on which he is patiently drying damp twigs, before arranging them in a tiny tepee shape on the earthen floor. He then places the lit candle into the centre of the tiny tepee and gently blows on the reluctant wood. Before long, a wisp of smoke lazily ascends, soon to be joined by dozens of dancing sparks. He keeps blowing gently, coaxing the tiny flames to lick the crackling twigs. Being satisfied that the fire is alive, he carefully places on more sticks, until it is burning brightly and radiating welcome warmth throughout the cold, concrete bunker. The smoke rises to the ceiling and gathers in a thick woolly cloud, politely queuing up to languidly escape through the narrow ventilation pipe.

The gang is gathered in a circle around the fire. There is love-struck Gary, who sits sullenly silent. Next to Gary, is Paul, the Chief Torturer, who has been at the Actors Orphanage since the age of four. Paul can attest that not one bomb has been dropped on the orphanage. He swears that he has seen dogfights overhead. He says he once saw a German plane, maybe a 'Focke-Wulf', which was hit. It went screaming and spiralling towards the ground, coming to earth about three miles away near the town of Chertsey. The pilot lived and was taken to the local police station as a prisoner of war. He was escorted by the proud, old men of the Home Guard, bravely brandishing their ancient Royal Enfield rifles.

Then there is Yvon, who is from Jersey, in the Channel Isles. He speaks of the German occupation of Jersey and the massive underground hospital complex that they constructed; it had its own electrical and water supplies. According to Yvon, this underground complex, was so big, it could easily house the entire population of the Channel Islands. To Yvon's left, sits Kurt and David, who try to tell their stories, but they can never complete a sentence, because they keep interrupting each other and speaking in unison.

Bobby is looking pensively into the fire, the flickering flames reflecting off his smoke-smudged face. The damp twigs, cracking and snapping, send sparks flying upward, to eventually peter out and disappear into the soft underbelly of the accumulating cloud of smoke above. Remembering the chaotic destruction wreaked by the Doodlebug, Bobby is intently watching each tiny explosion and following its upward trail. In this cave of dancing shadows, they listen as he tells his terrible tale of destruction.

*

The Commander is at his desk, in his study, composing further rules of punishment to enforce discipline on his unruly crew. The Orphanage Committee has been informed of the cruel canings he is administering to the boys, and told him, in no uncertain terms, to cease and desist. He seems to be perplexed by the maxim, 'The punishment must fit the crime'. He admits to himself that some of the punishment that he has meted out, like the beatings he inflicts on boys for talking after dark, is maybe a little too harsh for the transgression. On the other hand, he doesn't beat the girls, but just makes them stand outside his office, barefooted in their nighties for an hour, and then he will bellow them back to bed. This unevenness of punishment worries him. What is good for the goose must be good for the gander. He remains perplexed.

Searching for inspiration, he swivels his chair to face the French doors that look out onto that gentle, spring morning, hoping that the pleasant view will spawn the answer to his confounded problem. The furrows in his worried brow increase, as he notices a plume of white smoke rising in the vicinity of the sunken gardens. By standing on his chair, he can just see the rooftops of the two bomb shelters, and from one of them, he sees the origin of the white smoke. His sightless right eye starts twitching under the eye patch. Jumping off the chair, he throws open the French doors, so hard, that a pane of glass shatters on impact as it hits the stone wall, he swears bitterly. In this agitated state, he stomps down to the offending bomb shelter.

*

Bobby has just got to the part in his narrative, of the 2,000 pounds of high explosives slamming into the block of flats, when the Commander violently explodes the door of the bomb shelter open, so hard and fast, that the blast of the wind generated, forcefully scatters sparks and ashes from the fire, immediately producing great billowing clouds of smoke, which rapidly fill the cramped and already smoke-filled choking chamber. As the attacking smoke rushes through the open doorway, it completely envelops the Commander, sending him into a paroxysm of coughing, as he frantically rubs his one good eye. Seizing the opportunity of the temporarily blinded enemy, the boys lithely evade his groping hands and slither to the safety of the open fields where, under cover of the ever-expanding smoke screen, they make their escape. All of them that is, except for Bobby, who falls into the groping clutches of the coughing and wheezing Commander. Bobby is then frog-marched up the hill to wait, yet again, outside the old one-eyed lion's den, in anticipation of further punishment.

"Shafto, come in," the lion roars through the closed door. Bobby sheepishly enters the lion's den, and stands before his inquisitor, who is seated, with his back to Bobby, staring at the shattered pane of glass. He speaks in a controlled and icy voice. "Shafto, what were you boys doing in the bomb shelter?"

"Telling stories, sir," Bobby replies to the back of the Commander's head.

"And why did you light a fire?"

"Because, we were cold, sir." He feels the warmth draining from his hands and feet, in anticipation of the worst.

"Don't you know you could have burnt the building down?" snaps the irate Commander.

"No, that's impossible," Bunny emphatically replies.

Thrusting his finger under his eye-patch, the Commander energetically rubs his sightless eye. "What did you say, Shafto?" he roars, as he abruptly swivels his chair to face Bobby.

"It's elementary. It is impossible for the build-ing to burn down, because the fire was on the bare earth, and the building is made of re-enforced concrete; it is fireproof," Bunny shouts.

"Don't shout at me, Shafto," shouts back the Com-mander as he quickly rises and walks around his desk to stand directly behind Bobby. Reverting to his icy, controlled voice, the Commander hisses, "Shafto, you are an insolent little boy, and for that you deserve to be punished."

"Yes, sir," Bobby meekly replies, waiting to hear the swish of the bamboo cane.

"What punishment do you think you deserve?" the Commander asks in genuine interest.

"Not the cane, sir," Bobby hastily replies.

"I agree with you, Shafto," roars the Commander, "can-ing doesn't seem to correct your impudent behaviour."

"Thank you sir," he sighs in relief.

"Don't thank me, boy. I am putting you on Defaulters. You will not sit at your usual place in the mess hall. You will sit apart from the rest of the crew, at a separate table, and for a period of three days, you will be served nothing but dry bread and water."

This is more than Bobby could have ever hoped for. "Thank you, sir," he says with sincerity.

"I told you not to thank me. Now get out of my sight, and close the door behind you," orders the Commander, feeling almost certain that he has made the right decision, and fitted the punishment to the crime.

Bobby is smiling as he closes the door gently behind him.

Chapter Twenty-Three

You have to make the journey
to understand its meaning

At the age of seventeen, Bobby has reached his full height of sixty-two inches, and a weight of one hundred and thirty-four pounds; he will grow no more. It is time to put away childish things and start to earn his living. After an interview with the Actors Orphanage Committee, to discuss his career aspirations, it is mutually agreed that an occupation at sea will make a bigger man of him. So, without further ado, he is sent to the Gravesend National Sea Training School, from which he hopes to graduate to life aboard ship, as a deck hand in the Merchant Navy.

. As Bobby approaches manhood, he doesn't like to look over his shoulder. At this critical juncture in his life, he is not so much interested in the past as he is in the future.

Eleanor knows she is about to lose her son to the world and the time has come to tell him the truth about his father. Broaching the subject with some trepidation, she pours him a sherry. She is all too aware of her boy's eagerness to become a man, but it is crucial that he know the truth. She sits him down and embarks upon her revelation. "Bobby, Darling, the time has come for me to tell you about your father."

Bobby is eager to cut the umbilical cord, he loves his mum, but he is annoyed by her overprotective manner; he feels suffocated and wants to escape, his impatience is reflected in the bellowing of Bunny.

"We already know," Bunny, bawls, in that awefull voice that only a mother can ignore.

Eleanor persists. "This is very important, Darling; it is something you have a right to know."

"This is pointless; we have a train to catch. We told you, we already know," Bunny tetchily replies.

"How could you possibly know?" she demands in exasperation. "Who told you?"

"Nobody told us, we just know, that's all. We already know Mummy."

"But you can't know it all," she insists. "This is something that only your father and I know."

"Our father who art in hell is dead," shrieks Bunny.

Bobby feels a tightening of his temples. He can sense the dark energy rising, and knows he will find it difficult to debate with any recognisable construct, but the pressure forces the words, and Bunny continues to babble.

"I know, because cognitive conditions cannot be understood, because the malfeasance of mediocrity meanders through the process of an identical quintessence. Don't talk to me of mentors, when the world itself is an obfuscation of magnificent impudence."

The energy is accelerating and rushing through Bobby's lips, which are vibrating with *Bunnybabble*.

"Subtract, then you will arrive at two, divide, and you will become one. We are miniatures of what we know; look at what we don't know. Laugh uproariously in the face of phantoms, and smile like a giant. Disparage their translucent obviousness; that unholy fear of not knowing, of keeping together the Gordian knot."

Eleanor knows she can't stop the words gushing from his mouth, but she has to divert the torrent. It is imperative that she tell him about his father; she can remain silent no longer. "Bobby, I want you to listen to me. There is something that you have to know about your father"

Bunny will not listen, the torrent will not be stemmed, there is no damn way.

"The sum parts of my experience and knowledge are only attainable by and for myself. I want to taste, see, touch, hear, smell, and feel every sense and non-sense of each universe. I can't close my mind to infinite knowledge, for the peaks and valleys are there to explore not ignore. To be levelheaded is to keep the spirit on one plane; tilt it and chase the bubble. Don't stop, or you will falter and know that fear will return and crack you. Embrace encumbrances, recognise the hardness that is life, and walk gently on this tender earth, for the planet is seething underfoot. Look up and see the scudding sails of infinity and you will truly wonder."

Eleanor knows that Bunny is in control, she remains silent, for she can do no more. What she has to tell Bobby will have to wait.

With his mother's blessing, Bobby closes the door to 100 Elm Park Mansions behind him. He takes his first cautious steps alone; he has cut the cord and cast off, he is now floating freely.

It is a cold, grey day; the drizzle is making a point of persistently pecking at his new, navy-blue, Burberry raincoat. With his kit bag slung jauntily over his tiny right shoulder, he emerges from the block of flats on to Park Walk. Turning his face upwards into the drizzle, he sees the yellow, plastic kitchen curtains of the third floor flat flapping in the wind and rain; they act as an agitated frame for the serene face of his heavenly mother. She peers down with a wide smile and a nervous giggle, her beautiful set of false teeth out-shining her limpid, pale blue eyes. Those perfect white teeth don't quite belong in that wise old face. She has aged beyond her years; he knows that Bunny and he have been hard on her, and he wonders if he will ever see her again.

Behind him, he hears the squeak of a swollen wood-framed window being raised, and he immediately smells the hot, acrid energy that is emanating from within; it is Mrs Egan. The old crone has a habit of sitting inside her dirty, paint-peeled window, on a straight-backed chair, just staring out at the passing parade, whilst taking mental notes and muttering acerbic comments to all and sundry who dare to go by her black hole. She is privy to all the comings and goings of Elm Park Mansions, as the broken-down-bomb-damaged-soot-stained block of worker's flats is euphemistically called.

Mrs Egan is in her late eighties, house-ridden, and hungry for gossip. She is always attired in a grubby, faded, blue-flowered pinafore; her dirty, grey, wispy hair, dancing delicately on her scaly, steaming scalp. The room behind her is dark, dank, and dingy. It pushes out a sickly-sweet smell, the smell of the unwashed, the smell of suffering, the smell

of decay and impending death. Emanating from her tooth-
less mouth, he sometimes fancies that he smells the putrid
stench of a witch's breath.

"Where are you going, little Bobby?" her parched voice
rasps.

"Out, and I'm not little," he retorts.

"Out where? Yes you are," rebuts the hag.

"I'm going to sea. No I'm not."

"To see what? Yes you are."

"Not to see anything in particular, I'm going to sea."

"Hello down there, Mrs Egan," greets the angelic voice
from above. Bobby silently thanks his heavenly mother for
her timely intercession.

He spots a taxicab rounding the corner from Fulham
Road onto Park Walk, and stepping briskly off the kerb, he
flags it down. As the vehicle splashes to a halt, he shouts
over his shoulder, maybe a little too effusively, "Bye, Mum,
bye, Mrs Egan. See you in three months." With calculated
cool, he enters the heart of the purring beast.

With a flourish, as though pulling on the arm of a one-
armed bandit, the driver lowers the meter's flag, starting
the shillings and pence on their inexorable march to the
pound. "Where to, Guv?" asks the driver as he looks up at
his passenger's reflection in the rear-view mirror.

"Charing Cross and step on it," shouts Bunny.

"You don't have to yell, Guv," responds the driver. "My
hearing is not that shabby."

Bobby tries to control his inner voice, and with a little
effort, he apologises, "I'm sorry, I'll pay more attention in future." He turns around to peer out of the cab's rear window.
Disappearing into the distance, through the grey curtain of
drizzle, he can see the shapes of the rapidly receding, stink-

ing witch in her dark cave, and above her, a pale, saintly face, with gleaming white teeth, framed by plastic kitchen curtains, which resemble wildly flapping daffodil-yellow ears. He mutters tenderly, "Goodbye, Mum, I love you," again wondering if this will be the last time that he will see her.

"Faster, faster, faster," yells Bunny. The driver smiles, as if he knows.

At the bottom of Park Walk, they turn onto the busy Kings Road. Bobby settles back comfortably in the spacious cab and takes stock of his driver. There is a familiar essence about him, he can't quite grasp what it is, but the feeling is strangely reassuring. The driver sits like a seasoned warrior; tall, angular and proud, but bowed a little from the weight of his long campaigns.

They are heading east along the Kings Road, approaching the Chelsea Public Baths. The driver is deftly piloting the taxi through the busy London traffic, as effortlessly as a gondolier navigating his love-worn craft through the carnal canals of Venice. His face is entrenched with the wisdom of the universe. He is a distinguished looking man, except for his flaming red hair, which is greying at the temples, giving him the look of a clown out on the town.

It isn't until the taxi has negotiated its way around Trafalgar Square that the driver speaks again. "Are you going to sea for the first time, Guv?"

Bobby is somewhat taken aback by the suddenness of the question. "Yes, actually I am, well, I have to attend Sea Training School at Gravesend first. But, how did you know that I was going to sea for the first time?"

The driver smiles again, "Just a hunch, Guv. Let's just say that I can tell the ones who are just starting on their journey."

"Is it that obvious?" Bobby exclaims in mild alarm.

"Well, Guv, to me it is," answers the driver, "You have to make the journey to understand its meaning."

The front wheels of the taxicab kiss the kerb outside Charing Cross Railway station. Bobby alights and reaches into his inside jacket pocket for his wallet.

The driver raises the meter's flag and stares straight ahead and asks, "Where I picked you up, Guv, do you live there?"

"Well, yes," Bobby replies hesitantly.

"Do you live with your family?" persists the driver.

Bobby looks quizzically at him.

Turning to face Bobby, he says, "Look, Guv, I don't mean to be nosy, but you do look familiar."

"As a matter of fact so do you," Bobby declares. "I live with my mother, my father died when I was four."

The driver is silent for a few moments, before asking, "Are you sure your father is dead?"

"Of course we're sure, you raving lunatic. We were right there when he croaked. Robert succeeded Edward."

"I'm sorry, Guv, I mistook you for someone else. Please forgive me." Checking the fare on the meter and extending his right hand, he announces, "That comes to sixteen shillings and ninepence, Guv."

Bobby withdraws a pound note from his wallet, saying, "That's all right, no need to apologise."

As he tenders the money, he notices that the two middle fingers of the driver's hand are joined together. He looks up into the penetrating stare of his driver's eyes; each is of a different gem-like colour, like an odd-eyed, white oriental cat. His right eye is the colour of lapis lazuli, and his left, the colour of turquoise. Bobby feels a shiver of distant recognition running through his tiny frame. With a buzz of delicate excitement, he murmurs, "Keep the change." He turns slowly on his heel to walk into the steamy, cacophonous cavern of the train station that is Charing Cross.

"Thanks, Guv," shouts the driver, "ave a good journey, make sure you don't get into too much trouble. Maybe we'll meet again under a more propitious moon." The taxi peels away slickly from the kerb and is digested by the teeming London traffic.

"What do you mean trouble?" yells Bunny at the rear of the departing taxi, **"We are embarking on the adventure of our life, and you caution us not to get into trouble. I say, go for self-actualization, rebel against the authors of the rules that dictate your life. To do otherwise is to submit in supplication and lose your individual freedom. The primal prerogative is to live life to the lees. When at the bottom of the well, look up and you will see the light. Cast off your trappings, leap naked into the fast flowing river, and let the current guide you. Living in your own shadow will stunt your growth… Sorry, Bobby. Step into the light and blossom."**

Bobby's mind flashed back thirteen years, to those idyllic childhood days with Hobbs the gardener. Can this be that man? At first, there are just trickles of recollection, and then, the dam bursts and the memories come flooding back. His eyes were unmistakeable, but it was the first time Bobby had been conscious of Hobbs' webbed fingers. As a child, having webbed fingers himself, he had taken them for granted and hadn't noticed them. He was almost sure that his driver was Hobbs. How could he ever forget that wise and gentle giant?

Did Hobbs recognise him? And if he did, why didn't he say so? Why would he keep his identity a secret?

Turning towards the departing taxi, he whispers, "Under a more propitious moon, Hobbs." He makes his way into the crowded train station, anxious to phone his mother and tell her of the amazing news of his reconnection; he knows he is sublimely blessed.

*

Arthur Hobbs guides his taxi through the busy London traffic, with the sure knowledge that his recent passenger is Bobby Shafto. How could he mistake that tiny, trusting child with that awe-full voice, those wide-open eyes, and tiny webbed fingers? He wonders how much Eleanor Shafto has told her son about his father.

*

After paying for his train ticket to Gravesend, Bobby makes a beeline for the bank of A&B phones, situated next to the Railway Buffet. He is anxious to phone home and tell his mother about meeting Hobbs again. Inserting three pennies, he rapidly dials FLA-5624. After three double rings, his mother answers, he can tell that she has been crying.

"Hello, Mother," he whispers tenderly. "I love you."

Of course, this opens the floodgates again, and she sobs in reply, "I love you too, Darling. I am so glad you called. Are you all right?"

"I'm fine, Mother. Now stop crying, I have something wonderful to tell you."

"That's sweet, Darling, but I still want you to know something very important about your father."

"How many times have I told you? Father is dead," screams Bunny into the mouthpiece. Eleanor quickly pulls the phone away from her ear.

Precisely at this instant, a loud, booming voice explodes over the station's Tanoy system, ricocheting around the cavernous railway terminal. "The eleven forty-two to Gravesend, calling at Deptford, Greenwich, Bexley Heath, Crayford, Dartford and Gravesend, is now boarding at platform number twelve… The eleven forty-two to Gravesend calling at Deptford, Greenwich, Bexley Heath, Crayford, Dartford and Gravesend, is now boarding at platform number twelve."

During this announcement Eleanor is pleading quietly and intensely into the phone, "You must listen to me, Darling."

He can't hear his mother's voice over the loudspeakers. His train is about to leave, and he isn't going to miss it. He shouts into the phone, "I can't hear you, Mother. I have to go. My train is boarding. I just wanted to let you know that I am sure I saw Hobbs today; he was my taxi driver. Bye, I love you. I'll phone you from Gravesend." He hurriedly hangs up the telephone and dashes towards platform twelve.

Eleanor slowly puts down the receiver, her son's voice still reverberating in her ear. She is saddened and frustrated that she still hasn't been able to tell him about his father. She is also surprised and excited that Hobbs has possibly re-emerged after all these years, but Bobby could have been mistaken. How could Bobby be sure that it was Hobbs? Then again, how could anyone mistake a man like Hobbs? She is feeling strangely anxious about his reappearance, if indeed it is really him. She wonders how much he has told Bobby.

Chapter Twenty-Four

THE SECRET IS OUT

Hobbs retraces his route, and within the hour, he comes to a stop outside Elm Park Mansions. Keeping his motor running, he sits in the cab, trying to come to terms with his conflicting emotions. His mind travels back thirteen years, to the day that he was dismissed from the service of Eleanor Shafto. They had agreed they wouldn't see each other again, until she had told Bobby the truth about his father, and from what he could gather it is obvious that Bobby is still unaware.

Over the years, Hobbs had been true to his word, merging with the nameless masses of the great metropolis of London. For the last ten years, he'd been driving a taxicab. Soon he will be leaving England. He has already booked his passage, and is scheduled to sail on November 24th, on his old ship the 'RMS *Strathaird*', bound for Sydney, Australia. He is well aware of the irony of being a paying passenger on the very ship from which he was dishonourably discharged. On the way to Charing Cross, he was aching to tell Bobby the truth, but he could not betray a sacred trust.

*

After Bobby's phone call, Eleanor swiftly surveys the tiny flat. She pulls up the rumpled sheets on her bed and smoothes out the covers. Going into the living room, she empties the ashtray, dusts the bookcases, and puts all the loose books into tidy piles. Opening the glass door of the large bookcase, she is pleased to observe that there is an unopened bottle of Dry Fly Sherry, accompanied by three lead-crystal glasses. She lights the gas fire, setting it on low. Glancing over to the dining table under the window, she is moved by Bobby's parting gift, an extravagant bouquet of vibrant wild flowers in a Venetian cut-glass vase.

Feeling that she would have no time for a bath, she goes into the kitchen and turns on the hot water geezer, running some water into a chipped enamel basin. Undressing, she washes her body with a soapy flannel, and then rinses herself off with cold water. Back in the bedroom, she selects a modest, cotton print dress, a dress she hasn't worn for thirteen years. Having brushed her greying shoulder-length hair, and applying a minimum amount of makeup, she returns to the living room. To sooth her nerves, she pours herself a glass of sherry, and lights a cigarette. Seating herself in the armchair that faces the window, she expectantly awaits him, if indeed he will be paying a visit.

*

Mrs Egan, from her stinking cave on the ground floor, who has been keenly observing the stationary taxi, takes note of the approach of the imposing redheaded figure, striding purposefully towards the entranceway of the flats. She wonders who would ask a taxi driver to come to the door. She finds it odd, because she knows that London taxicabs will only stop if they are flagged down on the street. She will file this little bit of information away in the dark recesses of her acquisitive mind.

He gives a perfunctory nod to the old women in the ground-floor window, who he notices is staring intensely at him, and without hesitation, he walks through the front entranceway and climbs up the four flights of stone stairs, two at a time, arriving a little out of breath, at the front door of 100 Elm Park Mansions. He stands for a moment, straightening his tie, and rubbing the toe of each shoe on the back of his pant leg. Running his fingers through his mop of greying, red hair, he pulls himself up to his full height. With the knuckles of the two joined fingers of his right hand, he lightly knocks on the door, three times.

Although she has not heard that signature knock for thirteen years, she instantly recognises it; the measured beat of the knocks indicate a polite enquiry, rather than a rude demand. She stubs her cigarette out, dispersing the smoke with a rapid, sideways, fanning motion of her hand. Standing up, she smoothes out her dress, and looks in the mirror above the mantle-piece, fluffing her hair with both hands, and cocking her head from side to side, searching for reflected approval. Drawing a deep breath, she pulls herself up to her full height and with a final swift glance around the room, goes out to the hallway, and approaches the front door.

After what seems like an eternity, he is about to knock again, when he hears the soft footsteps approaching on the other side of the door. Through the transom, he notices the hall light flick on. He quickly lowers his arm and stiffens his spine, almost coming to attention. The door is unhurriedly opened, to reveal... her. She stands erect, her body is backlit from the hallway light, and he immediately recognises that dignified profile. It takes a second to adjust to the light and to see more clearly the graceful woman, whom he had once served those many years ago. In the half shadow, he imagines he sees an enigmatic smile playing around her lips. For a suspended moment, there is silence, and then time dissolves.

There he is, standing tall; the hall light behind her is highlighting his shock of greying, red hair. His noble face remains impassive, and he is wearing a conservatively cut, navy-blue suit, a crisp white shirt, and a black tie. His black peaked cap is neatly tucked under his right arm. He bows slightly and clicks his heels together. Looking in the direction of the sound, she notices the radiant shine on his shoes, and time fades away. "Hobbs!" she sighs, exhaling the word slowly in warm affection and relief.

"Your carriage awaits without, Mum," he announces, with due deference.

Without a moment's hesitation, she responds, "Without what, Hobbs?"

"Without wheels, Mum."

The old chestnut is roasted into their memories. Time reconnects and they laugh together; a rich, throaty, but cautious chortle rolls from deep within him, accompanied by a delighted, but tentative giggle from her.

"Please come in, Hobbs, I have been half expecting you."

"Thank you, Mum, and who told you I was coming?" enquires Hobbs respectfully.

She smiles, "Bobby phoned from Charing Cross Station. He said that he had run into you."

"Yes Mum, I was his taxi driver, I was wondering if I recognised me."

"Please don't stand on formalities any more, Arthur, please call me Eleanor." She steps aside to let him pass, and as he moves by her on his way into the flat, he ducks his head instinctually, and their left arms softly brush together, she feels a static tingle. "The sitting room is the first door on the right. Make your self comfortable, I'll be right there."

Quietly closing the door, she turns the key. The proximity of this gentle giant brushing against her has momentarily disarmed her. She stands holding the doorknob for support, whilst waiting to regain her composure. Entering the sitting room, she is apprehensive about her appearance and the impression she will make on him.

He is equally guarded, as he stands ramrod straight.

"Please be seated, Arthur," she orders, a little imperiously, directing him to the chair facing the window.

He seats himself stiffly, and places his cap on his lap. He then begins to emit intermittently, discordant grunts, awkwardly searching for words to broach the subject at hand.

She immediately regrets her imperious tone, and sensing his reluctance to engage in conversation, takes the initiative. "Please let me take your cap," she offers, a little more warmly. "I was just treating myself to some sherry before lunch, would you care to join me?"

He smiles appreciatively. "Thank you, Mum, I mean, Eleanor, I would be honoured."

She places his cap on the sideboard and pours two sherries.

The sherry begins to ease the tension between them, and the slight sinew of apprehension that remains is soon severed. How easily those gracious and refined gestures, and the mannered speaking, return to them; the cycle of time is affably turning.

After their second glass of sherry, and dealing with the necessary preliminaries of filling in the thirteen-year informational gap, they both fall silent, each knowing that the matter of Bobby's father has to be addressed.

He becomes aware of his own deep sighs as he attempts to pluck up the courage to ask for forgiveness. He is also acutely aware that he has broken his promise, not to contact her until Bobby knew about his father, and yet here he is, in her home, wanting absolution.

It is she, who broaches the subject again, maybe because she has consumed two glasses of sherry, and is beginning to feel mellow. She also wants to assuage his obvious feelings of guilt. "Dear, Arthur," she begins softly, reaching across the gap between them, to rest her hand on his. "It was a long time ago, and I don't hold you to that promise. You are here now, and I am glad you came. Being here with you is as though the circle has closed and we were never apart." She can see those odd-coloured, gemlike eyes glistening.

Turning his hand over, he tenderly rests her hand in his great palm, then covers it with his other massive webbed hand. He can feel the tears welling up as he struggles for control. "Eleanor, forgive me, I had to see you one more time before I left England. You see, I am migrating to Australia. And when I saw Bobby, it took all my will to restrain myself from telling him about his father. You see, I didn't know if you had told him or not."

Putting her free hand on top of his, she gives it a gentle squeeze. "Arthur, my dear, I feel so sorry for putting you through all of this, over these many years."

He tries to reassure her, "It's all right Eleanor, we both agreed."

Patting his hand, she gently reassures him. "No, please, let me finish. This morning, before we parted, I tried to tell Bobby about his father, but he wouldn't listen; or rather Bunny wouldn't let him listen. He left without knowing. He phoned from Charing Cross Station, to let me know he had met you after all this time. I again tried to tell him, but I was drowned out by the loud speakers in the station. He again left without knowing. I'm so glad you're here, because he promised to phone from Gravesend, which could be any time now."

Relaxing his shoulders, he leans closer to her. "When he phones, do you plan to tell him, Eleanor?"

She smiles with relief. "Yes, Arthur, I do."

Making an attempt to rise from his seat, he is restrained. "Eleanor, I should be going, so that you may talk to your son alone."

"Definitely not," insists Eleanor. "I want you to be here when I tell him, and I want him to talk with you, and that is an order," she commands, with mock severity. "Would you like another sherry?"

He chuckles. "I will, if you will."

She is on her feet, glasses in hand, when the phone rings. Placing the glasses on the side table, and looking enquiringly at Hobbs, she picks up the receiver.

"Hello?" she answers, the inflection in her voice rising a little too sharply at the end.

"Hello, Mother," answers Bobby's cheerful voice.

She laughs delightedly. "Hello, Darling, did you have a good train journey?"

"Yes thank you, Mother. What was it you were trying to tell me about Father? I couldn't hear, for all the noise. I'm sorry, but I had to rush to catch the train."

"That's all right, Darling," she quickly replies. "Before I speak to you about your father, there is someone here I want you to speak to, hold on." She hands the phone to Arthur.

"Hello, Guv, how are you doing?" He can hear the quick intake of breath on the other end of the line.

"Hobbs? Hobbs? Is that you?"

Arthur smiles, "Yes it is, Bobby. I had to contact your mother again. You see, I had to know if she had told you about your father. It turns out that you are still unaware, so I want you to listen very carefully to your mother, and totally accept what she has to tell you, because I know it to be the truth. After she has talked to you, I would like to speak with you again, OK, Bobby?"

"OK, Hobbs."

He hands the phone back to Eleanor. She accepts it with a tender smile. "Hello, Darling, where are you phoning from?"

"Gravesend, Mother."

"I mean where exactly are you? Are you alone?"

"Yes, Mother, I'm calling from a public phone box."

"Oh! That means that we only have three minutes to talk."

"Well yes, Mother, that would be correct. But if we need to talk longer, I do have a few more pennies."

"No, that won't do, Darling. What I have to tell you might take longer, and also, Hobbs wants to talk to you again."

"Well, Mother, the three minutes are almost up, what shall I do?"

"Listen, Darling. Put down the receiver, then ring back and reverse the charges, then we can talk as long as we want to."

"All right, Mother. Goodbye."

She replaces the receiver. Eleanor and Arthur burst out laughing. Collecting the glasses from the side table, she crosses to the bookcase. Before she can refill the glasses, the phone rings again and she answers it.

The operator is saying, "There is a reverse charge for Eleanor Shafto, from Robert Shafto. Will you accept the charges?

She exclaims excitedly, "Yes, yes, operator, of course I'll accept. Hello, Bobby, is that you?"

"Yes, Mother."

She sits down. "Bobby, what I'm about to tell you about your father may come as a bit of a shock and a surprise."

Bobby responds reassuringly, "It's OK, Mother I can take it, after all, he has been dead for thirteen years."

She hesitates before answering, "No he hasn't, Darling, he is still alive."

"What do you mean alive? We were there when he died. We saw him dead. We saw him buried," screams Bunny.

She sharply interrupts. "Bobby, please keep him quiet. It is essential that you know, and I can't deal with both of you right now."

"I'm sorry, Mother, he won't interrupt again. Please, go on."

During this conversation, Arthur has poured two sherries and he hands one to Eleanor. After consuming little more than a sip, she looks steadily at him as she addresses her son. "Bobby, Darling," She pauses and draws in a deep breath before revealing, "Edward was not your natural father."

There is a long silence on the end of the line before Bobby exclaims, "What, Mother? Are you telling me that Father was not my father? I don't understand."

She has committed herself; there can be no holding back now. "Bobby, I know you were only four at the time, but do you remember your daddy's dying words?"

"Yes I do, Mother," he replies, "I will remember them until the day I die, they were, 'I'm sorry, Bobby, I am so sorry, please forgive me, forgive me, please'."

"That's right, Darling. And do you remember understanding only two other words, before he apologised to you?"

"Yes, Mother, they were whispered and slurred, but they sounded like, 'after', and 'father'."

""Yes, Darling, that's right, and I think I know what he was trying to tell you."

"What was it, Mother?"

"He was saying, Arthur is your Father."

Bobby is silent for a few seconds, before exclaiming incredulously, "Mother, are you telling me that Hobbs is my father?"

"Yes" she replies, feeling relieved that at last the secret is out. "He is your *biological* father, we made love only once, and I became pregnant by him."

There is no immediate response from Bobby.

Eleanor took a long sip of sherry. "You see, Darling, Edward and I, couldn't have children. We tried to make love, but it seldom worked out; I think he was impotent. I suspect it was because of his heavy drinking." Before Bobby can respond, she quickly continues. "We both wanted to have children. I wasn't getting any younger, and I desperately wanted to bear a child of my own. I am ashamed of the deception, but the news that I was pregnant gave him so much joy, He desperately wanted to believe that you and Bunny were his sons. I didn't have the heart to tell him the truth."

Arthur is feeling a little weak at the knees and eases himself into a chair.

Eleanor goes on, "And when your father, I mean when Edward, was dying, with his last breath, he was trying to let you know, that he knew. How he knew for sure, I will never know. But, he was an intelligent man, and I suspect your webbed fingers would have tipped him off. However, despite this, he still wanted to believe that you were his son. He was a proud and stubborn man, to whom appearances meant everything. He kept this secret from you until his dying day. After he died, Hobbs left our employment, and we agreed that you were to be brought up as Edward's son.

We also agreed not to see each other again, until such time as you were old enough to know the truth about your father."

"But why didn't you marry Hobbs then?" Bobby asks in a confused voice.

"Because, Darling, I wasn't in love with him, I was in love with Edward, and beneath his cold exterior, I think he still loved me too."

"But he didn't even like Bobby; he even tried to drown him. He blamed Bobby for my strangulation."

She quickly pulls the receiver away from her ear. Bursting into tears, she cries into the phone, "I know, I know and I am so sorry, I tried to stop him pushing Bobby underwater. But, I didn't know what to say or do, I didn't want to argue with him, I loved him too much." She lowers her head and sobs silently, her shoulders shuddering, the phone hanging limply, by its cord, from her hand.

Coming quickly to her side, Arthur puts a comforting arm around her shoulder and relieves her of the phone. "Let me talk to him," he says quietly.

Bobby's panicky voice comes over the line, "Mother! Hobbs! What's happening? Mother, are you all right?"

With no trace in his voice of the cheery taxi driver, Arthur answers. "Your mother will be all right soon, Bobby. She is naturally distraught. This is very hard on her, and I imagine quite a shock to you too. Are you OK?"

Bobby is strangely calm. "Yes, Hobbs I'm fine, it seems that Bunny is more upset than I am. In a way, I feel relieved that he was not my real father. I was always troubled by Father's…, I mean, Edward's, deep feeling of resentment towards me. It must have been very hard on Mother."

Arthur nods sympathetically. "Yes it was, Bobby. Now you know the truth. I was always proud to be your natural father and at the same time frustrated that we couldn't live together as a family. But, we had some wonderful times together, didn't we?"

Bobby replies fervently, "The best, Hobbs, the best. I always loved being with you, it really felt like a natural bond."

Arthur is beaming. "It was Bobby, it was as natural as you can get. You have grown to be a fine young man, and I am sure you will do well in life. Now, I'll hand you back to your mother."

Bobby breaks in, "Hobbs, when will I see you again?"

His voice cracking, the big man answers, "I don't know, son. You see, I have already made arrangements to immigrate to Australia."

Bobby is silent for a moment, and then he quietly says, "Oh, when will you be going?"

Hobbs is uneasy about the turn of the conversation. "I plan to go very soon, Bobby, very soon. Now, here's your mother, she wants to talk to you."

Bobby won't let him off the hook. "Wait, Hobbs, I want to ask you one more question. Did you love Mother?"

Hobbs replies tentatively, "I think I did, Bobby, but, I was never sure. Here she is." He hands the receiver to her, their hands touching a little longer than is necessary. "Talk to your son, Eleanor, I think he is all right."

"Hello Mother, Dear," chirps Bobby.

She is smiling. "Hello, Bobby, Darling, I am so happy you are taking all this so well. And I am so sorry for all that I have put you through, you certainly don't deserve it, because you are a good and loving son."

"Thank you Mother," replies Bobby gratefully. "And I love you too. As I told Hobbs, I am relieved to hear the truth, and I feel elated that he is my natural father, I've always wished that he was my father. Obviously, I am disappointed that he is going away, but I am sure we will meet again."

"It's all in the past, Darling. What is important now is that the truth is out, and we can all get on with our lives. I will let you go now, please keep in touch, and tell Bunny that I love him too."

"Thank you, Mummy," shouts Bunny exuberantly. **"And I love you too."**

"Bye for now, Mum, I will phone again soon, I love you."

She looks candidly into Arthur's eyes. Again, she is the first to speak. "Arthur, dear Arthur, at last he knows."

The big man shuffles uneasily. "Yes, Eleanor he does, and what do you think we should do now?"

She stiffens a little. "We, Hobbs? We? What do you think *we* should do now? We don't do anything. It's not up to us, if only it could be so."

Taken aback by her formal tone, he asks. "What do you mean?"

"Please be seated, Arthur. You must see that I cannot betray the memory of Edward. You see, after all these years, I still love him, I just can't help it."

He slumps into the chair as she continues.

"I know Edward is gone, and I know you are Bobby's biological father, but I still love Edward and feel I always will. No other man could ever erase that love."

Arthur rapidly comes to terms with the situation. "I know that, Eleanor, I have always known that. What happened between us, at the time, was the culmination of many influences; the fatigue after a hard days labour, the warmth of the sun, the scrumpy, the story I was telling you, the camaraderie, and also a genuine attraction. I knew you were in love with Edward, and I had no intention of coming between you. Please forgive me." Rising abruptly, he announces, "I have to be going now, Eleanor. I will be leaving for Australia in a few months. I just wanted to see you one more time."

"Oh, Arthur, thank you for your unselfish wisdom, I am so glad you understand. Never apologise for that one wonderful moment, without which, Bobby would not be alive today. I know you must miss Janice and Hope. Is that why you want to return to Australia?"

"Well, yes and no. Yes, because I want to see them again, and no, because I don't want to come between Janice and her husband. But, I also had this romantic dream that after Bobby had learned the truth about us, you and I could renew our friendship."

"Bless you, Arthur, I hope we will always remain good friends, but you must understand we could never be together, my undying love for Edward would always come between us."

"I do understand, and subconsciously I knew this, maybe, that is why I booked the trip to Australia." He places his hand tenderly on her shoulder. She reaches up and grasps his webbed fingers. "Eleanor, there is one last question I would like to ask you."

Yes, Arthur, what is it."

"Have you ever told Bobby about the existence of my daughter, in Australia?"

"No I haven't, Arthur, I always saw it as a private matter, strictly between you and me. I haven't told anyone about Hope, not even Edward."

Leaning towards her, he kisses her gently on her forehead. "Thank you, Eleanor."

She stares out the window at the nondescript, soaking greyness of the gloomy London rain.

Retrieving his cap, he walks slowly across the room.

She can taste the salt of her tears trickling down her cheeks. "God speed, Hobbs."

He hears the quaver in her voice as she focuses her moist gaze on the rain-washed windowpanes. Turning at the door, he looks at her and notices the quiver of her shoulders; it breaks his heart. His body involuntary jerks, he feels a prolonged, sharp stab of pain in his chest. Waiting for the ache to subside, he leans on the doorknob for support. Then bowing imperceptibly, he clicks his heels and whispers, "Farewell, Mum," he then turns towards the hallway.

Listening to his broken-hearted footsteps retreating down the hallway, she stays sitting ramrod straight in her chair, and her chin starts to tremble. She hears the squeak of the front door, as it is slowly and gently, opened and closed, and then there is silence… Hobbs is gone.

Chapter Twenty-Five

IS THIS YOUR FIRST TRIP TO SEA?

On November 5th, 1954, at the age of seventeen, little Bobby Shafto proudly graduates from the Gravesend National Sea Training School. He ranks the second highest in his class for which he is awarded a Proficiency Badge. The citation reads, 'This is to certify that Shafto. R. has been granted a Proficiency Badge for outstanding ability as a Deck Trainee'. This achievement is duly noted in his newly acquired Seaman's Record Book and Certificates of Discharge.

Three weeks later, he marches up the gangway of his first ship, the SS *Egyptian*. She is moored on the Thames, just below Tower Bridge, and is bound for Hull, on the northeast coast.

He is wearing the smartly pressed uniform of The National Sea Training School, proudly displaying his Proficiency Badge on his left arm. His boots are glowing, an elegant testament to 'spit and polish'. He reports to the First Mate in his cabin, who is at his desk pouring over the cargo manifest. He is dressed in a well-worn uniform which is shiny at the elbows and knees. The three stripes of gold braid on each arm are of the brilliance of tarnished brass, his black shoes are scuffed, and he is unshaven. Clicking his heels and standing stiffly at attention, Bobby smartly salutes and barks, "Deck Boy Shafto reporting for duty, sir."

Hearing the young and eager staccato voice behind him, the First Mate is a little startled. He turns to survey his new recruit.

"Stand easy, Shafto, this isn't the Royal Navy; this is the Merchant Marine. This isn't a ship of war; we carry cargo. Now, report immediately to the Bosun."

"Aye aye, sir," Bobby sharply replies and relaxes his posture. "And thank you, sir"

"For what, Shafto?"

"For signing me up, sir."

"Welcome aboard Shafto. I hope I haven't made a mistake."

Grinning from ear to ear, Bobby retorts, "You haven't, sir, you'll see."

"Well what the hell are you still standing here for?" snaps the First Mate, good-naturedly. "Get the hell out of my cabin and report to the Bosun. I've got work to do."

Turning on his heel, Bobby heads aft, to where he knows the crew's quarters are situated. He is thrilled to walk the decks of his first ship, and he vows to make the First Mate proud of him.

He is descending the companionway to number five hold, just as a dock crane is loading a pallet of cargo. He notices that it is swinging a little too low and he watches it rubbing over, and then straddling, the hatch combing, threatening to tumble its cargo into the hold below. He sees this as his first opportunity to prove his proficiency as a seaman. Jumping down the remaining few steps of the companionway, he races across the deck, in an attempt to save the pallet from tipping. He has no sooner grabbed on to a corner wire, than he hears a thunderous voice behind him.

"Stand clear below." Bobby is still hanging on to the pallet. "Stand clear of the hatch, you fucking idiot. What the fuck do you think you is fucking doing?"

Bobby becomes painfully aware that the voice is booming directly at him. He hurriedly lets go the wire and steps back. Turning to face his inquisitor, he is confronted by a large, bearded, bear of a man, directing the crane driver to take up the slack on his hook, so that the pallet can clear the hatch combing.

He turns and glares at Bobby. "I asked you a fucking question, son. What the fuck do you think you is fucking doing? And who the fuck is you?"

Bobby is stammering; "I… I only wa… wanted to h… help, sir. I am… am the new Deck Boy and I am loo… looking for the B… Bosun, sir."

The crisis having passed, the big man has by this time, calmed down a little. He addresses Bobby in more measured tones. "Listen, son, don't ever fucking try that again, there is men down the fucking hold, and they could have been fucking seriously injured if that fucking pallet had fucking got away from you."

Bobby is brought back to earth, well, to iron; after all, he is standing on the deck of a cargo ship. "Sorry, sir, I'll be more careful in the future. Do you know where I can find the Bosun?"

"You're fucking looking at him, son, and don't call me fucking sir. Now get the fuck down below, find a spare fucking bunk, get out of that silly fucking uniform, change into some sensible fucking work clothes, and report back to me, then I will show you to your fucking work station."

"Thank you sir, I'll be right back."

The big man is obviously irritated. "Clean out your fucking ears, son. I said, don't call me fucking sir, I is not a fucking officer, I is the fucking Bosun. What's your fucking name, boy?"

"Shafto, Bosun, Bobby Shafto."

"OK, Bobby Shafto, welcome aboard. Just fucking remember this. On board a fucking ship, you have to be aware all the fucking time." With his mighty paw on Bobby's tiny shoulder, he turns him to face aft, and dismissively orders, "Now get the fuck out of here."

"Aye, aye, Bosun." Bobby swaggers to the stern of the ship, affecting the rolling gate of an old salt.

He is aware that since coming aboard, Bunny has not made himself known. This seems odd, as Bunny usually emerges in times of stress. Yet, Bobby doesn't really feel stressed, he is willing to accept this verbal abuse; after all, it is the language of the sea. At this moment, he is exactly where he wants to be, on board his first ship, and it sends shivers of excitement through him. Maybe, Bunny hasn't made himself known, because he is at peace with the world. Bobby can't answer these suppositions, but he knows that his twin brother is still within.

He reports back to the Bosun, wearing his shiny new dungarees. He is then taken amidships, to the sailors' mess. There, he is told that his duties consist of being a servant to the deck hands. He will serve them their meals, wash their dishes, keep their mess and pantry clean, and scrub out the heads and showers. He is bitterly disappointed at this turn of events; he was looking forward to being a real sailor, working on the open deck, splicing ropes, and climbing masts, not subjugated to being a servant in the sailors' mess. Bobby remains silent, but Bunny will not.

"What?" shouts Bunny, in that dark and overbearing voice. **"We were second to top of our class in Sea**

School, and also graduated with a Proficiency Badge. **Do you think that with these qualifications we are going to stoop to serve these undeserving ignoramuses? What do you take us for? We demand to serve on deck as is befitting our training.**"

The Bosun, for one stupefying moment, is both motionless and voiceless, and then he erupts. The blood rises to his cheeks, the veins in his bull neck are throbbing, as he bellows, "Listen to me, you fucking horrible little man. You will fucking do what ever the fuck I tell you to fucking do, or you go over the fucking side, do you under-fucking-stand?" Without waiting for an answer from the petrified Bobby, he continues. "I've got no fucking time for fucking upstarts like you on this fucking ship. This is your first fucking trip to sea and you want to fucking pick and choose what you want to fucking do? Who the fuck do you think you fucking is?"

Bobby stammers, "B.. bu.. but, Bosun."

.   The big man bellows, "Shut your fucking moaning cakehole, you poor fucking excuse for a sailor. I am fucking talking to you."

As the colour drains from his cheeks, Bobby remains speechless.

Seeing the effect he has on the tenderfoot and realising he is getting a little out of control, the Bosun draws in a deep breath and levels his voice. "Look son, every new fucking Deck Boy that comes aboard this fucking ship has to be fucking 'Peggy'. If you do well at the fucking job and another new fucking Deck Boy signs on next fucking trip, I might put you out on fucking deck permanently like. Until then, all I fucking ask is that you do what the fuck I tell you to do, to the best of your fucking ability. Fair e-fucking-nough?"

"Fair enough, Bosun, I'm sorry for losing control."

"That's OK, son, now get fucking scrubbing."

"May I ask you a question, Bosun?"

"Fire away, son, what's on your fucking mind?"

"Why is this position called fucking Peggy?"

"Well, son, in the days of fucking sail, there were a few fucking bad injuries, like you or those men in the fucking hold could have had, with that fucking cargo pallet. Well, it often fucking happened that a man would get his fucking leg caught in a fucking fast-moving rope or hawser, or have it fucking crushed by a fucking boom or hatch board. Then they would amputate his fucking leg, and replace it with a fucking wooden peg-fucking-leg. So, to keep the fucking man working, the fucking Mate would put him in the fucking sailors' mess. And that's why you are called fucking Peggy."

"Thanks Bosun, I won't let you down again"

"You be fucking sure you won't now," warns the big man, as he turns to walk out on deck. "By the way, son, you will have your fucking chance to work on deck, sooner than you fucking think."

"When the fuck would that be?" Bobby shouts expectantly.

"We sail on the fucking tide tonight. Report to the fucking aft mooring station, at 2300 hours."

Bobby springs to attention, smartly saluting. "Yes, sir," he barks with enthusiasm.

"I told you not to call me fucking sir, you crazy little fucker," the Bosun replies with mock anger as he goes out on deck shaking his head in amused disbelief.

*

At 2245 hrs, Bobby is at the aft mooring station. There are three deck hands leaning over the taff-rail, smoking and engaging in idle conversation. One of them turns around when Bobby approaches. He looks Bobby up and down, appraising this tiny young man, with the wide staring eyes, webbed fingers, new dungarees, new boots, a sea-school beret perched on his tiny head, and hanging from his belt is a shiny new, uninitiated deck knife and spike, encased in a stiff, spotless, brand-new, unmarked leather sheath.

"Hello kid, is this your first fucking trip to sea?"

"Yes it is. Is it that fucking obvious?" Bobby innocently asks.

The old sea dog, to the amusement of his shipmates, retorts. "Well, to me it is. I just fucking know, you know."

Bobby is reminded of Hobbs, and wonders why he doesn't keep in touch, he said he was migrating to Australia. Bobby wonders where he is right now. His thoughts are interrupted by a long, drawn-out blast of a steam whistle, from an approaching tug on the starboard quarter. A heaving-line from the tug is thrown up to the *Egyptian* and made fast to the ship's thick towrope, which is fed out through the fairlead to the tug below, then secured around the ship's big bitts. By this time, on the port quarter, the final mooring rope is already around the winch barrel. As the tug takes up the slack on its rope, the First Mate gives the order to slack off the stern line; it is thrown clear of the dock, and the ship's winch clanks into motion, pulling the mooring rope aboard, whilst the forward tug turns the ship's bow into the downstream current. This is a seminal moment for Bobby; the umbilical cord to his past life on land has been finally severed.

Under the direction of an A.B., Bobby is put to work, coiling ropes and heaving-lines, and battening down the hatches in preparation for sea. Before his work is completed, the Bosun tells him to go down to the engine room and ask the Chief Engineer for a long weight.

Bobby descends into the bowels of the ship, agilely slipping down the oily ladders of the engine room. He is reminded of a scene from one of those old, black-and-white illustrations of the interior of a factory, in the industrial revolution. The heat is oppressive, and he is confronted by the monumental dissonance of the growling of the ship's centre of energy; the massive pumping and thrusting din of the driving pistons, the sharp hiss of escaping steam, the brain-numbing clank of donkey engines, the shrill ring of the telegraph, and the tiny shouts of humans under the mighty cacophony of the massive engines. On the control platform, he recognises the Chief Engineer, by the four stripes on his open jacket. Edging his way past the banks of hissing valves, levers and dials, Bobby raises his tiny voice. "Excuse me, sir."

There is no reply. Bobby creeps right up to the Chief, who is standing next to the telegraph, looking, with a be-mused smile at the approach of this tiny foreign body. He bends down, to hear the boy better. 'Yes, son?" he yells, "What are you doing below?"

Bobby yells into the Chief's ear, "The Bosun sent me below to ask you for a long weight, sir."

The Chief shouts back, "OK, son," then he walks over to inspect some of the dials and talk to one of his crew. Half an hour later, he returns to where Bobby is still standing. "What the fuck are you still doing here son?" he yells.

Bobby is perplexed; perhaps the Chief had not heard him the first time. He opens his mouth to repeat the re-quest, but Bunny comes to the rescue; his voice blanketing the colossal clanking, whirring, and hissing of the mighty engines.

"I said, the Bosun sent me to ask you for a long weight, sir."

The Chief immediately takes two steps backwards, and staring down at this tiny man with the thunderous voice, he roars, "OK, son, you've been waiting long enough. Now fuck off."

This response brings gales of raucous laughter from the grease-smeared and sweaty engineers, donkeymen, and firemen. Bobby knows immediately that he is the butt of a long-standing joke, and it is all part of his initiation. He smiles feebly, and ascends the greasy steel ladders to emerge onto the open deck and breathe in the cool and silent river breezes.

By this time, the *Egyptian* has gathered enough steerageway, so the tugs are let go, and she is free to navigate under her own steam. He is too excited to turn in, so he walks along the iron deck to the bow of the ship, and leaning on the rail, under the starry November sky, he watches the twinkling lights of the ever-widening shoreline, reflecting off the placid river's surface. At last, he is heading out to sea, and the whole world lies before him. Looking up to the night sky, he lets out a little whoop of joy.

*

A few hours after leaving Tower Bridge, the *Egyptian* is passing Gravesend, where just three weeks ago, Bobby has graduated from The National Sea Training School. The river is widening, and soon they will be between the salt marshes of the Thames estuary, heading out to the North Sea. He is still leaning on the bow rail, not wanting to miss a moment. Ahead of him, he sees the brilliant lights of a large and stately passenger liner, slowly ploughing her way through the river, outward bound to some exotic destination in faraway, romantic lands. He is reminded of John Masefield's poem, *'Cargoes'*.

Bunny, who loves poetry, can't pass on this opportunity.

*"Stately Spanish galleon coming from the Isthmus,
Dipping through the Tropics by the palm-green
shores,
With a cargo of diamonds,
Emeralds, amethysts,
Topazes, and cinnamon, and gold moidores."*

The *Egyptian* is gradually gaining on the big ship ahead, and soon will be overtaking her. Bobby remembers Hobbs's stories of being a Quartermaster on the *RMS Strathhaird*. He knows he isn't yet qualified to serve on one of those wonderfully romantic ships, but in a few years, he will try and join the P&O fleet. In the meantime, he will have to be satisfied with being a fucking Peggy, on board a 4,000-ton cargo ship, plying the rugged North Sea coast of England.

*"Dirty British coaster with a salt-caked smoke
stack,
Butting through the Channel in the mad March
days,
With a cargo of Tyne coal,
Road-rails, pig-lead,
Firewood, iron-ware, and cheap tin trays."*

Arthur Hobbs is leaning over the stern-rail of the P&O passenger liner, *RMS Strathaird,* which is outward bound to Sydney, Australia, calling at Piraeus, Port Said, Aden, Colombo, Fremantle, and Melbourne. She has had two of her funnels removed after the war, and is now a one-class ship. To Arthur, it will be a familiar trip, except he will be out of uniform this time. He watches the running lights of a small cargo ship, gradually gaining speed as she approaches the Thames estuary. Soon she will be overtaking the *Strathaird*. He wonders if Bobby has signed up on a ship yet.

Harmonising with the reverberation of the big ship's churning, twin screws, Arthur hears the onomatopoeic cadence of his favourite poem. "*Dirty British coaster with a salt-caked smoke stack*," the memorable words are blending with the throbbing rhythm of the stern wash. "*Butting through the Channel in the mad March days*." Arthur hears again, the almost forgotten rhythms of ships and the sea. "*With a cargo of Tyne coal, road-rails, pig-lead, firewood, ironware, and cheap tin trays.*" Standing on that vibrating, stern deck, under the November night-sky, and breathing in the brackish, salty-sweet-water scent of the Thames estuary, he lets the hauntingly recognisable sounds seep into him.

In the widening estuary, at a distance of one hundred yards off her port beam, the *Egyptian* is passing the brightly lit passenger liner. Bobby looks across at the fairytale vessel, with her rows of brilliant lights reflecting in the water, and his stomach stirs.

 "**Hobbs,**" Bunny shouts.

"Yes," Bobby whispers, as he waves into the darkness.

As the little cargo ship passes on the starboard beam of the *Strathaird,* Arthur feels an unseasonably warm breeze washing over him. When the little ship has steamed by, the cold dampness of the river embraces him again; it is time to go below.

The two ships pass in the night.

Chapter Twenty-Six

THE REALM OF LITTLE WHITE LIES AND FANTASY

Lying in his bunk on E Deck, Arthur is listening to the turning of the screws. He feels the gentle vibration of the ship, gradually increasing speed as she heads out into the open water; he is lulled into reflection. He is now 68 years of age. It has been three months since he had closed the door on Eleanor and vanished into the night. He knows he can't remain in touch with her, it is plain that she is still in love with Edward, but he is glad that there was some kind of closure after all those years. He would've liked to have seen more of Bobby, but the time allowed was too short to re-establish any kind of meaningful relationship. Until that short taxi ride, he had not seen the boy since he was four years old, so he hardly knows him, he also doesn't want to come between Bobby and Eleanor. He has agreed to surrender any legal claim to Bobby as his son, it will be better to make a clean break. He also hardly knows his first family, Janice and Hope, but he feels, in a strange, compelling way, he needs some kind of rapprochement with them. So, he had quit his job, driving a taxi, and booked a one-way passage to Australia.

He hasn't been at sea since that fateful day in 1936, when he was dishonourably discharged from this very ship in Tilbury. Here he is again, eighteen years later, on the same ship, sailing from Tilbury as a passenger, and again his destination is Sydney. The voyage will take about five weeks. It will be very hot in Sydney at this time of the year. He will pay a visit to Bondi Beach, and who knows? Janice might still go there, and so might Hope. He wonders what Hope looks like now. She is sure to have her mother's haunting, dark brown, green-flecked eyes. He wonders …

*

When Arthur awakes for breakfast at 0800hrs, the ship is in the English Channel, just off Le Havre. The seas are starting to rise, and she is waltzing into a gentle roll. He is sharing a cabin with one other passenger who is not particularly enthusiastic about the thought of breakfast, and elects to stay in his bunk. Dressing in tan coloured, cavalry-twill trousers, brown loafers, a maroon crew-neck pullover, and making sure he is wearing his thin, black leather gloves with the two middle fingers cut open and then sewn together, he makes his way to the dining salon.

By 0830 hrs, he is seated at his allotted table for breakfast, it is a table for four, but this morning, he has just one other person for company. His fellow diner looks to be in his early fifties, short of stature, stocky and strong, in a pugnacious way. He is wearing blue denim jeans, white plimsolls, and a white shirt with its wide collar worn over a dark blue, V-neck pullover, contrasting effectively with his tanned face. Arthur notices his eyes, they are pale blue, and crow's feet are walking around the corners. The stranger smiles, displaying a perfect set of firm white teeth. His handsome head is crowned with slightly receding, closely cropped, and tightly curled, golden-blond hair. He presents an image that is too perfect, an effervescent picture of vibrant health, vitality, and confidence.

Arthur thinks that he probably presents a contrasting image to his handsome tablemate. Over the years, his large frame has lost a lot of its muscle-tone, his shoulders are slightly stooped, and his head bowed from the instinctual ducking under doorframes and other low obstacles. His shock of once flaming red hair has lost a lot of its glow, and the ashen colour of grey is sacrificed at his temples. His face has lost its firmness; his cheeks are taut no more, his teeth are only partially his own, but his generous lips remain firm and attractive, as are his enigmatic, odd-coloured, catlike eyes.

The too perfect, picture of health, vitality and confidence, expansively greets Arthur. Flashing his pristine teeth, he energetically exclaims, "G'day mate, how's it goin'?" Surveying the sparsely populated dining salon, he remarks in a strident and derisive voice, "It looks like most passengers on this here tub have lost their sea legs and can't face their tucker. Eh? Eh?" Congratulating himself on his bravado, he laughs coarsely. Thrusting his hand towards Arthur, he bellows, "They call me Ted, Ted Atherton. What's your handle, mate?"

Arthur, being in no mood for abrasive joviality, reluctantly grasps the meaty paw with his gloved hand. "Hobbs," he replies curtly, "Arch…" he stops short and swallows. Then correcting himself, he says, "Arthur Hobbs." Shipboard life all comes rushing back to him. He has subconsciously almost said "Archie". He doesn't want any of the crew to recognise him, and his webbed fingers would certainly have draw attention to himself. He has no intention of re-living that shameful period of his dishonourable discharge.

Ted has noticed Arthur's gloved hands. "Are you cold, mate?" he bluntly asks.

"No, I'm fine thank you." Arthur doesn't want to explain the reason why he is wearing gloves, but he suspects that if he doesn't offer an explanation, Ted will persist with this line of questioning. Holding his gloved hands under the table, he explains, "I wear these gloves, because I have a skin condition that causes my hands to become very dry and cracked. These gloves are lubricated and they help to keep my hands moist."

Ted seems to accept Arthur's explanation. "I'm sorry to hear that, Art. It must cause you some agro."

"No it doesn't, Ted. And I would prefer that you not address me as Art, my name is Arthur."

Ted doesn't notice the frostiness in Arthur's tone for he remains warm and cordial. "No worries, mate."

Arthur is beginning to feel a little depressed at the thought of sharing the table with Ted for the remainder of the voyage. The steward's timely arrival jerks him out of the doldrums.

Their steward is a sprightly fellow with Brylcreamed, gleaming, jet-black hair, slicked back flat on his head. He is dressed in an immaculate, freshly starched white jacket, fastened up to his neck, with silver coloured buttons. "Good mornin, gentlemen, my name is Vincent, I will be your table steward for the rest of the voyage. By the looks of this ere table, I can see that you two are the only ones that ave the stomach for breakfast. I reckon the uvers ave a touch of the old mal de mer. Know wot I mean? Know wot I mean?" He winks, but doesn't nudge them, as he surveys the dining salon. "I dare say arf the people who made it to breakfast today, won't be ere tomorra." He winks at them again.

Ted takes the bait. "Why is that, mate?"

"Because we will be in the bloody Bay of Biscay won't we? And it ain't arf rough this time ov the year, ain't it? Now, wot can I get you two gentlemen?"

"I'll have the mixed grill," said Arthur.

"Good choice, sir," Vincent says, and turning to Ted he asks, "and wot will your pleasure be today, sir?"

"What's in a mixed grill?" enquires Ted.

"You would like to know all the ingredients, sir?"

"From go to whoa, mate."

Vincent brings himself up to his full height and announces with solemn dignity and decorum, "Well, sir, it is a fine English delicacy, that I am sure you will want to partake of. It consists of blood puddin', sausages, pork chops, bacon, tomatoes, and eggs; all fried in their own delicious fat, and served with generous portions of fried bread."

In Arthur's perception, Ted's tan is beginning to fade. He watches in fascination, as Ted screws up his eyes in a twitching motion, making the crow's feet hop.

Ted remains silent for a moment, then gripping the sides of his chair; he remarks quietly, "No thanks, not now." Rising unsteadily from the table, and excusing himself, he manoeuvres through the sparsely populated dining salon, seeking fresher air.

Vincent pours coffee for Arthur, and bowing slightly, he winks and announces, "I'll be right back with your mixed grill, sir."

Arthur is left alone.

*

As Arthur knows, only too well, the fundamental nature of shipboard life is unique; you live only in the present. Your past life is left at your original port of departure; your future awaits you at your final port of call. Now, is all that exists, all that exists is now. Arthur also knows that his predetermined value-judgements of others become softened with each passing day, and at about the two-week point into the voyage, he will find himself in a peaceful non-judgemental frame of mind, thus, it is, between Ted and himself.

*

The day after leaving Colombo, they are in the Doldrums and expecting to cross the equator in about half an hour. The oppressive heat is hard to escape, and the best way to handle it is to do absolutely nothing at all, the less energy expended, the less intense the heat feels. After three weeks of daily conversation with Ted, Arthur, despite his initial cool reaction towards him, is starting to warm up to this extroverted Australian, As they lean over the starboard side rail of the Promenade Deck, catching what little breeze that is created by the ship's forward motion, he remarks to Ted, "Have you ever seen the equator Ted?"

Ted looks at him quizzically. "No, mate, I haven't. In fact I didn't think you could actually see the equator."

"Of course you can see the equator; I've seen it many times." 'Damn', Arthur thought, 'now I've let the cat out of the bag'.

However, Ted doesn't seem to make the connection. He simply states, "They say we'll be crossing it shortly. I can't see her, can you?"

Removing his binoculars from the case, Arthur's mouth creases in a sly smile. "What we see on the surface is no indication of what lies beneath. The equator can only be seen through these binoculars." Raising them to his eyes, he announces, "Yes, there she is, there's the equator, about half a mile ahead." Handing the binoculars to Ted, he offers, "Here, have a look."

"Give over, mate. Have you got a few roos loose in the top paddock?"

"I'm serious, Ted, the eye doesn't create a rainbow. See for yourself."

Ted takes the glasses and leaning on the rail with his elbows to steady himself, he intently stares through the lenses, and with an astonished gasp he exclaims, "Strewth! By jingoes, you're right, mate, I can just see her, she's a little blurred, but I can definitely see the equator."

Arthur took the binoculars back as Ted stares at the sea with his naked eye, looking vainly for that magic line of latitude. "That's amazin, mate, bloody amazin. Ere let me ave another gander.

Arthur smiles at his own conceit, and giving Ted little latitude, casually remarks, "Too late now, Ted, we have already crossed the line, didn't you feel the slight bump?"

"I dunno, I might have, mate, it's hard to tell." Ted's face spreads into a smiling, but puzzled frown.

Arthur is congratulating himself on his deception; after all, it is all in fun. Perhaps Ted will never know what he has really seen, and if he never finds out, he will continue to believe that he has seen the equator. What's the harm in that? Arthur knows that what Ted has really seen is the blurred image of a hair, superimposed on the water that has been inserted behind the lens of each eyepiece. Arthur will have to be careful; he doesn't want anyone to know that he has been to sea before, let alone on this very ship. His cleverness is beginning to get the better of him.

*

They are at the pool bar, watching some children, who are shrieking with delight as they stand on the rail and jump into the water, creating mighty splashes, and then climbing out again to repeat their entry. The kids are intent on making as much noise and displacement of water as is possible, and in the process, they are thoroughly enjoying themselves.

In the course of their conversation, Arthur and Ted are tentatively revealing a little about each other's background. Arthur learns that Ted is a sports journalist who has worked in radio for the Australian Broadcasting Corporation. He is now on his way back to Sydney after taking a BBC course in Television Journalism, in preparation for the 1956 Olympic Games, to be held in Melbourne.

A very white, dark-haired, gap-toothed, skinny little boy, who is in danger of losing his bathing trunks, throws a white inflated balloon at Arthur. Arthur, who is absent-mindedly watching this boy, whilst listening to Ted's narrative, deftly catches the balloon. He is intrigued with Ted's story, because he remembers that Janice had married a sports reporter with ABC Radio, but she never revealed his name. Arthur is unsure of which direction to take; he wants to ask Ted more, but thinks it prudent to put the matter in abeyance. He passes the balloon to Ted.

"And you, mate? What's your story?" enquires Ted brightly as he tosses the balloon back to the delighted kids in the pool, one of whom immediately bounces it back to Arthur, who enthusiastically punches it into the air and watches the balloon describe a perfect arc and fall into the midst of ten outstretched and eager hands, like a large insect falling into the inviting mouth of a Venus flytrap.

Arthur enters the realm of little white lies and fantasy. He regales his newfound friend with stories about his life with Eleanor and their eccentric little son; he omits to tell Ted about Bobby's webbed fingers, or even to mention his name. He paints a fanciful vision of the three of them living an idyllic life together, until their son has grown up and finally leaves home to become a sailor. He relates how Eleanor and he had gradually grown apart and finally separated, and reveals that he is now on his way to Sydney, to make a new life for himself. As he is relating this fairy tale, Arthur realises how one conceit can effortlessly grow into many, it is so easy to lie to a stranger. "Do you have family in Sydney, Ted?" Arthur asks conversationally.

"Yes, mate, I've a lovely wife and daughter. We've been together for twenty years now."

Arthur is reminded that it was twenty years ago that Janice had married the sports reporter from ABC. "That's wonderful, Ted. Were you with ABC when you met your wife?"

"Yeah, mate, I was in radio then, but now we are going into television, I want to be there, you know?"

"I don't blame you, Ted, I think you'll do just fine on TV." It could very well be that it *was* Ted that Janice had married, or the whole story could be a complete coincidence. Arthur is confused. He has woven a tangled web of deception, and he is not sure of how to escape. Should he lay it all out on the table and ask the questions he really wants to ask, or should he hold his cards until he is ready to play them? He rests his gloved hands on his lap.

"Thanks mate. Have you ever been Down Under?" Ted enquires.

Arthur is thrown off guard by the directness of this question. He is uneasy about the turn in the conversation; Ted might be digging too deep. "No," he lies, with a tight smile, "This will be my first time."

There is a loud *bang,* as the balloon bursts, which makes Arthur twitch, which is *f*ollowed immediately by shrieks of nervous laughter as they all watch the flaccid bladder floating limply on the surface of the pool. It strikes Arthur as the perfect symbolic punctuation to his bold-faced lie.

Ted laughs heartily, clapping Arthur on the back. "That's great, mate. When we get to Sydney, I want you to meet my family and we can show you around."

Arthur isn't sure why he has chosen this route of deceit, but he continues on the same path. "That is very kind of you, Ted, I'll be looking forward to meeting your family."

"Good on ya, mate," said Ted, "that's what cobbers are for."

The kids splash noisily out of the pool to drink beef tea, whilst Arthur and Ted order another cold beer.

Chapter Twenty-Seven

KEEP YOUR EYES ON THE HORIZON

Bobby's maiden voyage isn't turning out to be as romantic and adventurous as he had dreamed. Once out of the protected waters of Old Father Thames, the *Egyptian* heads out into the harsh winter of the North Sea, and sets a northerly course for Hull, an estimated twenty-hour voyage. They are soon battling gale-force winds, cold rain, and high seas. Bobby isn't used to the brutal, bucking movement of a ship in rough waters. On more than one occasion, he is brusquely awakened in mid-air as he is thrown out of his bunk; that night, he doesn't get much sleep.

The *Egyptian* is pitching fiercely; mountainous waves are smashing down on her foredeck, forcing her bow under and engulfing her in green seas. At the same time, her stern is thrust violently out of the water, causing her screw to spin wildly, sending dangerous vibrations throughout the full length of the hull, and shaking the ship to her very keel. As the valiant little vessel tries to climb to the peak of the next relentless wave, her stern is again slammed down into the trough.

At 0700 hours, it is time for Bobby to make his way amidships to serve the sailors their breakfast. Holding onto his bunk rail, he struggles into his oilskins and sea-boots. As he opens the cabin door, the violent motion of the ship rips the door out of his hand, slamming it hard against the bulkhead, then immediately whipping back again, to pound viciously into his left shoulder, propelling his little body unmercifully onto the heaving deck, and struggling to his feet, he makes his way topside. Fighting the enormous pressure of the wind, pressing against the heavy door that leads out to the open deck, he puts his tiny shoulder against it, and with all the strength he can muster, he manages to force the door open, he is unprepared for what he sees. Looking aft, as the stern comes crashing down into the trough again; he sees a towering wall of hard, green water. The wind is screaming under his oilskin coat, threatening to lift him bodily off the deck. The heavy rains are combining with the cold and stinging spray to lash painfully against his face. With no time to be frightened, and struggling to keep his balance, he grabs the safety line that is rigged along the open deck. As the little cargo ship heads into the next wave, her decks become awash with the seething seas. Hooking his arm over the lifeline, and fighting the tremendous force of the wind, the rain, and the seas, and desperately clinging on for dear life, he determinedly pulls himself; hand over hand, along the open deck. At one point, he loses his footing, as the roiling deck-wash upends him. By keeping his grip on the line, he recovers, and finally reaches the amidships accommodation, where he lurches safely inside. After he has successfully closed the heavy wooden door, a wave of relief sweeps over him, accompanied by a sharp realisation, that this is not a romantic dream, he is experiencing the real thing.

Bobby makes his way down the alleyway to the pantry, where he cranks up the steam on the boiler to make tea for the deckhands. The cooking smells of a greasy English breakfast are wafting through the galley's open hatchway.

The ship is dancing under him, as she tangoes through the exuberant seas. He struggles to set the table in the empty sailors' mess, and watches in frustration, as the plates and cutlery slide off and smash onto the deck. He raises the fiddles on the table edges, but the plates are still sliding wildly around with the high-spirited motion of the ship. With tears of frustration in his eyes, he hangs onto the table with one hand and tries to gather the pieces of smashed plates on the heaving deck.

He hears an affable voice behind him. "Wait, son."

Looking round, Bobby sees a tall, slim sailor, with thinning grey hair, and a craggy, weather-beaten face. He is dressed in blue denim, his deck knife and spike in their scarred, supple, dark-leather sheath, hang from a thin leather belt, which is loosely buckled around his waist. The tip of the sheath is tied with rawhide to his right thigh, like a gunslinger. He looks like a saltwater cowboy, and speaks in an easy, non-judgemental drawl.

"Look, son, get hold of all your dish towels and soak them in water, wring them out, and put them on the table, then you can put the plates on them and they won't slide around." Again, comes the observation, "I can see this is your first trip to sea, you'll get used to it. My name is Tom."

"I'm Bobby, and thanks for the tip, Tom. Would you like your breakfast now?"

"Yeah, I would, and a mug of tea," Tom replies.

The ship is still lurching wildly as Bobby makes his way to the galley-hatch. He asks the cook, a sweaty little man with a lighted cigarette hanging from his mouth, for one breakfast. Bobby watches in fascination, as the long ash from the cook's cigarette falls into Tom's breakfast. On the plate are two fried eggs, swimming in grease, three rashers of under-cooked bacon, four soft slices of fried tomatoes, and two slices of grease-soaked fried bread, the sight of which starts to make Bobby feel queasy. The cook removes the ash from the eggs with the corner of his grease-stained apron, and hands the plate to Bobby. Grasping the rail with one hand, and juggling the plate with the other, Bobby staggers back to the sailors' mess.

"Thanks, Peggy," says Tom, who enthusiastically digs into his delicious, greasy breakfast. "I'll have my tea now."

Bobby is beginning to feel woozy; his stomach is churning as he fights his way back to the pantry. When he reaches the water boiler, the cooking smells, the suffocating heat, and the wild pitching motion of the ship, become too much for him; he is suddenly overcome with nausea. Grasping the edge of the sink, he vomits violently, over and over and over again, until his spasming stomach is turned inside out. He is still retching, but there is nothing left to surrender, not even Bunny, who, in his delirious state, Bobby thinks he sees, lying in the bottom of the sink amongst the contents of his recently evacuated stomach. He turns on the taps and tries to flush the mess down the plughole, Bunny and all. His whole body is weak, he is shaking, his skin is clammy with sweat, his head is pounding, and his legs are wobbling; he can hardly stand.

Tom appears at the door of the pantry with half an orange. "Here, son, take this and go out on deck, keep your eyes on the horizon, and suck on this orange; the fresh air will make you feel a little better."

Grasping for stability, Bobby hoarsely whispers, "Thanks, Tom."

"Get goin, son, and don't forget to clean up this mess when you get back. I'll get my own tea and tell the rest of the lads they'll have to fend for themselves this morning."

Stepping out onto the heaving deck, and holding firmly onto a stanchion, Bobby turns his face towards the cold wind. Fixing his eyes on the tilting horizon, he sucks the juicy orange. In time, he begins to feel a little better, and is ready to return to his duties.

That night, they are in calm waters, in the lee of the land, steaming up the Humber River to their first port of call, Hull. The following night, he goes ashore to a dance at the 'Flying Angel' Seaman's Mission. Bobby has found his sea legs.

Chapter Twenty-Eight

AT LAST, MY HEART'S AN OPEN DOOR

After his maiden voyage, Bobby feels that he has truly tasted the sea and has saltwater flowing through his veins. For a little fellow on his first trip to sea, he has done well. Following his initial bout of seasickness, he quickly adapted to shipboard life. The Bosun and the First Mate were impressed with his enthusiasm and his ability to learn. He is given an honourable discharge and asked to return for the next trip. The *Egyptian* is scheduled to be away for six weeks, calling at various ports in the Mediterranean. Bobby is thrilled with this news, particularly as he will be working on deck permanently. He is told they will sign on another fucking Peggy. He is given one week's shore leave, before he has to sign up again. Bobby is feeling rather cocky as he walks on *terra firma*; as he adopts the rolling gait of an old salt.

After spending the first two days of his leave at the flat in Chelsea with his proud and loving mum, he decides to pay a visit to the orphanage. Phoning ahead for permission to visit, he is told by the Commander, who is proud that Bobby has chosen a career at sea, that he is welcome to stay as long as he likes.

Leaving Elm Park Mansions, he is verbally accosted by the scaly-headed Mrs Egan. From out of the depths of her darkness, she shrieks. "Ah! Little Bobby Shafto, where have you been all this time?"

"I'm not little," he states, with a touch of irritability. "I've been to sea."

"Yes you are," crows the old crone, "to see what?"

"No I'm not," he says, relaxing a little as he recognises the familiar banter. "To see the sea, Mrs Egan."

"God bless you, Bobby Shafto," screeches the witch, displaying a gummy smile. "Come here, sailor, and give a lonely old lady a big sloppy kiss."

He declines gracefully. "Goodbye, Mrs Egan, I've a train to catch." He hears her cackling laughter as he quickly walks towards the number eleven bus stop.

*

It is a mild, drizzly Sunday in early December. Polly Plowright, who has grown to be a very seductive sixteen year old, and her eternal suitor, Gary Roman, are in the assembly room of the Actors Orphanage, listening to the BBC radio program, 'Family Favourites'. Doris Day is singing.

> *"Once I had a secret love,*
> *That lived within the heart of me.*
> *All too soon that secret love,*
> *Became impatient to be free."*

They are staring out of the floor-to-ceiling windows, looking across the grey, rain-soaked lawns towards the front gates. They see in the distance, the hunched and shuffling figure of Bert the groundskeeper, admitting a visitor. At first, they don't recognise the little man, who is walking with a confident, rolling gait. He is wearing a duffel coat and carries a kit bag, slung over his shoulder.

> *"So I told a friendly star,*
> *The way that dreamers often do,*
> *Just how wonderful you are,*
> *And why I'm so in love with you."*

As the little man draws nearer, Gary hears a quick intake of breath from Polly. She points excitedly in the direction of the visitor, giving a little skip of joy, whilst audibly sighing. "Look, Gary, it's Bobby, he is back from the sea." She waltzes around the room singing along with Doris Day.

> *"Now I shout it from the highest hills,*
> *Even told the golden daffodils,*
> *At last my heart's an open door,*
> *And my secret love's no secret anymore."*

Running towards the French doors, she exclaims, "Come on, Gary, let's go and meet him."

Gary's heart sinks and all the old feelings of jealousy and resentment come rushing back to overwhelm him. He whispers through his clenched teeth, "Just when everything is going so well with Polly and me; why, oh why, does that little runt have to come back and spoil everything?"

Polly doesn't hear him; she is skimming across the field, bending the wet grasses like a warm Chinook wind as she eagerly runs towards her conquering hero. She is shouting, "Come on Gary, it's Bobby, it's Bobby." The little man grows bigger and bigger as she runs towards him; she is waving and screaming in elation, "Bobby, Bobby, Bobby."

Gary grudgingly follows her, moueing and slouching across the lawn, wincing at the sound of that accursed name.

He hates Bobby for shattering his fragile paradise; Bobby could never love her as much as he does. He experiences the visceral, churning emotions this desperate love generates. He feels the roiling turmoil, the obliteration of his common senses, the volcanic eruptions of torturous tumult in the pit of his stomach, the epicentre of his emotions. He feels the radiating of this uncontrollable energy that is coursing outward in vibrating waves, deep from within his inner core, to his outer extremities, to his groin, his legs, his heart, his chest, his head, right to the very surface of his skin, and to the tips of his fingers and toes. His entire being is excited with raw and tangible sensations; nothing makes any sense. He is so alone and unwanted, he is a lost soul, and he earnestly prays to be taken away from this unhappy place.

Bobby sees the ravishing Polly rushing towards him. He drops his kit bag and stands waiting to absorb her exuberant, headlong rush. In no time, they are together, her arms around his neck, and her sweet panting breath caressing his rain-kissed cheeks. They hold each other closely, urgently grunting tender little internal sounds of love that never have a chance to cross their lips. Their mouths meet in a full and shameless kiss. Bobby feels so alive and strong; he picks up his kit bag, and hoists it easily onto his swaggering little shoulder. In the gentle drizzle, the blissful couple walk hand in hand in a sublime dream through the long, wet grass, towards the resentful Gary, who has halted his forward progress to sullenly await their approach.

"Ahoy there, Gary," hails Bobby, "I hope you have been looking after my girl for me." Polly giggles bashfully; Bobby certainly knows how to rub salt in the wound.

Gary glares darkly at him and without a word, turns on his heel, and retreats slowly across the lawn. He shuffles back towards the house, a forlorn and defeated boy.

By this time, the rest of the kids have spotted the approaching sailor, and the adoring throng, like a fast-running stream around a snagged log, rushes past the humiliated Gary, to noisily greet the returning sailor.

For the next three days, Polly and Bobby are scarcely apart, they both wander aimlessly around, wearing the silly smile of love, oblivious to all about them.

Bobby is given a guest room, in the empty servants' quarters on the second floor. On his final night at the orphanage, when silence is floating down and smothering the hum of day, and the pale evening light is stealing across the fields, on its way to the other side of the world, Polly is tiptoeing quietly up the creaky stairs to his room. Under the protection of the cloak of gathering darkness, she knocks timidly on his door, which he swiftly opens. In the twilight, he silently holds her hand and gently guides her towards his bed. They coyly disrobe and slip between the cool, inviting sheets.

As they ardently embrace, feeling the wholeness of the moment, they tenderly explore each other's firm and virile young bodies. Rapidly, their timidity falls away, and with their nerve-ends dancing, they surrender to the intoxicating rush of their instinctual desires. She opens herself to him, and with amazing grace, he enters her, and she welcomes him. For the next few convulsive moments, they are thrust out of their young bodies, to be swept away, surging through the timeless universe, on an omnipotent tsunami of passion.

After the storm of their ardour has subsided, and their breathing becomes shallower, they lie in sweet embracement, and close their eyes in carefree repose. They swear their undying love and fidelity to each other, and blissfully drift off to sleep, blessed by the gentle hand of that first tender and pure love. But, first blood is drawn, they are no longer children; they have lost their innocence.

*

After breakfast the following morning, and in front of the assembled crew, the Commander requests that Bobby Shafto wait outside his study. When the old, one-eyed lion arrives, Bobby notices that Gary Roman is trailing behind him. In the ensuing confrontation, Gary, who is seething with jealousy, points at Bobby with a shaking outstretched finger, and accuses him of sleeping with Polly. Whether Gary actually knows the truth of his betrayal, Bobby is not sure.

"You are a has-been, Bobby Shafto," shouts Gary disparagingly.

"What does that mean, Gary Roman?'" Bobby replies icily.

"It means that you were, and never can be again."

"Then, how come I am standing here right now, Gary? Look at me, alive and throbbing with love. And look at you, rotting, and seething with resentment." Bobby is unafraid; a deep-seated, cellular anger is welling up from within. Bunny pours out his invective.

"You little wriggling worm, Roman, you Judas. Your vindictive jealousy has driven you to the ultimate duplicity of cowardice. Do you think that your betrayal will win back her love? There is a curse on your life. You are doomed to forever grovel and beg for forgiveness, which will never be fully forthcoming. Your soul is damned, Roman. You will live a long and brutal life, devoid of the only essence which you so desperately seek, deep and abiding love. My seed will haunt you for all eternity." Turning to the Commander, he sneers.

"You fat slimy slug Smith, you Pontius Pilate. Go ahead, wash your hands of us, banish us from your mansion, throw us on the mercy of the mob, crown us with thorns, and crucify us, so that we will be forever out of your miserable life. But beware, for we will rise again."

A taxi is immediately summoned, and when it arrives, Bobby is marched to the front door and told by the Commander, in no uncertain terms, "Never darken the threshold of this house again, on pain of being brought up on the criminal charge of rape." Both the Commander and Gary Roman are well pleased with themselves; the co-conspirators are only too glad to see the last of this vexatious little man.

*

The day following his banishment, Bobby phones the orphanage and asks to speak with his old friend, Paul Havers, the Chief Torturer. He wants to know what punishment has been meted out to Polly. Paul tells him that she was immediately expelled, but beyond that, he knows nothing. The next day, Bobby signs up for his second voyage on the SS *Egyptian*.

Chapter Twenty-Nine

What's in a name?

Four and a half days out from Colombo, the *Strathaird* is scheduled to cross the Tropic of Capricorn. Ted and Arthur are playing a game of deck quoits on the boat deck. Arthur notices that the Bridge Wallah, on the port wing of the bridge, is staring down at them. The game of quoits continues, and then Ted also notices that they have the attention of the Bridge Wallah. They both stop playing and stare up at him, which prompts him to turn away and direct his attention to polishing the brightwork.

A short time later, they see him sliding down the companionway to the officers' deck. From past experience, Arthur knows that he is on his way to alert the second officer, to prepare to take the next watch. Before opening the door to the officers' quarters, the Bridge Wallah, with a shining betel nut-stained smile, waves enthusiastically at them and yells, "Sahib! Sahib!"

Ted waves back at him shouting, "G'day, mate." The Bridge Wallah then disappears inside the officers' accommodations. "That's a friendly bloke," remarks the affable Ted.

"Yes he is, isn't he?" Arthur is a little nervous, hoping that he has not been recognised. However, what are the chances, after all these years, of the same Bridge Wallah still serving on the same ship? He has to admit to himself that the chances are good, because these Lascars have a great loyalty to their ships, as each crew usually comes from the same village and follows the same ships.

Ted interrupts Arthur's musings by saying, "Listen, mate, there's a Bridge visit scheduled for one o'clock, let's go and have a gander."

Arthur declines, "No you go ahead without me, Ted, I have to write a few letters that I have been procrastinating over for far too long."

"OK," replies the perennially sunny Ted. "How about meeting for a drink later, in the Veranda Lounge on B Deck? Is three o'clock OK?"

"Yes that'll be fine," Arthur hurriedly replies. "See you then." He quickly ducks out of view and disappears below.

*

At precisely 1500 hrs, Arthur enters the almost empty Veranda Lounge. Ted is sitting at a table for two, under a window on the starboard side. Arthur observes that Ted has almost finished his beer, on his way past the bar, he asks the steward to take two beers over to their table. As he approaches, he notices that Ted is staring pensively at the Brussels lace that is left on the inside of his nearly empty beer glass.

"Hello, Ted, have you been waiting long?" Arthur asks, with a twinge of apprehension. He is not used to seeing Ted with a cloud over his head.

"I thought I'd get here a little early," replies Ted soberly. "I've got a lot on my mind, mate."

"You do look deep in thought," said Arthur, feeling that the net was closing in. "Perhaps you'd prefer to be alone?"

"No, mate, I want to talk to you, but I don't quite know where to begin."

The steward puts two glasses of beer on the table and Arthur signs the chit. Raising his glass, he salutes Ted with forced joviality. "Cheers! What's on your mind, Ted? You know you can talk to me. After all, we are old friends; we've known each other for nearly a month now."

Ted doesn't touch his beer, or even acknowledge Arthur's weak attempt at humour; he is looking directly into Arthur's odd coloured eyes. "Let's get down to the duck's guts, mate, I went on that Bridge visit and…"

Arthur cuts him off bluntly. He is nervous about the direction the conversation might take. "That's good, and how did you enjoy it?"

"Enjoy, isn't the right word, mate, but I did find it to be very informative, that's a dead cert."

"That's good. What did you find most interesting?"

"Well, you remember that Lascar bloke that was staring down at us from the Bridge, when we were playing deck quoits?"

"The Bridge Wallah, yes, the one who yelled at me and you waved back?"

"How do you know he yelled at you?"

"What I meant was, he yelled and waved at both of us."

"Oh! OK. Yeah, well, that's him. Anyway, on the Bridge visit, he and I had a little chat. He doesn't speak English too good, but I understood what he was telling me."

"Did he tell you all about navigation? I thought the officers did that."

"He wasn't telling me about navigation, mate, he was telling me about you."

"About me? But I don't even know the man."

"He says he thinks he recognises you."

"How can that be?"

"Because he says, he would never forget you, because of what you did."

"What I did? What did I do?"

"He said it happened eighteen years ago."

"Eighteen years ago? Who is this Bridge Wallah? Is he some kind of mystical Eastern wise-man?"

"He says that your name is Archie."

"Archie? But, Ted, you know my name is Arthur."

"What's in a name, mate?"

"What do you mean, Ted?"

"Well, Archie or Arthur, or whoever you are, he says that he can never forget you, because eighteen years ago, you were a Quartermaster on this very ship."

"But…"

"Please let me finish, mate. He says that one night, when the ship was approximately, where we are now, near the Tropic of Capricorn, you fell asleep at the wheel and steered her way off course, putting her half a day behind schedule, and you were kicked off the Bridge. He said he'd never seen anything like that before or since."

"But that could have been anyone."

"But it wasn't anyone, Arthur, was it? It was you, Archie, wasn't it?"

"How can you be so sure?"

"Because, I've been adding things up, you remember that first day at sea, at the breakfast table?"

"Yeah."

"Well, when I asked your name, you almost said 'Archie'. You also seem to know a lot about what goes on, on board this ship. Furthermore, this ship used to call at Sydney twenty years ago."

"Go on."

"That's when my wife and I got married. She had just broken up with a sailor, whose name was Archie. He was the one who got her preggers. And after her daughter was born, she used to take her down to see him, every time the *Strathaird* was in Sydney."

"What's this all about anyway?"

"Beg yours? You know very well what this is all about. It's about you and me Archie, mate. You lied to me about never having been on this ship before, and you lied to me about never having been in Sydney before. You see, what I'm beginning to think is that you and my wife, Janice, used to be lovers. Moreover, I think that you are the father of her daughter."

"Are you actually telling me that you really believe that I was the lover of your wife, Janice and the father your daughter, Hope?"

"How did you know her name was Hope?"

"I don't know, you must have mentioned it sometime."

"No I haven't, so there's no point in denying it any more, mate. I'm no nong you know."

"I don't think you're a fool, Ted, far from it. You see, I wasn't even sure that you were the actual man that Janice had married, but now I know. Yes, you're right, Janice and I were lovers, and yes, I am the father of Hope."

"You've been lying all along."

"I didn't intend to Ted, it's just that I didn't want you to know, because it would only complicate things and serve no purpose whatsoever. My relationship with Janice was before she met you. I didn't know she was pregnant until after she married you. What could I do?"

"I dunno, mate, but I wish you'd been more up front with me from the start. You never gave me a fair go. Now, I don't know what I think of you or even if I trust you anymore."

"I understand, Ted, but it's all in the past. I understand what a shock it might be for you to meet your wife's past lover and the father of her child. But, this is now, Ted. What shall we do now?"

"We? What should we do now? We're going to do nothing now, mate. *We* are never going to do anything again."

The echo of Eleanor's voice rings in Arthur's ears.

Ted's voice grows in volume as he continues determinedly. "Now bite your bum and listen to me. When we get to Sydney, I don't want you to have any contact with my wife and daughter ever again. You hear? You may be Hope's biological father, but you gave up all claims to her eighteen years ago, when you buggered off. I didn't like it, but I respected Janice and Hope's desire to see you when your ship was in, but then you just buggered off. As for Hope, she doesn't even remember you. So leave em alone. You hear? I don't need anymore agro." Abruptly standing up, he looks down at Arthur and remarks dismissively, "I'll pay for the bloody beers."

Arthur is crushed and humiliated, he lamely offers, "No, it's OK. I'm going to stay for another one. It's on my chit."

Ted sharply replies, "Well take it off your bloody chit. I don't want to owe you anything. I'm fed up to the back teeth with you. You probably lied about your family in England too, didn't you?"

Arthur has no time to answer the question, before Ted immediately renews his onslaught. "You jelly kneed, lying bastard." He then turns on his heel, and over his right shoulder, he dismissively growls, "And take those bloody gloves off, they don't fool me. Don't you think I can see that the middle fingers are sewn together? It's obvious you have webbed fingers; just like Hope. G'day, mate."

Arthur resignedly watches as Ted walks purposefully away.

The bar steward, who is witness to this scene, tactfully busies himself, polishing glasses.

Looking out over the vast expanse of the Indian Ocean, Arthur stiffens as he feels an intense pain shooting through his right shoulder and across his chest. He also feels the jagged sting of isolation.

*

When the *Strathaird* arrives in Sydney on January the first, nineteen fifty-five, Arthur Hobbs is standing at the rail of the boat deck, looking down at the welcoming crowds on the wharf below. There are hundreds of people throwing streamers, waving, cheering, and shouting over the marshal music of the welcoming band; it is a typically enthusiastic Australian reception. The temperature is ninety degrees, Fahrenheit, and everyone is dressed appropriately, in thin dresses, shorts, T-shirts, and sandals. On 'A' deck, two decks directly below him, Arthur sees the tightly curled, golden-blonde head of Ted Atherton. They haven't spoken a word to each other since that painful conversation crossing the Tropic of Capricorn. Ted is scanning the cheering crowd, searching for his family.

Arthur is studying the jostling crowd, looking for a familiar face. Then he sees her; she must be about fifty by now. She is a little plumper, bronzed body, white dress, sandals, wide beaming smile, sparkling obsidian eyes, and still as sensuous as ever. Beside her, is a gum-chewing, twentyish wild-child; she is wearing skin-tight jeans, and a blue-and-white horizontal striped, figure-hugging T-shirt. Janice is waving exuberantly in his direction and he delightedly waves back, until he realises that she is waving at Ted, two decks directly below him. He remembers Ted's warning about not contacting them again, but no one can stop him waving, and he does so, energetically, perhaps unnoticed by Ted, or Janice, or the wild-child.

*

As they clear the Customs Hall, Arthur stands back and watches as Ted eagerly walks into the waiting arms of Janice. The wild-child hangs back for a while, and then hesitantly steps forward and joins them. As her arms unenthusiastically encircle Ted's back, Arthur notices her webbed fingers. Over Ted's shoulder, Janice seems to be looking directly at him, then her eyes flicker away, and she turns her head to welcome her returning husband. Arthur exhales deeply, as he watches them pick up their baggage and disappear into the buzzing crowd, with nary a backward glance; his already stooped shoulders, slump deeper into his emptiness.

Reaching into his inside jacket pocket, he pulls out his wallet. Opening it, he takes out the remains of the photo that Janice had given him; he has carried that photo with him for nineteen years. However, after a time, like their relationship, it has broken into pieces, and then the pieces have broken into pieces, until eventually, time has turned it into a flimsy representation of the original. Holding on to the Customs counter-top for support, he feels his chest tightening and breaks out into a cold sweat.

Chapter Thirty

Don't touch me

Janice's attention is drawn towards the tall, stooped, and bushy-haired man in the Customs hall. For a brief disarming moment, their eyes meet, then quickly disconnect. Her arms involuntary tighten around her husband; there is a familiarity about this stranger that disturbs her.

Her mind travels back to a night over twenty years ago, to when she had taken Archie to the beach. They had fallen in love immediately. For a while, they were spectacular together, and then it all had fallen apart, because she wanted a good life for the child she was carrying within her. She had never loved Ted in the same passionate way that she had loved Archie, but, Ted had offered her and Hope a secure future. When they were married, they moved into his house on Bondi Road, Waverly. It was a good place to bring up a child, away from the hurly burly of the inner city.

When Hope was born, Ted was very attentive to both of them, but he became a little irritated with her, when she would take the child to visit Archie, every time his ship docked in Sydney. Janice had told Ted who the biological father of Hope was, but Ted became suspicious that she still held a torch for Archie. To allay this suspicion Janice had removed Archie's Siamese silver locket from around her neck, and put it away for Hope, for when she would be old enough to understand who her real father was.

Janice remembered Hope, at the tender age of two, becoming withdrawn and unresponsive after seeing Archie for the last time. Hope, despite fully not understanding that Archie was her father, had loved and missed the gentle giant, and mourned deeply for his loss.

As time drifted by, Hope, knowing that Ted was her stepfather, became more and more resentful towards him. She would throw the wildest temper tantrums, yelling hateful abuse at him. Ted's reaction was always to yell back at Hope, and sometimes slap her hard on her behind, much to the chagrin and horror of her mother. Janice's response to this turmoil was to try and comfort Hope and give in to her demands, for Janice was weighed down with a great guilt, for the betrayal of Archie. However, her love for her daughter, and the concern for her future, remained steadfast. What was most disturbing was that deep within her heart, she knew she still loved Archie. It was not long before Janice and Ted grew apart.

Ted became more and more distant, spending most of his time at work, only coming home late at night, stinking of booze. Janice was careful not to criticize either Ted or Hope; she became the only conduit of their communication. Over time, Ted's resentment of Hope grew, he was resentful that she was the progeny of another man, who, in his absence, exerted some strange power over his wife and daughter. These thoughts would send Ted into blind rages, which he took out on Hope in the form of verbal and physical abuse.

By the time Hope was fifteen, the family was just going through the motions, with Janice trying to hold it all together; it became an impossible task. Janice would spend most of her dark days alone, walking aimlessly around the empty house, sobbing despondently. What little love that once existed in that home, had packed its bags and walked out the door a long time ago.

Hope sought love and approval outside of home. After school, she and her friends would head down to Sydney docks and watch the big ships arrive and depart. They flirted outrageously with the sailors, who would inevitably invite them aboard and ply them with booze. Hope learned to be a woman far too soon.

*

On the night of Hope's seventeenth birthday, Ted was returning home, after spending the evening at a bar with friends from work. He had just pulled into the driveway, when he heard the piercing squeal of tires. He saw the headlights of a car, swerving crazily down the street towards him, its radio was going full blast, and the occupants were 'hoot'n and holler'n'. As the car screeched to a sudden stop, right in front of him, the door was thrown open and Hope fell out onto the road in a drunken stupor, eliciting guffaws of laughter from the remaining occupants of the car. The car door was quickly slammed shut, the engine gunned, and the machine screamed away; the raucous voices of its occupants streaming back through the once silent night.

Hope was hopelessly trying to stand up, but her legs kept collapsing under her; she was alternatively moaning and giggling. Ted looked down at her, in disgust and anger, and brutally tried to yank her to a standing position. But, as drunk as Hope was, she kept resisting his efforts, pushing him away and screaming at him, "Don't touch me. You are *not* my father. Don't you dare lay a fucking hand on me. Just rack off and leave me alone."

This violent reaction further enraged Ted, and he yelled back at her. "Don't you fucking yell at me, you ungrateful, drunken whore. You fucking spoiled, selfish slut. Get the fuck up off your knees and into the fucking house right now."

This commotion immediately woke up the neighbourhood, who instantly responded by slamming their windows shut.

Janice rushed out of the house, screaming at her dysfunctional family. "Shut the fuck up, both of you. You've woken up the whole godamn neighbourhood." She helped her daughter to her feet, and with Hope drunkenly sobbing on her shoulder, took her inside the house.

Ted determinedly stomped after them, and viciously slammed the front door behind him, shattering a pane of glass on impact. He swore bitterly. He was totally out of control, and was still yelling abuse at Hope. "You listen to me, you fucking good-for-nothing tramp. You do as I say, or I'll give you a fucking beating you won't ever forget until your dying, fucking day."

Through the thick haze of her inebriation, Hope immediately became sharply focused. She stared steadily at him and pointing a warning finger in his direction, she screamed at him. "If you lay a fucking hand on me one more time, you'll be fucking sorry."

His raging anger, fuelled by alcohol, incited him to rush towards her, and   swinging his arm back, with his tightly clenched fist, he delivered a brutal roundhouse punch to her right ear, which instantly dropped her to the floor, where she lay in a crumpled heap, quite still, with blood trickling from her rapidly swelling ear.

Janice's protective, maternal instincts instantly clicked in. She proceeded to take control, screaming at Ted, "Get the fuck away from my daughter, you stupid fucking drunken arsehole." She slammed him against the wall, and bent down to help her daughter. With a cursory examination, she was relieved to see that Hope was still breathing, but blood was still oozing from her bruised and swollen ear. She ordered Ted to open the front door, and with reserves of strength she didn't know she had, lifted the limp body of her brutalised daughter, and carried her out to the car, then frantically drove her to the Royal Women's Hospital in Sydney. There, they staunched the flow of blood, and after x-rays were taken, Janice was told that Hope had a badly ruptured eardrum, and would probably have very little hearing left in her right ear.

When they returned home, Ted was mortified and full of remorse; he tearfully pleaded for forgiveness and promised that he would never raise a hand against Hope ever again, and he would make it up to them and become a good husband and loving father.

Hope, who by this time was conscious and had quickly sobered up, didn't say a word. She couldn't bring herself even to look at Ted. He moved towards her, in a gesture of reconciliation, but rapidly shaking her head in revulsion, she shivered and shrank from his presence. She gently kissed her mother on the cheek and, without even acknowledging Ted, slowly and deliberately climbed the stairs to her room, and with a sense of finality, she firmly closed and locked the door behind her.

*

That night, as Janice and Ted lay together, they didn't speak, and they didn't touch. Ted rose early the following morning and, without waking a soul, he meekly left the house. When he returned home, directly from work that evening, Janice informed him that Hope had left home to stay with her aunt in Woollahra, and would not be returning.

Hope remained living with her loving aunt in Woollahra, where she steadily regained her emotional strength. Janice would frequently visit her, and they would often talk about Archie. It was on one of those visits that Janice gave Hope the Siamese silver locket. Hope gradually pulled her life together and pursued a career in nursing. She would not see Ted for another three years, when he returned from England on the *Strathaird*, on that hot and sultry New Year's Day, in 1955.

*

In the intervening years, Ted had sought professional help and guidance, and to a great extent had come to terms with his feelings of anger, jealousy, and inadequacy. Janice and Ted's relationship bore the strain of Hope's absence, but in time, maybe because of her absence, they tentatively healed their wounds. It took a lot of persuading on the part of Janice to reconcile her daughter with Ted once more, and meet him on the dock that day.

*

Ted is touched and thankful for their rapprochement, and fearful of the threat of reliving the violent anger and resentment of the not too distant past, he purposely neglects to tell his family that Archie is in town. After all, as Archie had said, in their final conversation, in the Veranda Lounge, "It would only complicate things and serve no purpose whatsoever."

Chapter Thirty-One

YOU ARE TOO DANGEROUS TO LOVE

On his nineteenth birthday, Bobby has been paid off from the SS "*Egyptian*" and is waiting for his next ship. He is staying at his mum's flat in Chelsea, and is becoming increasingly concerned for her health. Not being able to get any work in the theatre any more, and still mourning the death of her long departed Edward, she has retreated into seeking solace in books and booze. She rarely ever ventures out, preferring the hermetic existence of a recluse. For days on end, she will lie in her bed, only bothering to get up to go to the toilet, or open a can of stew. Once a week, she will get dressed and leave the flat, to exchange her library books and shop for her meagre supplies.

Her only income is from an Actors Equity pension, and the monthly allotment that is deducted from Bobby's wages. Her alcohol and tobacco consumption has reached a point where she can't live without her bottle of sherry and two packets of cigarettes a day.

The interior walls and windows of the flat are coated with the greasy, yellow stain of nicotine. Bobby has made a Herculean effort to wash down the wallpaper and clean the windows. As he removes Edwards' paintings to clean the greasy film of nicotine from the glass, he can see the sharp blank shape of the picture frame imprinted on the wall where it had hung, revealing the original bright colour of the patterned wallpaper of a bygone age.

Having spent three days cleaning the flat, he feels the need to escape from this decaying world of booze and smoke and capitulation. He needs to taste the fresh and natural world of trees and flowers and grass.

On April eighteenth, 1956, Bobby rides the Tube on the District Line from Sloane Square to Kew Gardens. There, in that magnificent 300 acres of flora and fauna, he walks alone in peace and contemplation. Eventually he finds himself at the Temple of Aeolus, overlooking the Palm House pond and Woodland Gardens. On the steps of the temple Bobby rests, and absentmindedly looks out over the nodding daffodils.

Tending to be influenced by his immediate surroundings, he remembers the myth of Aeolus and Odysseus. Aeolus was a minor Greek deity, who was the keeper of the winds. He lived on one of the rocky Lipara islands, close to Sicily. In the caves on this island were imprisoned the winds. Aeolus, directed by the higher gods, let out these winds as soft breezes or gales.

When the Greek hero, Odysseus, visited him, Aeolus received him favourably, and on the hero's departure, presented him with a bag, containing all the adverse winds, so that Odysseus, on his voyage back to Ithaca would always have smooth sailing. However, in sight of his homeland Odysseus, having been untroubled by foul weather, fell asleep, and his men, not being able to contain their curiosity, opened the bag, thus releasing all the fierce winds, creating such a violent storm which blew their ship far off course.

Bobby is lost in a mythological fog, when he hears a voice calling him back to the present; the voice is soft and hesitant.

"Bobby, is that you?"

At first, he thinks it is the Sirens in his dream calling again. The voice persists. "Bobby, Bobby, can you hear me?"

Emerging from his trance, he turns in the direction of the voice, to see a young woman holding onto a pram, in which there is a young child. Standing apart from her, at a distance of about twenty yards, he notices a young soldier, who is staring in their direction. Bobby immediately recognises the young woman. They haven't seen each other for about a year and a half; it is Polly. Her smile is as radiant and welcome as the spring sunshine. He stands up, and crossing the narrow gap between them, he takes her hand. The soldier takes two steps towards them, before coming to a halt. "Polly!" exclaims Bobby, his wide-open eyes opening even wider. "What a surprise. Where have you been? You look wonderful," and indeed she does. Nodding in the direction of the pram, he asks, "And who is this? Are you a Nanny? Where are you living?" His words come tumbling out. He can't restrain his joy at seeing her again. Leaning into the pram, he extends his little finger, which the sleeping child's perfect little hand instinctually grasps.

Polly smiles wanly. "Oh, Bobby, so much has happened in the last year and a half. When we were expelled from the orphanage, I was sent to work in Harrods, stuffing Stilton cheese into jars Gary found out where they had sent me, and he came to me and told me that he loved me and wanted to look after me. I was so lonely and so grateful to him, we started to live together, and when we found out that I was pregnant, he asked me to marry him, and we now have a daughter; I named her Joy." She looks over her shoulder at the soldier.

Bobby is taken aback by this sudden turn of events. "You married Gary? You and Gary have a child? But, Polly, I thought that we were in love with each other. I thought that you loved me."

Polly stands erect, her eyes squinting in vexation and her lips are pursed. "I did, Bobby, but I had to marry Gary. I was pregnant with Joy, and he didn't care whose child it was, he wanted to marry me. You know very well he has always been in love with me, and he is a very kind man, I am quite contented with him." Again, she turns and looks at the soldier, who starts to march towards them; he stops when she shakes her head.

Nodding his head in the soldier's direction, Bobby asks, "Is that Gary? I don't recognise him in his fancy uniform."

"Yes, it is," she replies. "Please, Bobby, don't make this difficult, he doesn't want to talk to you."

As he stares at Gary, Bobby whispers icily, "The feeling is mutual, I assure you. Then whose child is it?" he abruptly enquires, with a twinge of jealousy.

"Gary's and mine, Bobby, Joy is seven months old now."

He refocuses his attention on Polly; his stare is cold and hard. "I know you and Gary are the legal parents, what I want to know is, who is the father?"

Polly returns his stare, and a dark cloud of anger crosses her brow. "She could be yours or she could be Gary's, what difference does it make Bobby? You just ran away to sea, as far away as you could get from me. I gave up hoping I would ever see you again and just shut you out of my life." Her voice is rising and Bobby feels her palpable pain and anger. "You are too dangerous to love, Bobby. I loved you so much because you were so romantic, so confident, and so different from other people. Now I'm content with Gary, because he is a reliable and constant husband, and a good father to our child; now, I have become comfortably numb."

"I'm sorry, Polly, I didn't know where they sent you, I tried to find you, but I had to be on my ship the next day."

"No need to apologise," she retorts coldly, "we are doing fine, thank you. Gary has just completed his first year of National Service, and he is already a corporal, and wants to enlist in the Regular Army. He is going to be sent to Cyprus, as part of the British Peace Keeping Forces, and I am going with him. We'll be stationed in Nicosia and I'm going to train to be a nurse at the Military Hospital there, and… and… and…" She starts to sob, her body shaking; she looks so broken and vulnerable. He puts his arms around her and she sobs and sobs on his tiny shoulder. "Damn you, Bobby Shafto. Damn you. Damn you. Why did you leave me?"

With firm and determined steps, Gary marches towards them.

Polly quickly pulls away from Bobby and turns to face her husband. She shouts through her tears, "No, please, Gary, I told you, I have to do this alone."

Gary comes to a halt, and then quickly and impatiently, starts pacing back and forth, kicking stones.

All Bobby could think of saying is, "I'm so sorry Polly, I truly am, please forgive me."

Polly straightens up and dries her tears. Stepping towards the pram, and bending down, she lifts up the child. As Joy opens her eyes, Bobby gasps, and his mouth shoots open in amazement as he is immediately drawn to her enigmatic eyes; each is of a different gem-like colour, like an odd-eyed, white oriental cat. Her right eye is the colour of lapis lazuli, and her left, the colour of turquoise.

Joy points to the daffodils and smiles. Holding her daughter lovingly in her arms, and snuggling her nose into the nape of her neck, Polly coos, "Yes, darling, daffodils. Aren't they pretty?"

Joy looks at Bobby, pointing in his direction.

"Do you know who that is?" enquires Polly, with a small smile.

Joy wrinkles her brow in a slight frown.

Polly whispers, "Would you like to meet him?" She passes Joy over to Bobby for him to hold.

Gary stops pacing and stares intently.

Joy and Bobby look into each other's eyes, and his heart melts. "Oh my God, Joy is my…." is all Bobby is able to say, as he recognises the eyes of his father.

Polly cuts him off, sealing his lips, by putting the soft pad of her forefinger firmly on that little cleft under his nose. Then taking Joy from him, she puts her back in the pram and says, "Wave bye-bye to Bobby."

Bobby stands forlornly watching Polly and Joy waving goodbye. "But Polly," he pleads.

Polly remonstrates. "Don't say another word, Bobby; I don't know if I could keep my composure."

He moves towards her, his arms extending in an invitation to hug, but she quickly withdraws and says firmly, "Goodbye, Bobby, Please don't try and contact us. I wish you well in your life, I will never forget you." She turns and wheels the pram towards her waiting husband.

Rooted to the spot in stunned amazement, Bobby lamely whispers. "Nor me you, Polly." He watches dejectedly as little Joy waves from the departing pram, her cat-like eyes gleaming with delight. Bobby can't bring himself to wave back. Polly doesn't look back.

As the pram approaches him, Gary stands to attention and barks in a disconnected voice, "Shafto, you are dismissed." He then sharply about-turns, and falls into step with his wife and child.

Bobby watches desolately as Joy is wheeled away. He remembers Bunny's prophetic words to Gary: *"My seed will haunt you for all eternity."* He thought of Hobbs his father, they had been so close at one time, and now, they were so far apart. He felt that he needed to reconnect with him. Should he embrace the future and embark on the epic voyage in search of his father? Or, should he endeavour to reconnect with Polly and their daughter? But, how can he travel that road, when Polly is married to Gary? What right does he have to come between them? How can he come to a decision, when he doesn't even know what direction to take? Standing on the steps of the temple of Aeolus, he is reminded of Odysseus, when all the adverse winds are released from the bag, and he is blown way off course. He is confused and out of his element.

"Do not grieve Bobby. This is meant to be."

Deep down, he knows his first mistress is still the sea. Once again, he hears the song of the Sirens.

Chapter Thirty-Two

HEY, SAILOR, ARE YOU NEW IN TOWN?

Bobby had served on the *Egyptian* for two years, calling at many ports around the Mediterranean Sea. During his travels, he had seen his share of trouble-spots.

Cyprus, in 1955, EOKA was demanding union with Greece. Bobby and a few of his shipmates were in a café in Famagusta, when a homemade grenade was tossed in from the street, it failed to detonate, but the boys exploded out of there in a hurry.

Algiers in 1955, the Algerian Uprising was in full force; the Algerians were trying to oust the occupying French. As the ship was docking, a Cabin Boy was hurling insults down at the men on the wharf; he went ashore that night, and never returned. Also in Algiers, Bobby was chased along the wharf by a knife-wielding Arab, who wanted a piece of his little white arse. Luckily, he made it to the safety of the ship, just in time for his shipmates to scare off his pursuer.

The Suez Crisis, in 1956, when the British-French-Israeli Alliance were fighting with Egypt for control of the canal, his ship was requisitioned by the British government, and armaments were mounted fore and aft; they ran guns and ammunition to Israel.

Now, he is about to embark on the most dangerous encounter of all, it is Strait Street, dubbed, The Gut, in Valletta, Malta. The Gut is a pedestrian street, roughly a quarter of a mile long. In the sixteenth century, the Knights of St John used to duel for their honour in this street. In 1955, foreign sailors are getting drunk and trolling for sex. The Gut is lined with bars and restaurants, standing cheek by jowl along the whole length of the street. The challenge for sailors on shore leave is to start at the top of The Gut, and emerge from the other end of the street, walking, and unscathed; many a brave man has attempted this heroic feat and many have failed. This legend does not deter little Bobby and his shipmates from trying.

The first bar they visit is aptly named *The Egyptian Bar*. It is a dark and smoky place, right out of a Bogart movie. After a couple of whiskies, Tom, the affable saltwater cowboy, introduces Bobby to Gerry, a bargirl.

"Hey, Sailor, are you new in town?" enquires Gerry invitingly.

"Yes as a matter of fact I am," Bobby answers, matter-of-factly.

"Then let's dance," invites Gerry temptingly as she steers him onto the tiny dance floor.

This brings applause and cheers from his shipmates. Gerry and Bobby stand and vibrate for a while, and then she asks him if he would like to go home with her. Flushed by the booze and aroused from the dancing, he capitulates. On the way out of the bar, Tom calls out, "See you in little while little Bobby, we'll be waiting here for you."

"Don't bother waiting, I won't be back." Bobby laughs boastfully.

.   "Oh yes you will," shouts Tom tauntingly, and the whole table of his shipmates breaks into appreciative laughter and applause.

To the bemused stares of the local girls and other sailors, the prospective lovers walk, arm in arm to the top of The Gut. There they hail a horse-drawn gharry.

With his prospective lover by his side, and listening to the rhythmic clop, clop, clop, of the horse's hooves on the cobblestone streets, Bobby is luxuriating in the heady romance of a sultry Mediterranean evening. The gharry has travelled about a hundred yards along the narrow winding street, when Bobby makes his move. He buries his nose in Gerry's cleavage, kissing the small mounds of her breasts, and it isn't long before his hand is exploring her thighs, and not long after, his hand closes around an engorged penis. He freezes, sits bolt upright, and Bunny lets out a blood-curdling scream that goes straight to the very heart of the terrified beast, which breaks into a frenzied gallop, pulling the swaying and shaking gharry behind it, its frightened occupants hanging on in desperation, as the driver heaves frantically on the reins. Bunny is shrieking at Gerry.

"Who are you? What are you? Are you a man? Are you a woman? Are you both? Are you neither? What kind of monster are you? What are you going to do to us? You have deceived us. You have despoiled us. You have stolen our innocence. You have stolen our trust and you have stolen our money. You are incongruous in the extreme. No more of this perversion, no more." Bobby hastily jumps from the dangerously, fast-moving carriage as he yells, **"Geronimo!"**

He hits the cobblestones and rolls over and over, until he comes to a stop in front of rapidly gathering crowd of astonished spectators. One of them comes to the aid of the bruised and battered little sailor and helps him to his feet. He can still see the precariously swaying gharry and its panicking occupants, the driver still frantically heaving on the reins in a futile attempt to stop the terrified horse, as they disappear down the narrow cobblestone street.

A little the worse for wear, Bobby eventually arrives back at *The Egyptian Bar*, to the tumultuous applause and laughter of all his shipmates, who recklessly ply him with further libation. As the ribald crew drags little Bobby from bar to bar, it only gets worse. In the *Sunset Bar*, where Bunny tries, unsuccessfully, to sing 'Rock Around the Clock', he is booed off the stage. By the time, they reach *Dirty Dick's*, the little sailor is almost unconscious. His shipmates can only revive him by sticking his head in the toilet and pulling the chain. After a few more bars, he gives up singing, and his mates give up trying to revive him. For the rest of the evening, they drag the unconscious little Deck Boy with them, from bar to bar…'You never leave your shipmate's body behind for strangers to desecrate.'

When they finally return to the ship, which is at anchor in Grand Harbour, they still have Bobby in tow. They drunkenly drag him up the gangway, feet first, his head bobbing and knocking against each step on the way up. Eventually they throw him onto his bunk to sleep it off.

The next morning, on opening one bloodshot eye, he is assaulted by the pounding of ball-peen hammers inside his head. As he lies there, trying painfully to remember the previous evening, he realises he is still fully dressed. His brand new, blue suit from Burtons is torn, stained, and stinking of vomit. He is unable to work that morning, so he is deducted a day's pay.

Chapter Thirty-Three

TOO MANY SHERRIES

In the early morning of November 1956, Bobby arrives home on shore leave. People are emerging from Elm Park Mansions on their way to work, wrapping their coats around them, and raising their brollies against the cold and the rain of an inhospitable London winter. Approaching Mrs Egan's ground floor flat, he notices that the window is closed and the curtains drawn, there will be no good-natured banter this morning.

He climbs the four flights of stone steps to his mother's flat and puts down his bag. Not seeing the hall light through the transom, he suspects that she is still sleeping. Reaching through the letterbox, he feels the familiar string that is attached to the front-door key. He pulls on the string, which seems to be caught on something, but eventually he is able to free it and fish the key through the letterbox, and insert it in the keyhole. Unlocking the door he gently pushes, but is met with some resistance. He exerts a little more force and manages to open the door ajar. "Mum," he calls softly, "are you there? I can't open the door." There is no answer. Thinking it might be the hall rug that is stuck against the door, he pushes a little harder and shouts, "Mum, could you help, the door's stuck." There is still no answer. With his little shoulder, he gives the door an almighty shove. There is a soft whimper from the other side of the door. He anxiously yells, "Mum, is that you? Are you all right?" He is answered with a slightly louder cry. He knows then that she is lying on the floor on the other side of the door. "I'm here, Mum, it's Bobby. Try and move away from the door so I can open it a little." He is starting to panic. "Mum, I am going to try again, so see if you can move just a little away from the door, OK?"

There is a sharp intake of breath, and she replies painfully, "All right, Bobby."

He pushes the door slowly open, just far enough for him to enter the flat. Squeezing through the gap, he sees the shape of his semi-conscious mother, sprawled on the floor against the door, which is jammed against her contorted body. Switching on the hall light, he bends down to help her. With a perfunctory examination, he notices there are clots of congealed blood in her hair and her right leg is hideously folded under her frail body. Closing the door, and easily lifting her in his arms, her leg grotesquely dangling, with her foot scraping the floor, he carries her to her bed. "Mum, can you hear me? Tell me what happened." She can only groan in reply. "Don't worry, Mum, I'll get help." He doesn't know what else he can do to help her, so he immediately phones for an ambulance.

She seems to revive a little and tries to whisper something. He moves closer, to better hear her. She is whispering, "Sister … Hope."

Right away, he thinks of the convent. "That's all in the past, Mum."

"Bobby, we love you,"

"I love you too, Mum. Now save your energy, I've called an ambulance, and help will be here soon."

She resumes her whispering in a painfully dry and parched voice. "Bobby, don't let them take me away, I can't bear to leave this place. This is my home, I can't leave my books, they are my friends, I can't leave Edward's paintings, I can't leave my home; it's a second skin around me, Please, Bobby, please let me stay here."

After, what he feels is a painfully long time, he hears the wailing of the approaching sirens, and he turns away from her, tears stinging his eyes. He can hear the ambulance attendants pounding up the stone stairs and the sharp rapping on the front door. He lets them in, and watches as with cool efficiency, they quickly assess his mother's injuries. They lift her on to the stretcher and strap her in.

She looks over to Bobby, pleading plaintively. "Please, Bobby, don't let them take me away, please don't leave me. Please, please."

Her imploring look is breaking his heart. "It's all right Mum, I'm coming to the hospital with you."

As the stretcher is carried past him, she is crying, "No, no, no, please. Bobby, please let me stay please, please, please."

Against her protestations, he follows them out of the front door, down the four flights of stone steps, out into the cold London drizzle, past the drawn curtains of Mrs Egan's deathly silent window, and into the waiting ambulance.

When they arrive at the emergency entrance, of St Stephen's Hospital, on Fulham Road, his mother is immediately admitted, and he is told that there is nothing more that he can do. He is advised that it would be better if he went home and to come back the next day.

The next day he returns to St Stephen's, and learns that his mother is in critical condition. She is drifting in and out of consciousness and is very weak and dehydrated. When he goes to see her, she manages to relate that when she had fallen and broken her leg, perhaps she had had too many sherries. She was standing on a rickety chair, by the front door, in the half-light of the hallway, in the process of putting some shillings in the gas meter, when she had lost her balance and struck her head against the door, knocking her unconscious. She must have fallen awkwardly on her right leg and broken it. For three days, whilst lying on the floor, she had drifted in and out of consciousness, unable to move or call for help.

He is told by her doctor that her right tibia is severely fractured, her knee and hip are dislocated and she will require extensive surgery, but in her weakened state, it will be too risky to perform the operation now. The doctor suggests that she remain in hospital, whilst she regains her strength, until such time as it is safe to operate. Knowing that she is in caring hands and there is nothing more that he can do, he returns to his ship.

*

Seven days later, the SS *Caslon* is one day's run from St. Johns, Newfoundland, where she is scheduled to load a cargo of newsprint. It is late November and they have come through a rough Atlantic crossing.

Bobby is forty feet down number four hold, cleaning it out in preparation for her new cargo. He has collected a pile of dunnage, and yells up for a heaving-line to be thrown down, so that he can make it fast around the scrap wood and have it hauled topside. As he stands looking up, the heaving-line comes spiralling down, but unfortunately, a three-pound spanner, which is entangled in the line, comes free, hitting him square on the top of his head, splitting it open. He doesn't pass out, in fact there is hardly any sensation of pain; the top of his head feels numb. He carefully makes his way over to the vertical steel ladder, which is welded to the forward bulkhead of the hold, and with blood streaming from his scalp, and running into his eyes and mouth, he blindly tastes the unmistakable, cloying sweetness of life. He slowly climbs up the forty feet, rung by rung, to the open hatch combing. There, he is helped onto the open deck by willing hands, and seated on a chair brought out from the sailors' mess. There being no doctor on board, it falls to the Chief Steward to stitch up Bobby's scalp. Bobby is told to down the glass of dark rum that is proffered, and then a lighted cigarette is stuck between his lips. With a ring of curious crew members around them, the Chief Steward sews up Bobby's head with fifteen even stitches. Apart from leaving a little ridge on his scalp, the result would have done credit to a royal seamstress sewing the Queen's wedding gown.

He is halfway through his second shot of rum, when the Radio Officer hands him a transmission from company headquarters in London. It reads, "*To Robert Shafto, A.B. SS Caslon. We regret to inform you that your mother, Eleanor Anne Shafto, passed away at 2.00 a.m. Nov. 21, 1956, at St Stephen's Hospital, Chelsea, London.*"

When the *Caslon* arrives at St Johns, Newfoundland, Bobby phones St Stephen's Hospital. He is told that after his departure, his mother's condition had become gradually worse, complications had set in, and she had contracted double pneumonia, from which she never recovered.

The hospital had informed his Aunt Theresa and Uncle Jasper of his mother's death, and they had made arrangements for her cremation and burial in the grave of Edward, next to their lost son, Bunny, in the old village of Wilmington. Eleanor was finally with the man she loved.

*

On December 14th, when he returns to England, Bobby goes straight to Wilmington. In the dead of night he stands over their graves, bareheaded, under the cold light of a full moon. With his tiny shoulders shaking, he silently weeps. Bunny says a requiem for his mother..

"Oh Mother, welcome to this cursed plot, at last you are with us again. But, why did you surrender? Could you not live without him? Did you love him that much? Did you love him more than your sons? More than our father? Did you love him more than your very self? Your love for him was all-consuming. You loved him too much. You will be remembered, Mother. You will not pass away; you will continue to live through your progeny."

Eleanor Shafto wasted away at the age of fifty-six, the same age, and from the same causes as her beloved Edward; in *simpatico*, she drank herself to death.

Bobby can take only so much grief. The time has come for him to process the anguish, take on the spirit of those he has loved and lost, and fold them into himself. He turns his back on England's green and pleasant land, and returns to the heaving bosom of the sea.

Chapter Thirty-Four

PHANTOMS IN HIGH HEELS

Bobby is proudly wearing a uniform for the first time; his dream has come true. He is now, at the age of twenty, a Quartermaster on the P&O passenger liner, SS *Himalaya*. She is a beautiful vessel of 28,000 gross tonnes, 171 feet in length, a 90-foot beam, and a cruising speed of 22 knots. The *Himalaya* is on an epic six-month world cruise, following the familiar P&O Australian run, through the Mediterranean, the recently re-opened Suez Canal, Aden, India, Ceylon and Australia. Then on to Tasmania, New Zealand, Fiji, New Guinea, Indonesia, the Philippines, Hong Kong, Japan, Hawaii, the west coasts of Canada and America, and back to Hawaii. From there, she returns to Australia, before retracing her outward-bound route back to England.

In the sultry Australian summer of 1957, the SS *Himalaya,* successfully completing the first leg of her world cruise, arrives in Sydney. She'll be in port for a week, whilst some passengers disembark, others board for further destinations, cargo is unloaded, new cargo is taken aboard, and she is re-supplied and refuelled.

Bobby is looking for his father, and he remembers that Arthur Hobbs has migrated to Sydney. Except for that brief taxi ride in 1954, he hasn't seen Hobbs for sixteen years, not since he was a very little four-year-old boy. Yet, after all those years, he can still recall those invigorating times with that gentle, redheaded magic man.

Bobby shares a cabin with his watch-mate, Brian, a twenty-five year old, strong, good-looking, slightly balding fellow, who has the reputation of being a bit of a ladies' man. Brian has served on the *Himalaya* for about two years. Bobby and he have become firm friends. Brian knows the ropes, and when in port, shows Bobby the best places to go for any kind of entertainment. When he wants to meet girls, Brian doesn't do the usual bar scene. He telephones the nurses' residences, attached to the local hospitals, and invites the girls to visit the ship. There is always someone who is interested, and tonight is no exception.

Bobby is standing the eight to midnight gangway watch, he is due to be relieved in about half an hour. Brian has made the phone call, he has already changed into his civvies, and is expecting the two student nurses to arrive at any moment; he has arranged for the passes and is keeping Bobby company, until they arrive. The plan is that Brian will show the girls around the ship and end up at the cabin, and by that time, Bobby will be off duty and will join them. The boys will then ply their guests with copious amounts of alcohol and then they all will go ashore for a night out on the town. After that, nature will take its course. At least, that is the plan.

Fifteen minutes later, they hear the syncopated, tap dance of heels clicking on concrete, they watch in delicious anticipation as the girls draw nearer. Like phantoms in high heels, they are floating through the ghostly pools of light that are projected onto the dock from the floodlights above. As they approach the gangway, they are walking arm in arm and giggling loudly in nervous anticipation. Bobby and Brian are smiling expectantly as they silently appraise their guests.

As the girls step onto the gangway, the boys are afforded a closer look at them; they both appear to be in their early twenties. Bobby is immediately attracted to the one in the lead, who seems to be the bolder of the two. She lifts her arm and waves at them, her hand moving quickly from side to side in a blurred cinematic motion. She is wearing an off the shoulder, emerald green, cotton dress, with a silver chain and locket around her neck. She is about five-foot-six, with a trim, lithe figure, moving with the sensual grace of a cat. With each step she takes, her jet-black hair rises and falls in natural waves against the shores of her tanned shoulders. Her eyes are a deep burning brown; her generous lips are parted in a playful smile. Her following friend is a tall, full-figured, blue-eyed, suntanned, blonde goddess, wearing a low-cut, royal blue, figure-hugging, satin dress, accessorised by a chunky pearl necklace. She is giggling nervously, and having trouble negotiating the gangway in her high heels.

Brian graciously steps forward to offer her a helping hand. "Hello, you must be Yvonne and Hope. My name is Brian and my friend in uniform is Bobby." By this time, they are all standing at the head of the gangway; in 'D' deck Foyer.

"Hello and welcome aboard" greets Bobby, rather formally.

"G'day, Bobby, I am Hope, and this is my mate, Yvonne," says the confident one, who is the first to reach him. She is wearing an exotically arousing perfume, which immediately sweeps him away.

Collecting his senses and proffering his right hand, he says, "Pleased to meet you, Hope. Hello, Yvonne, Brian will show you around the ship, and I'll join you when I get off watch in a few minutes."

Looking down into his iridescent blue eyes, Hope smiles teasingly, "I'll be looking forward to it, Bobby."

Whilst still maintaining his hold on her hand, his wide-open eyes are in direct line with the silver locket she is wearing around her neck, he is somewhat taken aback, as he notices that it is engraved with a webbed hand. With a bemused smile, she pointedly looks down at their coupled hands. He releases his grip, feeling her reluctance to let go. Looking down at their interlocking fingers, the green flecks in her eyes are sparkling, and her smile widens as she continues to hold his hand. Quickly following the direction of her gaze, his stomach rolls over as he notices her webbed fingers.

By this time, Brian and Yvonne are becoming acquainted. "Let's go, girls, it's show time," yells Brian as he protectively shepherds the captivating Yvonne through the foyer.

Hope and Bobby reluctantly release their grip, their webbed fingers unhurriedly stroking apart. She looks once more into his now gleaming eyes and gently whispers "Hooroo, Bobby."

Whilst her gaze still lingers, she reaches down and takes off her shoes, and turning away, she pads, with feline grace, after Yvonne and Brian, who are about to enter the lift. "Hey hang on you two, wait for me," Hope yells. Before disappearing into the lift, she hesitates in her stride, and with a playful smile, glances over her shoulder. He becomes conscious of his heart racing, his cheeks are flushed, his breathing is deeper, and he becomes aware of the voice.

"It's all right, Bobby, it's all right. This is meant to be."

After Bobby has completed his watch, he returns to the cabin and changes into his civvies. He has brought a tray of ice cubes from the Quartermasters' mess, the gin and tonic is here, and so is the beer. As he is quickly checking, to see that all is shipshape, he hears them approaching. He is excited and nervous about the night ahead, particularly about Hope, whom he is definitely attracted to, but he is a little disturbed by her webbed fingers.

After the preliminary surface chatter of the Hows, Wheres, Whens, Whos, Whats and Whys, and after having knocked back their first two drinks, maybe a little too quickly, they are now relaxing and chatting amiably. The conversation is swirling rapidly and enthusiastically around the tiny cabin.

Brian, the always suave host, and the voluptuous Yvonne, are sitting in the two chairs. Bobby and Hope are sitting on the bottom bunk. Little Bobby has plenty of headroom and he is able to drink his beer sitting up straight. However, Hope, in order to take a sip of her gin and tonic and to avoid knocking her head on the upper bunk, has to bend her neck a little and lean forward. To accomplish this, each time she takes a sip, she steadies herself with her left hand on the bunk, Bobby is aware of an almost tactile energy emanating from her.

Before long, they have found a common denominator, and the conversation is swimming effortlessly around the small cabin. Bobby has drifted closer to Hope, she leans forward once more to take another sip, and her left hand reaches out again to steady herself. It rests on, and grasps Bobby's thigh, and a convulsive force shoots through his body.

They look at each other, each recognising their mutual magnetism, and Hope says demurely, "I feel like I'm goin' to chunder, I think I need some fresh air."

Bobby immediately puts his beer down, and taking her hand offers, "Here, hold on to me, I'll take you out on deck for a while, the fresh air will make you feel a little better."

"Ta very much," says Hope timidly.

Bobby opens the cabin door and guides Hope through, saying to Brian and Yvonne, "We won't be too long, see you later."

"No hanky panky now," laughs Brian, and Yvonne giggles.

Holding her hand, Bobby guides Hope up the companionway to the foredeck. There, on that, warm summer's night, amongst the clutter of winches, vents, anchor chains and mooring ropes, they lean over the ship's rail and look out at the twinkling lights of Sydney harbour.

It is Bobby who first breaks the silence. "Feeling a little better now, Hope?" She doesn't answer. He touches her arm again and repeats, "Are you feeling a little better now, Hope?"

"Beg yours?" she replies. "I'm sorry, I can't hear too well out of that ear." She then moves around to Bobby's right.

"Oh, I'm sorry," said Bobby, raising his voice. "I said; are you feeling a little better now?"

"There's no need to shout Bobby, I can hear fine out of my left ear. Yeah, I'm feeling a lot better thanks. You see, I wasn't really feeling sick from the gin or the stuffy cabin, I just wanted to talk to you, alone."

"Me too," says Bobby earnestly, feeling a strange and different warmth creeping through his body. Taking her left hand in his, he squeezes gently, saying, "Apart from my father, I've never met anyone else who has webbed fingers."

Returning the pressure she turns to face him and Bobby reaches out and takes Hope's other hand in his. They both stand on the cluttered foredeck, in the faintly illuminated darkness, holding hands, their webbed fingers uniting them in a common bond.

The blast from a distant tug coaxes them out of their trance. "Bobby, you just said that your dad had webbed fingers."

"Yes he did, Hope, did yours?"

"My mum said he did."

"Oh! Have you never seen your father?"

She withdraws her hands, as though reluctant to continue. Between her fingers, she rubs the engraving of the webbed hand on her silver locket, she turns, and for a long moment looks out into the night, before answering, "Yes I have seen him, but I don't remember very clearly what he was like. He left us a long time ago. I do remember that I liked him very much; Mum said he was a legend. When I was very small, she used to bring me down to the ship to see him. I have a very hazy recollection of this big, grinning, giant of a man, with magical eyes and a mop of unruly red hair. But then, everyone looks like a clown, when you are only two."

A shiver of recognition runs through Bobby. "What is your family name?" he asks quickly.

"Atherton." Hope replies, "And yours?"

"Shafto." Bobby answers.

"Shafto?" exclaims Hope with a wide smile as she starts singing.

"Bobby Shafto went to sea,
Silver buckles on his knee,
He'll come back and marry me,
Bonnie Bobby Shafto."

"Yeah, yeah, I think I've heard that one before. But coming from you, Hope, it seems to hold more promise."

Hope laughs, "Well, who knows? Maybe you will come back and marry me one day, Bobby Shafto."

Bobby leans on the rail and looks up dreamily into the night sky, and Bunny breaks the tranquil silence.

"Have you been out with many sailors?"

Hope steps back sharply, almost tripping over a mooring rope. "Crikey! What the fuck was that? I told you, there's no need to shout, mate."

Bobby reaches for her. "I'm sorry, Hope, he wells up now and again, I'll try and keep him submerged."

Hope withdraws from him and clasps the top-rail for support. "He wells up? You will try and keep him submerged? Who the fuck are you talking about?"

"That was Bunny, my twin brother, who I think I strangled in the womb, he's always with me, and we are indivisible. He was sacrificed in the womb, so that I may live, we now walk together, we are one, he is my other self He is a little possessive, I'm sorry, but he emerges at the most inappropriate moments."

Keeping hold of the rail for stability, Hope stares incredulously at Bobby and laughs. "You are one fucked-up Pom, Bobby Shafto." Nevertheless, she is fascinated with the concept of Bobby having an alter ego, another self, who expresses himself so blatantly. "And what is upsetting him now?"

"He doesn't want to see me hurt, that is why he asked the question."

"What question?"

"Have you been out with many sailors?"

She shouts back, "All right, all right, I heard you the first time." Then she looks away and continues quietly, "If you really want to know, yes, I have been with a few."

"I'm sorry, Hope; it really is none of my business."

"No it isn't, Bobby, but I don't mind him asking." That teasing smile is playing around her lips again. "I think you are a little jealous."

"Me jealous? Of course not. Well, maybe I am, just a little."

"That's OK, I like that." She rests her forearms on his shoulders, clasping her hands together around the back of his neck. "Is it all right if I ask you a personal question?'

"By all means."

"You're sure your twin brother, Bunny won't mind?"

"No, it's fine, he doesn't emerge when I have conscious control. What do you want to know, Hope?"

"Tell me about your dad."

"You know, it's funny; well, not funny ha-ha, but funny peculiar, my father used to be a sailor too, his name was Arthur. I knew him for the first four years of my life, but I didn't know he was my father until I was seventeen, just three short years ago, and then I only saw him for a brief taxi ride. Now he is gone again, he told me he was immigrating to Australia, in fact he said he was going to live in Sydney, I was hoping he might still be here. And what about your father, Hope? Why did he leave you?"

Hope unclasps her hands, but keeps her arms on his diminutive shoulders. "Well, it was Mum who left my father, without telling him she was pregnant, and married Ted, who is now my step father. I don't know where my real dad is now. All I know is, he was a sailor and his name was Archie, and he buggered off when I was two. I never asked Mum what his surname was. I think that I would really like to meet him again."

Bobby steps back a pace, his unblinking eyes opening wider as he stares at Hope in amazement. In a stage whisper, he asks, "Hope, do you think they are one and the same?"

"Who?"

"Archie, Arthur, your father, my father, our father."

"You mean we could have the same father?"

"Yes, Hope, that is exactly what I mean."

"You mean, because we both have webbed fingers and our fathers had webbed fingers?"

"Not only the webbed fingers, but also your description of him, and he was a sailor who came on a ship from England. You said your father left when you were two, what year was that?"

"I was born in 1934, so it was in 1936."

"That's amazing, because that's the exact same year that Arthur Hobbs started working for my family. It was the year before I was born."

"But my father's name was Archie."

"Don't you see? It's too much of a coincidence. Syndactily is hereditary, he had webbed fingers, we have webbed fingers, and also, the year 1936 fits perfectly, and he could easily have changed his first name."

"If he is the same person, why didn't he ever tell you about me?"

"I don't know Hope, all I know is that he didn't tell me and neither did my mother, I have no idea why they didn't."

"That is amazing. I have his picture in this locket, which he gave to mum the last time he saw us, in1936. I don't recognise him, but mum says it is Archie."

Bobby whispers excitedly, "Let me see. Let me see."

Hope opens the locket; Bobby is faced with a black-and-white photo of a middle-aged man, in a sailor's uniform. He immediately recognises the younger Hobbs, with his generous smiling mouth, his glinting eyes, one of which was darker than the other, and his mop of unruly hair. It is an image that is indelibly etched on Bobby's mind.

"It's him. That is a picture of my father, Arthur Hobbs. That is how he looked when I was very young."

"But Mum said it was Archie."

"That is what I am getting at; he *must* have changed his name."

"Then if he is your father, and he is my father, and we both have different mothers that would mean you are my half-brother and I am your half-sister."

Now he understands what his dying mother was trying to tell him. *'Sister … Hope'.* "My God, Hope, I don't know whether to be happy or sad."

"Be happy, why be sad?"

"Because we are related, and I am attracted to you in another way."

Reaching for his hands, she says, "Don't let the fact that we are related stand in the way of what we want. I am attracted to you too, Bobby. I know this sounds peculiar, but, now I know that we are related, I feel closer to you already."

"I feel that way too, Hope. I want to get to know you, I want to be with you. But what do we do about it now?"

"Do? What do we do about it now? We do absolutely nothing. On paper, we are unrelated. We come from two unrelated families, living in two different countries. You are Bobby Shafto from England and I am Hope Atherton from Australia. If we want to continue seeing each other, which I know I do, just remember that nobody knows we are related, and nobody must know, not even my mum or Ted. Do you agree? Please say yes, Bobby."

'Of course I agree, Hope. Yes, yes, yes and yes."

She let go of his hands, and slowly reaching upward into the night, extends her lithe and sensuous body in a luxurious and lazy, catlike stretch. "Bobby, we both seem to be in the same boat; we are attracted to each other, we have the same father, we don't really know him, or know where he is, or even if he is, but wouldn't it be wonderful if we did find him?"

The question requires no answer.

Moving closer to him, she rests her arms on his shoulders, and looking down into his shining eyes, she says softly, "Do you want to join Yvonne and Brian now?"

He is again under the spell of her erotic perfume. As she slowly and rhythmically breathes, he can feel her stomach moving against his chest. The proximity of Hope is overpowering, he wants this sensation to last forever. "I'll tell you what I really would like to do," he answers fervently.

Taking a step back, she laughs, "Whoa, boy, take it easy."

He regains his composure. "You're funny, Hope. What I really meant was, let's go ashore for a long walk, where we can be alone and talk to our hearts content."

"I'd like that, Bobby; I'd like to go for a walk-about. Have you ever been to Bondi Beach?"

"No I haven't, in fact I haven't even stepped ashore in Sydney yet, but I'm game. That sounds great to me."

Taking him by the hand, she suggests, "Let's go down to the cabin and tell Yvonne and Brian that we are leaving."

Before going ashore, Hope advises Bobby to change into his jeans, T-shirt, and flip-flops. She plans to stop by her aunt's place in Woollahra, to also change into more casual attire. They say goodbye to the irrepressible Brian and Yvonne who are hitting it off famously, and are planning to go to the Palladium nightclub in Kings Cross.

As they drift down the gangway, she turns to him and asks, "Are you sure you want to do this, little brother?"

He answers without hesitation, "Yes, big sister, I am very sure."

Chapter Thirty-Five

IN THE IMPRINT OF THEIR FATHER

Arthur had settled in to a relatively contented routine in Sydney. On his time off from his job as a janitor at the Kings Cross Hotel, he liked to walk along Bondi Beach in the dead of night. Memories of that magic, moonlit night, when Janice and he first lay together over twenty years ago, would flood back to haunt him. He would think of the times when his ship was in, when he, Janice and little Hope would go to Bondi to walk and play.

Some days he would get into his trusty 1953 Holden FJ, and drive around Sydney and its suburbs. Many times, without conscious thought, he would find himself on the Bondi Road, driving through Waverley, where he knew the Athertons lived, hoping to catch sight of Janice or Hope. It had been easy to find their address from the Greater Sydney City Directory, but, he didn't want to stir the pot again, so, he kept his promise to Ted, not to make contact with them, and would always drive right on by. Except for one day, when he did phone, but Ted answered, and Arthur thought it wiser to say nothing, but still, that little ache persisted.

*

It is one of those warm and humid December nights, in the summer of 1957, the soggy heat bringing everybody outside to sit on their porches to cool off. On Bondi Road, by two in the morning, most people have retired to their beds. As Arthur drives by the Atherton's' house, he sees the lone figure of a woman sitting on the porch, in a wooden rocking chair, she is faintly lit by the dim porch-light above her. He slows down and watches her leisurely rocking back and forth, back and forth. It takes all his resolve not to stop, but he keeps on going until he can no longer see her in the rear-view mirror. Then he stops the car, turns off the engine, and rests, until the tight squeezing chest pains have subsided, and the ache in his back and shoulders has faded. Then, he turns the ignition key, and resumes his journey into the humid night, through the treeless landscape, to the edge of the continent, to walk yet again, alone, through the shifting sands of time, on the lip of the Tasman Sea.

*

Janice can't sleep; she is sitting on the porch, rocking with her memories, hoping for some relief from the oppressive humidity. In the dark of the night, she notices the Holden FJ, cruising slowly by the house. She thinks someone is probably looking for a street address. It is a little late to be paying a visit, but then again, it could be some young buck in lust and love. About a hundred yards down the street, she sees the car come to a halt and douse its lights. Then, about ten minutes later, it comes to life again and she watches its luminous red taillights disappearing into the velvet, black night. Her thoughts return to Archie and the life that might have been.

*

They take the Bondi Road to the beach, and as they approach her mother's house, Hope asks the taxi driver to slow down; she wants to show Bobby where she has lived. Letting go of his hand, she points. "Look, Bobby, see that house with the porch light on, that's where my mum and Ted live."

As the taxi creeps by, he peers out of the window. "Who is that sitting on the porch?"

'That's, Mum."

"Don't you want to stop?"

"No. I don't think so; I'd rather be with you tonight."

He repossesses her hand and is well pleased.

When they arrive at the Bondi Pavilion, there is only one car parked by the building. The full moon is at its perigee, flooding the sandy beach with its ghostly light. It is as though the universe is turning inside out, and they are walking on the face of the moon. As they slip off their flip-flops and walk past the pavilion onto the silky sand, they notice, in the half shadow, an old man standing on the Jerusalem steps. He is tall and stooped, with his head bowed into his body; in the vaporous half-light, he looks headless. He wears sandals on his feet, and a bright, white, long-sleeved shirt, which comes down to his knees, giving the impression that it is his only garment. Preferring their own company to this wraithlike apparition, they venture out onto the deserted, moonlit beach.

Bathed in the moon's monochromatic light, the old man watches the young lovebirds glide away. She is a little over a head taller than he, and has her left arm draped over his shoulders, his right arm lovingly encircles her waist. They both wear jeans and T-shirts. Their bodies move with the supple rhythm and grace of the immortal young. A slight sliver of recognition pierces him.

Bobby is carrying a bag that holds a blanket, towels, and their flip-flops. He puts the bag down by the water's edge and stands facing Hope. They gently embrace and hold each other for a long, long time, feeling each other's hearts beating as their breathing gradually finds a mutual rhythm. Reflecting the full moon, his bright eyes look up into the dark eyes of Hope. She tilts her head and hungrily tastes his generous lips. He feels her warm sweet breath on his face and his toes curl in the sand. Peeling his T-shirt from his small but well-toned body, she purrs in his ear, "Bobby, do you want to go swimming?"

"I would love to," he murmurs, as he reciprocally turns Hope's T-shirt inside out, exposing her small, firm breasts.

They hurriedly unbuckle their belts, and slip out of their jeans and underwear, revealing their faultless young bodies, washed by the moonlight; they stand silently facing each other in naked wonder. She removes the locket from around her neck and drops it on top of the pile of hastily discarded clothes. He is becoming aroused by the sensual beauty of Hope.

"That'll have to wait until later, mate," she laughs, as she takes his hand. Running into the sea, high stepping through the shallows of the receding tide, and shrieking with delight, they plunge into the invigorating surf. With sure, strong strokes, they swim out beyond the breakers, into the calm of the welcoming sea. Turning on their backs and holding each other's hands, they stare into the face of the full moon. Except for the shallow surf, stroking the shore, the world stands still. His feet find the firm sand beneath the water, and she invitingly entwines her legs around him as her arms lovingly encircle his neck. Their bodies meld into a salty embrace, and their eager lips explore and caress every line and contour of each other's firm and vibrating body. He has never before experienced such supernatural emotions.

Under the wide expanse of the southern skies, bathed in the bright light of the watchful moon, caressed by the warm waters of the ocean, and enveloped by Hope, he surrenders. From deep inside him arises that passionate voice.

"I want to be within you, Hope. We are joining you. Two into one will go."

The words soar into space and skitter across the surface of the placid sea, and the lovers join. Hope marvels at this overwhelming voice, she readily accepts him and is unafraid. Clinging tightly to Bobby, she feels him enter her and she welcomes him.

From his position on the Jerusalem steps, the old man has been watching the young lovers as they eagerly shed their clothes and run into the sparkling sea. He hears that outlandish voice. The tightness in his chest returns, and feeling as though he is carrying the whole world on his stooped and aching shoulders, he breaks out in a cold sweat. With the veins in his legs throbbing, he painfully makes his way across the beach, to where they have left their clothes.

Their bodies are as one with each other, entwined and interlocked together; they are thrashing in ecstasy. Illuminated by the sparkling phosphorescence, they resemble one glorious, glistening, two-headed, mythical sea-creature. Riding their orgasmic waves, they come together, and with one voice in perfect harmony, they sing.

"A-h-h-h-h-h! O-h-h-h-h! A-h-h-h-h-h! O-h-h-h-h! A-h-h-h-h-h! Y-eh-eh-h-h-h-ssss"

As the climactic waves sweep through them and gradually subside, their bodies palpitate and slowly shudder to tranquil contentment; for a silent eternity they float in their love.

The old man hears the primitive and familiar voices, and looking out at the flotsam of love, he is well pleased. He bows his head in contentment and sees lying on top of the hastily discarded pile of clothes, a silver locket, from which, he is temporally blinded by the reflection of the moonlight. He slowly bends down to pick it up, and gazes upon the engraved image of the webbed hand and presses it to his lips. Opening the locket, he sees, by the light of the moon, the dim reflection of his bygone self, confidently staring back at him.

A wave of nausea sweeps over him. With a vice-like grip, the agonizing chest pains return with a vengeance. His head is swimming with dizziness, his back is pierced with an intolerably sharp pain, his neck and jaw become rigid, his right arm is becoming numb, his legs fail him, and he falls hard upon the soft and forgiving sand. Knowing that his time on earth is exhausted, his mighty heart cracks, and he surrenders his soul.

As he lies there, rigid and still, with the open locket's silver chain loosely wound around his webbed fingers, and with those magic eyes blindly staring into the face of the full moon, his spirit is released from his corporeal form. It skitters across the silky sand, and skims across the shimmering surface of the silent sea, to gently embrace the moonlit, satiated and glistening, supine bodies of the young lovers, before winging swiftly and freely out into the vast and omniscient universe.

For a lingering moment, they feel a cool breeze caressing them, causing a simultaneous shiver to shudder through their bodies, bringing goose bumps to the surface of their skin. They cling tightly to each other for warmth and love. Gently disengaging, hand in hand they wade back to the beach to where they have left their clothes.

There, they are faced with the lifeless body of the old man, lying inert on the grey sand, his milky, vacant eyes reflecting the emptiness of the full moon. His white shirt is glowing, and the fingers of his outstretched left hand are entwined with the chain of the open locket. They are both reluctant to approach him in their nakedness. Turning their backs on the ethereal spectre, they hastily dress; coy in the vacant stare of the blind eye of death.

At first sight, noticing the open silver locket in his hand, she takes him for a thief, but as she bends down to retrieve her locket, she notices his webbed fingers. With a startled little cry, she drops to her knees. Bobby is by her side instantly, and as they look into the old man's face, they see his fading, gem-like, odd-coloured eyes. Under the ghostly pale of the moon, they stare into the grey and gentle face of their father.

"Archie," Hope whispers.

"Arthur," Bobby gasps.

"Hobbs," Bunny yells. Remembering their father's last words to them, as his taxi drove away, **"Maybe we will meet again, under a more propitious moon."**

Hope immediately feels Hobbs's neck for signs of a pulse, but there are none. Dry-eyed, she draws her hand over his unseeing eyes, eclipsing the reflected moon. Bobby gently releases the chain from the webbed fingers of his father's outstretched hand, and closing the locket, he places it around the neck of Hope.

As the first grey light of dawn diminishes the brightness of the moon, Hope walks back to the pavilion to phone her mother, to tell her the tragic news and ask her to call an ambulance.

*

The rosy hue of 'morn creeps over the southern sea, transforming the cold monochromatic grey of the sand into a warm and vibrant tint of orange, but, not even the sun, that gigantic burning star, the genesis of all earthly life, can imbue the gentle giant's ashen face with living colour.

When Janice and Ted arrive, Hope and Bobby are kneeling in silent contemplation beside the body of their beloved father. Hope looking up to her mother asks, "Mum, is this Archie? Is this my father?"

Janice and Ted exhale sharply as they see the lifeless form of the man that has so influenced their lives. Janice, recognising the old man at the docks as her departed lover, drops to her knees, and throws herself over his body weeping uncontrollably. Bobby puts a comforting arm around her shoulders and she, seeing the webbed fingers of that consoling hand, emits a little startled cry, and lovingly kisses them.

Hope and Bobby sense that Ted instinctually knows, from the intimate way they are touching, and looking, and whispering to each other, that they have made love. Ted stares accusingly at his wayward ward; that cold, hard stare.

Violent memories of humiliation and degradation are stirring up within her. Bunny is now within Hope, and from out of her depths, pours forth that dreadful voice.

"You are forever doomed to be without Hope. Do not ever look to harm her again, for you will do harm to me, for we now exist within Hope; we are a trinity, we are indivisible, we are one."

Ted is standing in stunned disbelief, rooted in the slow sand.

Janice cradles her departed lover's head in her lap, sobbing quietly.

Mingled with the wailing of the approaching ambulance sirens, the voice of an angel is heard; Hope is sweetly singing a requiem for her father.

 "I'll be seeing you;
In all the old familiar places;
That this heart of mine embraces;
All day through."

Ted stands alone disconsolately. Janice is washing Archie's ashen face with her tears of grief and remembering.

 "In that small café;
The park across the way;
The children's carousel;
The chestnut tree;
The wishing well."

Through the emptiness of that lovely summer's morn, they hear the mournful wail of the sirens warble into silence.

 "I'll be seeing you;
In every lovely, summer's day;
And everything that's bright and gay;
I'll always think of you that way;"

At the age of seventy-three, Arthur, Archie Hobbs lies still. They bear away the lifeless body of the gentle giant, and leave his imprint in the golden sand.

  "I'll find you in the morning sun;
And when the night is new;
I'll be looking at the moon;
But I'll be seeing you."

The song of Hope transmutes into the sharp sucking sound of silence.

Grief stricken, Janice follows the remains of her true love, her chastised husband is trailing dejectedly behind.

On the deserted beach, in the golden glow of the rising sun, Bobby and Hope lie with each other, in the imprint of their father.

*

The autopsy reveals that the cause of death is a massive heart attack. The obligatory arrangements are made and the mortal remains of Arthur, Archie Hobbs are cremated at the Rockwood Crematorium.

*

As the red-eyed sun squints over the horizon of the Tasman Sea, Janice, Hope and Bobby, return to Bondi Beach to scatter Hobbs's ashes, Ted preferring to remain absent. In his mortal life, Arthur had heeded Ted's warning not to contact his family, but in death, they embrace him. Ted will forever be haunted by the lover of his wife and the father of his child.

Silently they carry the urn to the spot where he had lain; the out-going tide has already reclaimed his imprint. Janice scatters some of Archie's ashes on that sacred ground, knowing that the sea will again repossess him. Hope and Bobby carry the urn into the ocean, and where they had consummated their love, and felt the presence of their father's departing spirit; they scatter his remaining ashes on the water's surface and float in his essence.

Bunny whispers,

"Our father, who art in heaven, hallowed be thy name."

Chapter Thirty-Six

THE GARDEN OF EMPTINESS

The sun-washed streets of Kobe, Japan, are a stunning display of pink and white cherry blossoms. All around him, Bobby sees people sublimely strolling, nodding, and smiling to each other in tranquil contentment, but his heart is not at peace. Although he feels exhilarated by his love for Hope, he despairs at the loss of their father. Fixed between the magnetic poles of joy and sorrow, his compass is unbalanced; he is confused and losing his direction; he needs to be alone.

He arrives in the ancient, capitol city of Kyoto in the late afternoon and heads straight for the Ryoan-ji Temple. Within the temple gardens, overlooking the Garden of Emptiness, there is an elderly Japanese man and woman, quietly resting on their haunches, on the floor of the veranda. Bobby sits apart from them, in a cross-legged position, and quietly observes the garden.

The Garden of Emptiness is only about ninety feet long and thirty feet across. Fifteen rocks of various sizes are arranged on small white pebbles in five groups. They are arranged in such a manner, that no matter what angle the garden is viewed from, he can only see fourteen of them at any one time. It is said that only on attaining spiritual enlightenment, as a result of a revelation, can you see the last invisible fifteenth stone.

The longer he sits, the more he becomes imbued with the spirit of the garden. He gazes at the branches of the cherry trees, bursting with bright pink blossoms, beyond the earthen wall with its peculiar but natural designs. In the light of the golden hour, they cast fantastically long shadows over the white pebbles and the moss that fills the pocks and spaces in the rocks. The straight-raked lines of the pebbles flow into many circles around the rocks, and where they touch the circular patterns, they stop without a single misplaced stone, and then resume, unchanged, beyond them. Although the rocks don't move, Bobby sees something enigmatic about the spaces between them. He is reminded of a tranquil sea, swirling gently around remote and uninhabited rocky islands; he lets it all wash over him and feels sublimely peaceful. He gradually becomes aware of the tension draining from him, until ultimately, his body disappears, and his mind relaxes into a state of nothingness.

There is no blinding flash or sudden epiphany; but rather a dawning awareness of the emergence of a guiding entity in his life. He is beginning to understand that the broad path of his life is predetermined, however, he does control the way he walks on that path. He observes the Japanese characters carved into the stone water basin, which translate into, *"The knowledge that is given is enough."* Perhaps, he is destined never to see that elusive fifteenth stone.

The tranquillity of his meditation is rudely shattered by the loud, harsh, and grating voices of two strutting Caucasian tourists as they aggressively tromp onto the wooden veranda.

"Geez!" exclaims the cigar-chomping man, "They call this a garden? It looks more like a quarry. It's nothing but gravel and rocks."

"Yeah, Hon," guffaws the woman, "where are all the flowers? I guess they haven't started planting yet. Should I take a picture anyway?"

"Save your film, Babe, there's nothing to see here but emptiness. Let's get out of here and grab something to eat."

As they stomp their way out, the male of the species arrogantly throws his lighted cigar-butt into the Garden of Emptiness. Bobby kneels, and leaning over from the veranda, without disturbing a single pebble, he carefully retrieves the offending, imperialistic symbol, and pinching it out between his thumb and forefinger, puts it into his shirt pocket. The Japanese man and woman, further down the veranda, who have also been obscenely shaken out of their meditation, notice Bobby's act of reverence, they smile and bow to him in appreciation, acknowledgement and acceptance.

On the way out of the temple, Bobby notices that the Buddha also has webbed fingers.

*

The *Himalaya* has just tied up in Yokohama, when a typhoon warning is issued. All ships are ordered to leave the harbour and head out to sea to ride out the storm. It will only be in open waters where they stand the best chance of survival, for to stay in port runs the risk of being smashed up against the wharves by the ferocious winds and torrential rains. Bobby has experienced storms at sea before and feels confident that he will survive another.

Eight hours after leaving port, the *Himalaya* is in rough seas, on the leading edge of the typhoon. The next day, the storm rapidly intensifies and soon reaches winds of 140 mph. The beleaguered ship is bouncing precariously through the pounding seas and high winds, which blow with such force that they rip the gangway from the starboard side of the ship as effortlessly as brushing a matchstick from a table-cloth. Two lifeboats are ripped from their davits and hurled into the voracious, dark maw of the turbulent ocean. On the second day, the storm intensifies to 165 mph winds. The ferocity of the sea is peeling large patches of white paint from the hull, exposing the subcutaneous surface of the ship's shining, steel plates, and the foredeck rails are twisting as effortlessly as sticks of liquorice.

Bobby is at the helm, trying to keep his body from being thrown violently around the wheelhouse. He is wearing a lifejacket that gives him no protection from the jousting and jolting they are experiencing, and certainly would have been totally ineffectual, if he was thrown into the gigantic 90-foot waves of the not so Pacific Ocean. At one point, he thinks they are going down as the bow of the ship is thrust high above the water, and then slams violently down, hitting the hard seas with a crashing jolt. "This is it," he thinks, as the helpless vessel suddenly rolls more than 45 degrees to port, threatening to dip its funnel into the raging waters. On the dance deck, the grand piano breaks its moorings and goes careening and twanging across the deck, in a *dance macabre*. Gathering momentum, it smashes discordantly through the fragile windowed, wooden partition, to break its legs on the ships railings, and is hurtled tunelessly into the raging seas. Below, in the galleys and dining rooms, pots, plates, glasses and cutlery are thrown around like hard peas in a tin can, striking up a strident crashing, smashing symphony of inharmonious noise that would have made Wagner proud. At the last instant, the ship is miraculously saved by another huge wave that lifts her out of the jaws of obliteration, and sets her on an even keel again. They endure hours and hours of relentless, soul-destroying helplessness and despairing fear. Neptune is out of tune.

On his twenty-first birthday, for two brief hours, he finds himself in the eye of the typhoon. The ship enters an area of about half a mile in diameter, a space of beguiling and extraordinary calm. A steely grey light falls on the debris that litters the water's surface. On the port side, at a distance of about one hundred yards, Bobby sees a wounded cargo ship, seeking respite from the storm; its bow has been smashed in by the pounding waves. Walking out to the wing of the bridge, and examining the distressed vessel through his binoculars, he is taken aback as bathed in a ghostly, steel-grey glow, he recognises his first ship, the *Egyptian*. She signals that she is still seaworthy and will ride out the storm.

Looking up through the massive funnel of tumultuous wind and water, Bobby is confronted with the swirling, satanic blackness of the monstrous storm, and his heart freezes. He is struck with the clear and uncompromising realisation that he is only a tiny, inconsequential mote in the eye of the storm. For the first time since leaving the convent, Bobby prays for deliverance… there are no atheists in a Typhoon.

As he is staring upwards in fearful awe, he sees, shining down on him, the shimmering angel that was reflected off the bottom of his pool, when he was four years of age.

 "What do you see, Bobby?"

Not being sure, whether he is alive or dead, he cries, "I see cosmic darkness, penetrated by a halo of turbulent, liquid light that is surrounding a shimmering angel."

 "Do you know what it is that you see?"

"It is the angel on the bottom of the pool, just before Edward tried to drown me. I'm scared, Bunny, what does it all mean?"

"**Don't be frightened, Bobby. What you see is your Guardian Angel.**"

"My Guardian Angel? How can this be?"

"**Do you remember your near-death experience in that pool? Do you remember being reborn?**"

"Yes, I do, and it was Hobbs who saved me. Please help me Bunny, I am lost."

"**You were born with your own individual soul and your own defining image or character. Your soul has selected the path of your life, and the angel is your guide. It protects and channels your character, which nobody can alter, not your parents, your teachers, your friends, or even your enemies**"

Bobby is apprehensive and still perplexed. "I don't understand. Am I actually looking at my own Guardian Angel?"

"**Yes Bobby, you see your very own Guardian Angel, it is the carrier of your destiny.**"

"Is Hobbs my Guardian Angel?"

"**The knowledge that is given is enough.**"

The vision dissolves into the dark, whirling mass of wind and water. Before long, they are steaming out of the centre of the typhoon, and the beguiling calmness is shattered; the seas are roiling again and the wind returns to its adamant ferocity. The wounded ship is pitching, rolling, shuddering, splintering, and shattering as it fights to survive. The typhoon relentlessly maintains it's intensity for the next eighteen hours, before weakening and drifting north-west to Japan as it gradually dissipates.

Two days before reaching Honolulu, the Himalaya emerges from the trailing edge of the storm, the winds gradually die down, and the sea returns to its welcome pacific nature. Bobby is thankful to be alive, and he knows he is sublimely blessed.

Chapter Thirty-Seven

You will live in Hope

Three and a half months after leaving Sydney, the battered *Himalaya* returns. Hope is on the wharf to greet Bobby; needless to say, he is overjoyed. He is not scheduled to be on gangway duty for another eight hours, so he rushes down to the dock to greet her. It is like one of those slow-motion scenes in a Hollywood film, where the two lovers are edging their way towards each other, struggling against the heaving crowd of a major South American revolution. They are being tossed forward, and then back, and then forward again, until a sudden surge propels them into each other's outstretched arms, where they cling desperately to each other, in fear of being ripped apart again by the turbulent sea of bodies swirling around them.

Bobby and Hope stand holding each other, until the pressure of the multitude has subsided; then, arm in arm, they walk away from the agitation of the great white vessel, towards the tranquil green of Hyde Park.

That perfect April morning, Bobby Shafto and Hope Atherton, their feet hardly touching the ground, feel that they are the only souls walking on the face of this blessed earth. Through the early morning traffic, they glide in silence, blissfully unaware of their surroundings. Their fathomless love for each other is radiating from the pit of their stomachs, and out to the very tips of their tingling extremities; their touch becomes electric.

They come to rest on a bench under the shade of a massive fig tree, which is part of the impressive Avenue of Fig Trees that slices through the park. Hope is glowing with contentment; the green flecks in her deep brown eyes are luminous. For a seeming eternity, they remain on that bench, swimming through the depths of their love, until eventually, Hope surfaces.

"Welcome home, Bobby."

"If only this was my home, Hope."

"It can be, if you really want it to be."

Bobby is a little taken aback by the suddenness of the suggestion. "Hope, as you know, I am very much in love with you, and I desperately want to be with you, but don't you think that we need a little more time together, before making a decision of this magnitude?"

She gently withdraws her arm from around his shoulders and turns to look down into his iridescent blue eyes, leaning forward she whispers lovingly in his ear. "There is not much time left, Bobby."

He sits bolt upright, in alarm. "What's the matter, Hope? Are you all right? Are you sick? What's wrong?"

"Nothing's wrong, I'm fine my love, I've never felt better. You see, Bobby, we are going to have a baby."

Bobby is a little stunned by this unexpected news. This is his first trip on the *Himalaya*, and before he swallows the anchor, he was expecting to do many more. Then, he remembers the Garden of Emptiness and that his life, to a large extent, is predestined. He remembers the heart-numbing terror of the typhoon, and Bunny's revelations of soul and destiny, and most of all he remembers his Guardian Angel.

His mind snaps back to when he was a little boy of four, sitting at the gatehouse at the bottom of the driveway of his home in Wilmington, rapt in awe, as he listened to the wise counsel of Hobbs the gardener. *"As you grow up, you will have many adventures, and you will see many different places and meet many different people. Some will be your friends and others will want to harm you, but never be afraid. Remember, wherever you are, whomever you meet, and whatever you do, you must believe in yourself, trust others, and respect the natural world. If you do these three things, you will always be protected. You will live in Hope."* Bobby Shafto eagerly embraces his destiny.

No sound comes from his parted lips as he leans forward to gently embrace her. He holds her head in his tiny webbed hands, and kisses her eyes and mouth, over and over again. Tears of joy co-mingle and wash over their ecstatic faces.

"Oh! Bobby I am so happy."

"So am I, Hope. So am I."

For the remainder of that morning, the half-siblings sit in the shade of the towering fig tree, wrapped in their love, and planning their future.

Epilogue

On his return to England, Bobby Shafto applies for, and receives, his Australian immigration papers. He arrives in Sydney as a landed immigrant, in late September of the same year. At 2.00 a.m on Sunday October 5th, 1958, at the Royal Women's Hospital in Sydney, Hope gives birth to a healthy baby boy; he weighs six pounds. Except for his size, he looks the spitting image of his father; a perfect little bastard, right down to his tiny webbed fingers and unblinking, wide-open eyes. The only imperfection on his tiny body is a scar encircling his neck, resembling a cord-burn; they name him Bunny.

Out of the mouth of this miraculous child, issues forth an intensely powerful and magnificent voice, which reverberates around the walls of the room with such force that it shatters the windows, and escapes into the warm night, winging swiftly and freely out into the vast and omniscient universe. He is twice born.

"Time has no beginning or end,
It turns in a never ending cycle."

Bunny Shafto 1941.

Printed in the United States
69437LVS00001B/4-102